TWISTED HEARTS

A DARK ENEMIES-TO-LOVERS MAFIA ROMANCE

DARK HEARTS
BOOK FOUR

JAGGER COLE

Twisted Hearts
Jagger Cole © 2023
All rights reserved.
Cover and interior design by Plan 9 Book Design
Photography by Wander Aguiar

❀ Created with Vellum

PLAYLIST

all the good girls go to hell - Billie Eilish
I Want It All - Cameron Grey
Heart-Shaped Box - Nirvana
Vigilante Shit - Taylor Swift
Heathens - Twenty One Pilots
Feel It - Michele Morrone
Panic Room - Au/Ra
Born To Die - Lana Del Rey
Friends - Chase Atlantic
War Of Hearts - Ruelle
Sex, Drugs, Etc. - Beach Weather
Mount Everest - Labrinth
Sweater Weather - The Neighbourhood
Grace - Jeff Buckley
I Could Give You All That You Don't Want - The Twilight Sad
Call Out My Name - The Weekend
Roll The Credits - Danielle Ponder
The Upswing - Bell X1

The Lighthouse - Halsey
Swim - Noah Gundersen
Electric Indigo - The Paper Kites
Don't Take The Money - Bleachers

Listen to the playlist on Spotify!

TRIGGER WARNING

This book contains darker themes and graphic depictions of past trauma, as well as mentions of SA. While these scenes were written to create a more vivid, in-depth story, they may be triggering to some readers. Please read with that in mind.

EILISH

I REALLY HATE SURPRISES.

A twisting sensation knots in my stomach as the elevator begins to rise. My throat works as I swallow nervously, my eyes squinting in an effort to see through the blindfold, even if technically that would be cheating.

I like plans. I like schedules. I like to know what's on the other side of a door before I walk through it. I'm going to have to force myself to swallow all that back tonight if I'm really going to go through with this.

And I *am* going to go through with it. I might not usually do surprises. But I also don't "do" breaking and entering or theft, either.

And, well, here we are.

"You look like you're going to puke."

Britney sneers, the only other person in the elevator.

"I'm fine."

"I mean, I would have thought that committing a crime as part of your initiation would be as easy as breathing for you, Eilish. But if you want to back out, now's your—"

"I said I'm *fine*, Britney."

She snickers. "Sure. If you say so."

The elevator keeps rising higher and higher, just like my blood pressure as it thrums in my veins. My hands fidget with my phone in the front pocket of my hoodie.

Her joke isn't anything new to me. Yeah, har-har-har, my family, the Kildares, are effectively the royal family of the Irish Mafia here in the US. And yeah, my Uncle Cillian runs the whole show. Like I haven't heard every possible joke and snide remark involving my family's criminal connections since I was in kindergarten.

Someone's juice box is missing? Well, you know who Eilish's family is. A teacher is out sick? Gosh, they probably crossed the Kildares.

Don't piss Eilish off, or she'll have you whacked.

I gave up trying to tell me people that my family name doesn't define me years ago. Because they were actually right: being a Kildare *did*—and obviously still does—define me.

So instead, I threw myself headlong into being "good".

I aced every test. I was top of every class. First chair cello in the New York Youth Symphony. Valedictorian with honors at NYU with early acceptance to Columbia School of Business.

But it doesn't matter how high you soar. It doesn't matter if there's never a single hair out of place or a single piece of lint on your clothes.

Names matter.

Family matters.

Blood matters.

And mine is inescapable.

Not that I *want* to escape my family. I truly don't. For all their involvement in what is categorically "bad"—i.e., crime—my family is amazing, flaws and all. My sister Neve, with her chaotic energy and heart of gold. Our broody, grumbly, overly protective bodyguard Castle, who at this point is effectively our big brother. Even my uncle Cillian, the lethally cold and vicious head of the Kildare empire, who is a literal, actual psychopath—at least, with his enemies. With us and his new wife, Una? He'd kill for us.

He *has* killed for us.

It's not just them. In the last year, my family has basically doubled, after Neve married Ares Drakos, head of the Greek mafia Drakos family. Now I have four new brothers-in-law, not to mention a sister-in-law, Callie, who's quickly become my best friend.

Yes, a lot has changed in a year.

I've changed, too. And I know it hasn't gone unnoticed. I know my family is worried about me. Three and a half months ago, when the combined Kildare-Drakos forces almost went to war with the Reznikov Russian Bratva family, a bomb tore through the bar that Neve, Callie, and I had been working our butts off to open.

3

I've been different since then. A little reckless, maybe. A little aimless. A little feeling like I'm just bouncing around, waiting to crash into something.

Neve, Callie, and the rest of them assume it's because of the explosion that sent me to hospital with fragments of my new pub embedded in my shoulder and thigh like so many cruel, wooden bullets.

That's a lot of it, of course. But in the almost four months since that night, my body has healed. And I've mourned our family friend, Sean Farrell, who died shielding me, Callie, and Callie's grandmother Dimitra from the worst of the blast.

But I'm still not the same.

When we were little kids, before Castle became our body-guard, an older, grizzled street brawler named Eoghan used to watch over Neve and me. We used to sit together in the kitchen of our family home and listen while he told what I now realize as an adult were *horrifically* inappropriate stories for children—tales of his various battles, fights, shootouts, and brushes with the law. And one thing he said back then always stuck with me in particular: when warriors die, they meet the ghosts of those they sent to Heaven or Hell before them.

It was only a terrifying story when I was a little girl.

Now I know it's true.

Because when I was in that hospital bed getting emergency transfusions as they rushed to stitch up the nicked artery in my leg, I got closer to whatever happens after life than I ever had been before.

And I saw the ghost of the one I sent there first.

The crime I've buried for more than a year. The crime that no one knows about.

Everyone looks at me and sees "the good one". The little angel who's always played by every rule, charmed every teacher, and aced every test.

When I look in the mirror? I see a darkness.

A killer.

I'd shut it away before the bombing, somehow. I'd kept it buried, hidden in the blur of day-to-day life and my friends and family finding their own happy-ever-afters—Neve with Ares, Cillian with Una, my friend Elsa with my brother-in-law Hades. But when I saw that ghost leering at me, pointing an accusing finger at me, all the walls I'd built around that one act of evil came crashing down like Jericho's.

And now they won't go back up. Even though I know what I saw was just the morphine and blood loss talking. Ever since, it feels like I've been slowly speeding faster and faster toward a cliff.

Aimless. Just bouncing around. *Reckless*, after spending my entire twenty-one years on the planet avoiding risk at all costs.

Hence, me being here—wherever "here" may be—with Britney Torres, a blindfold on my face, and a mission to steal something of value in about two minutes.

The mission is part of my initiation into the very exclusive, very secretive Crown Society—a club for "excellent students with driving ambition" at Columbia Business School. It's sort of like Yale's Skull and Bones, or the almost mythological Kings and Villains at Lords College in London.

The list of Crown Society alumni allegedly includes Senators, members of Congress, heads of major corporate entities and tech behemoths, and no less than *five* former U.S. Presidents. Needless to say, being a member opens doors to a world and opportunities most people can only fantasize about.

The downside is, you have to deal with absolute *cunts* like Britney Torres—a senior member of the Crown Society, and unfortunately my "pledge adjudicator", aka, the bane of my existence over the last three weeks of hazing and initiation tasks.

But honestly, you know what? I've been shot at, threatened, declared war upon, and blown up. Britney's going to have to bring her bitchy mean-girl schtick up about a hundred notches if she thinks she's going to get to me.

With a ding, the elevator doors finally open. Wherever we are, it's pretty high, given the length of time we were in the elevator.

"Still feeling fine?" Britney jeers as she leads me out into a cool, air-conditioned space. It smells clean and *rich*. I frown under my blindfold, trying to think where we might be, so I know how to prepare.

A year and a half ago, the Eilish everyone knew wouldn't have *dreamed* of doing any of this. Tonight's task—the final test before being confirmed as a member of the Crown Society—involves "proving you're ready to take on the establishment by taking what's theirs for your own".

Which is a sort of overly dramatic, overblown way of saying I'm supposed to break into the office of some rich, powerful head of a major company and steal something of sentimental and usually monetary value to them. Apparently, the current recordholder is a pledge from five years ago who managed to steal one of Napoleon's *actual* swords from the office of the CFO of Blackpool Financial Group.

"Yep," I mutter back at Britney. "Still fine."

She snickers. "If you say so."

I shiver, and it's not from the air conditioning. Wherever we are, the established members of the Crown Society have prepared the place, which includes paying off guards, looking for blind spots to sneak in, and hacking into the building's security system to make sure the crime I'm about to commit doesn't lead to my imprisonment. There's still obviously risk involved—a lot of it. But they don't want or need their prospective pledges going to jail.

"Okay, Kildare," Britney murmurs, moving closer to me after we've just walked up a staircase of some kind. "Your clue is 'if you want to make an omelet'."

My brow furrows. That's the other thing: I don't know what it is I'm supposed to steal. And I *won't* know until I get into whatever office I'm about to walk into and hopefully figure it out.

"Got it?"

I nod. "Got it. Can I take this off now—?"

My phone rings, making me jump.

"Jesus fucking Christ, Eilish!" Britney hisses. "Are you actually serious?!"

Shit shit shit. I must have turned the ringer back on by accident when I was fiddling with my phone in my pocket. I quickly jam my hand inside to silence it.

"Sorry," I mumble.

"Fuck," she sighs. "I really thought you'd be better at this—"

The phone rings again before I can turn it down. My face twists.

"I'm so sorry. Can I just check to see if it's an emergency?"

Britney groans. "Fuck. *Fine*. Knowing your family, it's probably someone needing bail."

Yeah, fuck you, too.

"Okay," she mutters, grabbing my arms and shoving me back. I jolt as my knees hit the back of a chair, toppling me into it. "You have one minute."

"Can I get some privacy?"

"No."

My teeth grind as I pull my phone out of my pocket and I frown again under the blindfold. "Uh, can you…"

"Oh my *God*, the fact that you're even being considered for the Crown Society is mind boggling to me. Here. It's someone named Callie. Not a fucking *word* about what you're currently doing, as if I need to say that?"

I can feel her hand brush mine as she taps the answer button. Then I raise the phone to my ear.

"Hey, Cals, this isn't really a good time—"

"Are you fucking serious, Eilish?!"

I wince at the abrasively loud tone in her voice. Which is saying something, considering "abrasive and loud" is sort of her default setting.

"Um…about?"

"Don't fucking bullshit me!"

"This is *really* not a great—"

"Do you even have *any* idea what the fuck you're doing?! Breaking and entering?!?!"

Shit.

"*Who fucking told you!?*" I hiss into the phone.

"Dahlia."

Goddammit. Dahlia is one of my closest new friends from business school—a good enough friend that I might have maybe spilled the beans about my initiation tasks to her. In fucking *confidence*, I might add.

She had plenty of concerns, obviously. And apparently when I ignored those concerns, she passed them straight up the chain to Callie.

"*Dude—*"

"I have to call you later, Callie."

"Can we appreciate the fact that *I* am being the voice of reason right now, and by extension how serious that makes this?"

"Duly noted. Call you later."

"No! Eilish, don't you fucking dare—"

Her voice cuts off abruptly as my thumb finally manages to tap the button to end the call.

"Did you want to plan your Christmas vacation and maybe do your taxes while you're at it? Or are you ready to fucking do this?"

I glare through the blindfold in the direction of Britney's obnoxious voice.

"I'm ready."

"Great."

I jolt as she grabs my wrists, pulling me out of the chair and maneuvering me forward. I hear a door opening, and then she's pulling me through it.

"You remember how this works, right?"

I nod.

"We're in the office. I'm going to head back to the elevators and leave. You, count to thirty before you take the blindfold off, find your object, take it, and then get out of the building without being caught. You got all that?"

"Got it."

She snickers again, the sound drifting away from me as she steps out of the office.

"Good luck, Kildare."

The door shuts behind me. I almost rip the blindfold off immediately, but stop myself just in time. Britney is a petty enough bitch that she'd do something like stay in the room and just make it *sound* like she left so she could catch me breaking the rules so that she could boot me.

So I wait and count in my head, my pulse thudding in my ears.

...Twenty-nine, thirty.

Swallowing, I reach up and pull off the blindfold. Even though it's dim to the point of darkness in the office, I still blink as my eyes adjust from the total blackness of the blindfold.

Holy shit. Where am I?

First of all, the office is *huge.* And gorgeously decorated, albeit in a very masculine way. High ceilings, slate stone walls with black and dark wood accents, and an enormous glass wall overlooking all of midtown Manhattan with a partial view of Central Park.

Even though whatever security system there is in here has been disabled, I still instinctively pull the hood of my sweatshirt up around my face. I walk quietly across the dark-stained hardwood floor and elegant area rugs toward the mammoth, all-black desk. Behind it, elegant built-in shelving frames a huge open space on the wall, where hangs what looks like an *amazing* replica of one of Monet's Rouen Cathedral paintings.

My eyes scan the built-in shelves, looking for family photos, diplomas, anything that will give me a hint about *who* I'm about to steal from. But there's nothing.

Not a single picture. No kids' drawings. The desk itself almost looks like it's been staged, as if no one actually uses it. The laptop is perfectly squared. Two silver pens are completely straight and in line next to it. There's even a bottle of still water with a crystal tumbler next to it, *with a fucking paper cover* on top of it, like in a hotel room.

Great, I'm stealing from a serial killer with OCD tendencies.

I prowl around the desk, repeating the clue in my head.

If you want to make an omelet...

My brows knit as I raise my gaze to the wall opposite the desk that I ignored when I walked in because I was too distracted by the view and the Monet replica. There, sitting on a shelf under a glass box, is a gorgeous, delicate, incredibly detailed, black and gold, oversized....

...you gotta break a few eggs.

Oh, fuck me.

Not just any egg, I realize as I walk over. It's a *Fabergé* egg. As in the House of Fabergé, the 19th-century firm famous for the jewel- and gold-encrusted eggs and other priceless decorative works of art they created for the Tsars and the other ultra-wealthy of pre-revolutionary Imperial Russia.

Like the Monet, it could be a replica. But judging by the glass case around it, not to mention the other opulent wealth clearly on display in this office, I'm guessing it's the real deal.

I'm also sure that *this* is what I'm supposed to steal.

Fuck. Me. Sideways.

Forget Napoleon's sword. This thing has to be priceless. It also has to be under the protection of an alarm. But again, that's one of the assurances made by the Crown Society concerning this task: all alarms and other security measures will be turned off during the theft.

My pulse races as I reach out with shaky hands, letting my fingers graze the glass of the case. No alarms. I wince, lifting it up as gingerly as I can.

Still no alarms.

I exhale slowly as I set the glass box down on the shelf next to the egg. Then I just stare at it sitting on its delicate, understated black wire stand mounted on an ancient looking wooden base. I mean it's *gorgeous*—a matte black egg girdled in gleaming gold with lines and swirls of what I think are yellow diamonds all over the surface.

It's simply beautiful. And for a second, I hate that I have to take this, even though I know that within a week, an anonymous courier will bring it back to this very office with a note of apology on paper bearing the seal of the Crown Society. Apparently, a lot of the "targets" that get picked for these initiation ordeals are either Crown Society alumni themselves or have otherwise heard of the ritual. Even the guy who had his Napoleon sword stolen apparently laughed about it once it was returned.

But fuck me, I have to walk out of here with *this*? A priceless, old, not to mention *fragile*, decorative freaking egg? Ideally without, you know, smashing it into a million pieces? Great.

I take a deep breath and ready myself to touch it. When suddenly, my gaze drops to the tiny slip of paper next to the egg glued to the dark wood base banded with brass that itself looks like an antique.

A slip of paper with beautiful, neat, masculine handwriting on it.

In Russian.

Moyemu synu. Vsya moya lyubov'.

I took two levels of Russian literature in undergrad. It was basically only enough to feel smug when discussing Tolstoy. But it's also enough for me to know that the note reads "To my son. All of my love".

My gaze drifts to the letterhead on which the little note is written, which includes the name of this benevolent father giving his son a freaking Fabergé egg as a token of his esteem:

Vadim Tsarenko.

It takes me half a second. Then cold, naked, razor-sharp fear stabs right through my heart.

Holy. Fucking. *Hell*.

Tsarenko. As in *Gavan fucking Tsarenko*, the co-head of the same Reznikov Bratva we almost went to war with four months ago. The same Reznikov Bratva whose captain, Leo Stavrin, blew up my bar and killed Sean. The same Reznikov Bratva who we might not openly be at war with, but whom we *certainly* are not "at peace" with.

I'm in Gavan Tsarenko's office at his massive holdings and acquisitions company, Ironclad Capital.

This is *horrifying*.

I shouldn't be here. I shouldn't be within five freaking blocks of this entire building. And I *definitely* shouldn't be stealing a priceless heirloom that he got from his father.

My heart races into overdrive, my ears ringing as my throat opens and closes reflexively.

Run. You need to run, now.

I know I should. Old Eilish would. Old Eilish would already be halfway down the block by now. But new Eilish is apparently fucking *insane*. Because before I know what I'm doing, my hands are raising again, reaching for the gorgeous black and gold egg.

My pulse skips as my fingers touch the gilded gold and yellow diamonds. I gently cradle it in my hands as I lift it from its wire stand and gaze at it with wide eyes, holding my breath.

Now, to get you safely out of the building—

"What the *fuck* do you think you're doing!?"

My heart almost stops as the deep, slightly Russian-accented voice roars behind me. As huge, powerful hands grip my arms fiercely. As the black power of the voice's owner rolls over me like a thunderhead crashing into a shore. As the heady, intoxicating scent of bergamot, wood, and *man* invades my senses like a drug.

I flinch as he grabs me, like I've been zapped with a taser.

My hands spasm.

My fingers release.

Oh God—

It doesn't happen in slow motion. It takes merely a fraction of a second for the priceless, gorgeous thing to slip from my hands and *explode* against the hardwood floor.

"You *little. FUCKING—*"

My reaction is instantaneous. When Gavan's grip tightens on me, the self-defense moves Castle has spent hours and hours drilling into me come to the fore without warning. It doesn't matter that this isn't some random mugger in the park. It doesn't matter that the man grabbing me is the single most powerful, dangerous man in New York.

I just react.

My foot stamps down on the bridge of his foot. And just as he hisses in a mix of pain, shock and surprise, I throw my heel back *hard*, my foot kicking all the way back and up until my shoe connects with his balls.

The bruising grip releases from my arms as he groans, and I *bolt*—flinging myself out the door of his office and rushing headlong down the halls of Ironclad Holdings. I skip the elevator and take the stairs first two and then three at a time, almost blind with the dizzying fear and adrenaline roaring in my veins like napalm until I go crashing out a doorway into a side street.

Then I turn and run into the night, the scent of bergamot and wood still in my nostrils, the feel of his grip still tingling on my skin.

2

GAVAN

WHEN THE SENSATION of wanting both to puke and curl into a ball finally abates, my eyes drop to the floor.

Mother. *Fucker.*

Everything goes silent as I stare at the shattered remains of what was once the "Imperial Shield" Fabergé egg that Vadim left me. The room continues to spin, and the throbbing pain in my balls lingers as I slowly close my eyes and suck in a slow breath.

I could chase her. At least, I *think* I could chase her, given the swollen state of my fucking nuts right now. But she's already gotten a head start, and I know she's fast. So I let her run, knowing she's not actually getting away for good.

My eyes open, my gaze taking in the smashed pieces on the floor. Fury begins to swirl like molten fire in my chest. My vision tunnels, teeth gritting as my lips curl into a silent snarl.

There's no going back. There's *never* been any going back for me. Only forward. Only upward, until I burn in the fucking sun like Icarus.

Leaving the pieces where they are, I turn and walk slowly toward the bar cart in the corner of the room. I pour a *very* heavy splash of vodka and bring it to my lips as I move to the window, glaring out at the city below.

It never ceases to amaze me that this is where I stand now, a king and vengeful god high above it all.

It wasn't always like this. Not for me, the product of violence and cruelty. A bastard son that a man I didn't deserve took in and cared for as if I were his own flesh and blood.

My mother was Kristina Reznikov. She was also the mother of the half-brother with whom I now rule this empire. Konstantin and I don't share a father, but we both were victims of our fathers' malignant cruelty when they were still alive.

It was Semyon Belsky, a rival Bratva king, who raped my mother twenty-five years ago. When she found out the assault had left her pregnant, she hid it from her husband, Konstantin's father, the unimaginably heartless Antin Reznikov. Antin, being the callous and merciless piece of shit that he was, would have seen—and eventually *did* see—the assault as infidelity on my mother's part.

So she carried me to term and gave birth to me in secret. And then it was Vadim, one of Antin's top *avtoritets*, who raised me like a son. Not just because he loved my mother from afar, in his own secret way. But because he was a good man.

My mother spent the rest of her sad life interacting with me as if I were Konstantin's best friend. As if I was "the brother

her son never had", even though in truth I *was*. Unable to openly love me in the way she wanted to, for fear for both of us.

Vadim taught me how to be a man, as well as the ways of the world and of the Bratva. But when Konstantin and I discovered the truth about my parentage six years ago, my life changed. Vadim, being a top captain whose loyalty had always been to Konstantin over that piece of shit Antin, was wealthy enough. But suddenly, as the rightful co-head of the entire empire, I was worth *billions*, and became more powerful than I could have ever imagined.

Now, Konstantin and I run the Reznikov organization like the brothers we are. But I've kept the Tsarenko name.

My Reznikov blood honors my mother. My last name honors the man who loved her, and who raised me as if he were my true father.

Two years ago, Vadim died at the hands of Declan Kildare.

Something lethal and vicious stirs, snarling inside me as I slam back the rest of the vodka and glare out over the city. I've always had a darkness in me—from the evil in which I was conceived, from the lies that were told to me to "protect" me as a child. From the pain and horror that were inflicted on me later in my teens that Vadim never knew about.

And ever since he died, that darkness has grown. It's taken root in me, and surged, until its black roots are firmly tangled around whatever heart I have left, strangling it.

Almost a year and a half ago, I went out one night to avenge my father. To kill Declan Kildare with my bare hands. Instead, I saw something I was never meant to.

I saw *her*.

Eilish Kildare.

And I saw what she did. I saw her secret sin, her darkest moment.

I've been sitting on it ever since.

Waiting. Letting it simmer. Biding my time until I could use what I saw that night to destroy her family.

I've spent almost a year and a half being the shadow she never even knew she had. Learning her every dark secret. Witnessing each private moment, hearing each whispered hope.

And tonight, she walked right into the fucking lion's den.

My skin tingles, my blood hot and close to the surface as I turn and stride back across the room to the shattered fragments of the Imperial Shield. My lips curl menacingly as I glare at the shards with malice in my eyes.

Gently, using a file folder and my fingers, I scoop up the pieces of the egg and then reverently cradle them in a decorative bowl from another shelf. The safe behind my desk opens to my code and thumbprint, and I deposit the bowl and its precious contents there before plucking out the little plastic baggie and holding it up, examining it thoughtfully.

The baggie with the bullet casing of a blank in it.

My lips thin to a hard sneer.

I saw what you did, solnishka.

But the simmering feeling in my veins isn't just from hatred and anger. It's the lingering heat from the proximity to her. From touching her. From feeling her wriggle and writhe against me, and from listening to the choked way her breath caught at the sound of my wrath. From the tumble of blonde, and the scent of Chanel No. 5, and *her*. From the flash of green in her eyes as she glanced back, right before she bolted from the room.

Tonight, Eilish has set things in motion that cannot be undone.

Things I will not *allow* to be undone.

I saw what she did. Now, her fate rests in the palm of my hand.

And I'm going to fucking *squeeze*.

3

EILISH

HE DIDN'T SEE YOU.

You had your hood up.

The cameras were disabled.

He does. Not. Know.

I've repeated these four lines to myself over and over like a mantra ever since I ran down 5th Avenue last night. I breathed them in and out fervently, like a prayer, as I lay wide awake in my bed all last night in the Upper East Side brownstone where I grew up. They've been on a constant loop all day today as I went to morning classes.

It hasn't done *a thing* to help.

My hands are shaking. My skin feels too tight for the pressure in my veins. My eyes dart side to side with every step, as if I'm constantly waiting for Gavan to lunge out at me from behind every tree or corner to murder me for smashing his father's priceless egg.

I shiver as I replay the stabbing jolt of pure fear when he grabbed me, and the terrible, sick-making sensation of the egg slipping from my fingers.

To my son. All of my love.

Dread pools in my stomach as I shuffle out of building that houses the market strategies class I just completely zoned out through. This is *not* good. Like, it could start an all-out war not good.

Except, he didn't catch me last night. He wasn't waiting for me at my house, or at school this morning, because—

He didn't see you.

You had your hood up.

The cameras were disabled.

He does. Not. Know.

I keep saying it as I head off to go meet Callie and Dahlia for lunch. It still doesn't do a thing to calm the jangling, twitchy feeling of impending doom screaming inside my head.

I'M a block away from the restaurant Calliope on the Upper West Side, Callie's all-time favorite Greek spot in New York that she swears isn't due to the fact that it's literally her name, when my phone rings. I glance down, my brows drawing together when I see my uncle's name on the screen.

"Aren't you supposed to be on your honeymoon?"

Though they were technically married—for the second time —six months ago, Cillian and Una are just now finally taking the time to escape for a real honeymoon. Currently, they're about a week into a month-long stay at a castle somewhere in Ireland.

Of course those two wouldn't go to a beach resort like normal people. Of *course* Mr. and Mrs. Donnie Darko are spending their honeymoon in a 13th-century tower somewhere out in the middle of nowhere, in County freaking Kildare of all places.

Cillian chuckles. "I just wanted to check in. Everything good?"

I swallow thickly. "Mm-hmm. Great."

"Great." He clears his throat. "Actually, I'm not just calling to chat. We need to talk."

My heart drops. I can feel my face go white. A naked chill rips down my spine as I come to a dead stop on the sidewalk.

"*Oh?*" I choke.

Oh God, he knows. He knows I've basically thrown our family into war with the freaking Reznikovs by breaking into—

"Do you and Brooks McKinnley still talk at all?"

The panic from a second ago evaporates. Or rather, is *drowned* in the tidal wave of disgust and churning anger simply hearing that fucking name brings out in me.

"What?" I blurt, my vision dotting. "No," I mutter coldly. "Not at all."

Not since that night, four years ago.

"You dated for a while in high school."

It's not a question. He knows this.

24

Cillian didn't raise us. He didn't even live on the same continent as us. Nor is he remotely the warm and fuzzy type of uncle who keep up with things like boyfriends and goings-on in our lives because he wants to chat about it. No, he keeps up with those sort of things because he's a methodical, calculating machine more than he is a man. The most human I've ever known him to be is since he's been with Una.

Even so, he was more of a father to Neve and me than Declan —*may he burn in hell*—ever was.

When I don't respond, he continues.

"You know his father, obviously?"

I swallow. Yeah. I know him. As if it would be possible to know Brooks McKinnley and *not* hear—usually from him, repeatedly—about his father. Senator Harrison McKinnley is *very* wealthy, *extremely* powerful, and a favored probable pick for a presidential candidate in another election cycle or two.

He's also, by all accounts, just as much of a slimy douchebag as his son.

"I do."

"And have you heard that Senator McKinnley has recently assumed the chairman position on the newly minted Senate Committee on Organized Crime?"

I nod to nobody in particular. "Also yes."

"I figured as much." I can hear the slow intake of air as he draws on the vape he's been using lately to quit cigarettes.

My brows knit. "So...what's up?"

"I want you to know it kills me a little to have to even bring this up to you, Eilish."

25

He sighs heavily.

"Brooks and his father reached out to me last night to posit the idea of you and Brooks marrying."

The breath leaves my body in a rush. My knees buckle, the very ground under my feet sways, and it feels as if a knife has been jammed between my ribs.

"Eilish."

"Yeah, I'm here," I'm finally able to mumble.

"This is a question, not a decree. I just want to get a read on how you might feel about this. That's *all*."

I nod, my mouth dry as the events of that awful night rush through my head. As my body remembers, and curls in on itself. As fury rises like bile in my stomach.

I clear my throat, shoving the nightmares from my head.

"With Harrison being the chair of the organized crime Senate committee, it's either a threat, or an olive branch," I begin.

"I agree," Cillian growls.

"And given Brooks' and my…" I squeeze my eyes shut, fighting back the urge to puke. "*History*, I'd bet on the olive branch."

"You should know this isn't the first time this idea has been floated."

My mouth twists with nausea. "Seriously?"

"Yes. It came up before, when you were still in high school. Something tells me Senator McKinnley is more than a little interested in aligning himself with a family like ours."

"As a shakedown, or for mutual benefit?"

Cillian grunts. "I'm guessing the latter. He's ambitious to a fault. Guys like him are never satisfied. Even being a goddamn Senator and Presidential favorite in a few years isn't enough. I don't know if it's ego, greed, a lust for power, or all three, but I think the good Senator wants to get his hands a little dirty. And given the position he's just moved into, and the sort of information he may be able to offer us—"

"It makes sense," I blurt out, mechanically. And suddenly, armor, mask, and all, I'm slipping right into the role I play in my family: the smart, good, crossed T's and dotted I's, *logical* Eilish.

Cillian sighs. "You really are the business-minded one, aren't you."

"I'm just looking at it objectively. To align our family with that sort of power, especially if he's probably going to be president? That's just smart."

Cillian doesn't say anything for a full fifteen seconds.

"To be clear, I am *not* asking you to do this."

"I—"

"And this isn't a decision we have to make today. I just wanted to float it in your direction. We can talk more about it later. Even if 'later' means after Una and I get back."

I nod in a daze. "Yeah. Sounds good."

"Everything's fine, though?"

"Mm-hmm!" I smile wryly. "Say hi to Una for me."

"Will do. Talk to you soon."

After I hang up, I stare at the phone for another few seconds.

This is my fate. After all, despite all my schooling, and excellent grades, and early acceptance to a prestigious business school, I *am* still at my core a mafia princess.

And *this* is the fate of mafia princesses: marriage as a bargaining chip. For power. For peace. For allies.

I mean, Neve did it, out of a sense of duty and loyalty to our family, marrying Ares to stop a war between us and the Drakos family. I should do the same.

The difference is, Ares turned out to be Neve's soulmate. Brooks McKinnley is not, and never will be, that to me.

He'll always just be the man who hurt me.

Cillian's words and flashes of the Brooks nightmare are still churning in my head as I step into the restaurant.

"Over here!"

I turn to the voice, quickly shoving all of that somewhere into the recesses of my mind as I smile at Callie and Dahlia and head over to their table.

Dahlia gives me a weak smile as she pushes a plate of baklava my way. Given that the sticky dessert is *legendary* at this place, I know it's a peace offering for ratting me out to Callie.

"Mate, I'm so fucking sorry."

I could try to stay mad. But honestly, it's a little impossible to do that when you're talking about Dahlia Roy. The daughter of a French housekeeper and a Saudi billionaire who abused and impregnated said housekeeper, she's honestly a force of nature of a human being—fearless, unshakable, and *very* smart. She's also absolutely gorgeous, with her mother's green eyes and freckles and her father's dark hair and tan complexion.

She's also even smaller than *I* am, which is saying something, and when that's combined with that posh little English accent of hers, it's almost too cute to stand.

All the same, I glare at her as I sit across from them, because I feel I should at least make her squirm *a little*.

"Honestly, I dragged it out of her," Callie shrugs, sipping her overly milky and, knowing her, probably *way* too sweet iced coffee.

"Bullshit."

"No, really—"

"It was me," Dahlia pouts, ever truthful to a fault. "I was just really worried about you."

"Well, she's not in jail," Callie mutters, eyeing me. "You didn't get arrested, right? You never texted me back about that."

I roll my eyes to cover the chill that ripples down my back. "No, I wasn't arrested."

Dahlia chews on her lip. "Did you...I mean, the initiation..."

"It was a bust," I mumble. I haven't actually heard from Britney today. But given that I never checked in with her last night, or sent her any proof about the egg, I think it's safe to say she's used my application to the Crown Society for toilet paper by now.

"Good," Callie glares at me. "That was seriously fucking stupid. And again, I want us all to appreciate that this is *me* saying that."

I sigh, but then drag my eyes back across the table to Dahlia. "Okay. You're forgiven."

She visibly relaxes as I pluck a square of baklava from the plate.

"But only because of this."

She grins. "Best in the city."

"Pfft," I shrug, nodding my chin at Callie. "Her grandmother's is better."

Callie's lips twist. "I dunno. Tough call, actually."

Dahlia smiles at me. "You're really not still mad at me?"

"Nah, we're good."

She exhales as she stands, shouldering her bag. "Thank you."

"Off to class?"

She nods. "Yeah. Venture capital risk analysis."

"Wow, sounds like a blast," Callie drawls.

Dahlia leans down to give me a quick hug, then she's out the door. Callie and I stay and each lunch, mostly talking about the grand re-opening of The Banshee—our Irish pub in the West Village that was blown to smithereens on its soft opening night. The building itself took a ton of damage in the attack, and we're now in the process of buying the entire property piecemeal from the condo owners above the bar, who have obviously all moved out. Our new plan involves using all four stories of the building for a bar, a small venue stage, and a restaurant. But it's going to mean a lot of time and paperwork before we can even start that rolling.

After that, Callie brings up the subject of her impending arranged marriage, which she usually hates talking about since her betrothed is Luca Carveli, a disgusting troll of a west coast mafioso who's also thirty years her senior. But as it gets closer and closer to her twenty-first birthday, when "the arrangement" comes into effect, she and I have been discussing the subject a lot more.

So gross.

After we're done gabbing and eating, Callie suddenly looks around and frowns. "Wow, this place sure cleared out."

My brow furrows. She's right. It was jammed when I arrived, and now we're the only table here, aside from three guys having coffee in the corner. I don't even see our waitress anywhere. Or *any* waitstaff, for that matter.

Callie winces as she glances at her phone. "Shit, I gotta go. I'm supposed to meet Elsa to go over our permit applications."

In addition to being Hades Drakos' recent fiancée, Elsa Guin is also an extremely hotshot lawyer at Crown and Black who counts our family among her clients. She's been helping Neve, Callie, and I with the Banshee stuff, ever since we first came up with the insane idea of opening a bar together.

"No problem, take off," I shrug. "I'm not on a schedule for the rest of the day. I'm going to take my time finishing my coffee."

She frowns, glancing around at the weirdly empty restaurant. "Still, it'd be really great if we could pay—"

"Cals, I got it. Really. Say hi to Elsa for me."

She nods. "Okay, okay. I'll get the bill next time. Oh, and I still want all the juicy details of your escapades as a cat burglar."

I smile weakly. "Honestly? It was pretty boring. I chickened out."

She rolls her eyes at me. "Lame. All right, later tater."

When she's gone, I sit back in the chair, finishing the last of my coffee.

He didn't see you.

You had your hood up.

The cameras were disabled.

He does. Not. Know.

I shiver and force myself to take a breath.

It's going to be okay. *I'm* going to be—

A clicking sound in the almost silent restaurant yanks my attention to the front door. My face pales.

One of the three guys who was drinking coffee has just dead-bolted the door from the inside. Another one is pulling the shades down over the big front windows, hiding us from the sidewalk outside.

Holy fuck.

My chair crashes over backward as I leap from it and bolt for the side door. But I barely make it four steps before two of the men grab me hard by the arms and yank me back, making me scream.

"Take your *fucking* hands off her."

I freeze immediately when I hear the voice.

His voice.

Instantly, I shudder as the same cold sensation from before tickles down my spine. My stomach clenches painfully, my heart thudding against my breastbone as the two men release me. The third man is already locking the side door when slowly, my tongue wetting my lips, I turn.

And I tremble.

Gavan is sitting alone at one of the empty tables, drumming his tattooed fingers on the top of it. His men are in simple black suits. Gavan, however, is dressed like a king.

Or a Tsar.

He's in an impeccably tailored and fitted three-piece suit—gunmetal gray to match his piercing gray eyes. His shoes are polished and stylish. He's wearing gleaming silver cufflinks. He's even got one of those tie-bars across his collar—also silver, to match the cufflinks.

Even if you don't know who and what he is, Gavan cuts an imposing figure. Well over six feet tall, with long legs and broad, muscular shoulders. The suit tightens across a powerful chest and bulging biceps, and I flush as I stare right back at the cold, calculating gray eyes boring into me.

I tense as I take in the high, aristocratic cheekbones, the jaw that could cut glass. He's got a dark, swarthy scruff of stubble covering his chin, and keeps his hair longish, but styled.

It is outrageously unfair that a man as terrifying and lethally dangerous as Gavan Tsarenko should be so ridiculously attractive. Heat courses through my system alongside fear as his eyes burn malevolently into me, and as the power almost literally radiates off him.

"Leave us," he growls quietly, addressing his men even as he keeps staring right at me. Slowly, he raises a hand, two fingers beckoning me in a "come here" motion. I swallow the lump in my throat as the three men in suits file out through the door to the kitchen.

"I thought we should have a little chat," Gavan murmurs, his eyes still locked on mine.

I see his men leave in my peripheral vision. Then I'm bolting for the front door. But I barely make it a few steps before Gavan grabs me, and I scream. His muscular, powerful arms circle me like iron bands, unyielding, lifting me off my feet, my back to his chest as my legs kick helplessly. He marches back to the table and unceremoniously drops me to my feet again before sitting back in his chair.

I glance sharply at the door again. He just sighs.

"We can play this game all fucking night if you'd like, Eilish," he rasps darkly. "Or you could simply *sit*, as instructed."

I purse my lips and look away.

"Where is everyone?"

"Gone. I own this place."

I shiver.

"Now—*sit*."

I briefly contemplate running for it again. But it's a stupid idea, and it's just going to make me look even guiltier, not to mention foolish. So, pulse roaring, I drop into the chair across from him.

"Good girl."

I simmer. My gaze rips to his, narrowing into a glare. Gavan just smiles a thin, cold smile.

"Do they know?"

I swallow and remain silent.

"Eilish, we can sit here with you insulting me by pretending I'm an idiot. Or we can *talk* like two adults. Do. They. Fucking. *Know*."

I quail under the fierceness of his gaze and the power emanating from him.

"Look, I…I'm sorry," I stammer. "I am *so* sorry. I shouldn't have gone in there."

"No shit."

I wince. "It was a stupid hazing thing for this club—"

"I'm well aware."

There's a dark violence rippling just beneath the surface. But outwardly, he's perfectly calm as he sits further back in his chair.

I smile weakly. "Look, I know it's irreplaceable. But I can pay for it—"

A cold, mirthless laugh rumbles in his chest.

"Oh, I very much doubt that."

I actually spent an hour last night researching the price of Fabergé eggs. They're not cheap by any means, but at around forty thousand dollars, which most of them seem to be, it's doable. It's going to sting. But I've got money in my trust fund.

"No, honestly. I can pay you back. Here…" I twist, reaching over and plucking my bag off the chair next to the one toppled to the ground. I pull out a pen and my checkbook as I turn to smile weakly at the venomously gorgeous and completely terrifying man sitting across from me.

"Let's settle this, okay?"

Gavan smiles as I open the checkbook to a blank one and pop the cap on my pen.

"If you insist, Ms. Kildare," he growls with a cruel curl to his lips. "You can make it out to Gavan—that's two A's. Tsarenko. T, S—"

"I know how to spell your name."

"I'm honored."

I ignore his biting sarcasm as I finish writing out his name before moving my pen to the dreaded "amount" line.

"And the damage?"

I'm ready to write "fifty thousand", which is ten more than the auction evaluations of most of the Fabergé eggs I saw online, just to smooth things over, when he clears his throat.

"One hundred and twenty-four million dollars."

My pulse skips. The pen goes still in my hand as my throat closes.

Hold up. Fucking *what*?

I raise my eyes to his, swallowing. "It's not worth that much."

"It is. It was actually recently appraised at one hundred and twenty-four million, five hundred thousand, but I'm feeling fucking *charitable*."

I stare at him, a horrible whining alarm sound slowly rising in my ears.

"I—no," I shake my head. "No, Fabergé eggs—"

"*Known* Fabergé eggs. Yes, they're cheaper. But what you destroyed last night like a rhinoceros in a fucking cutlery shop was one of the *lost* Fabergé eggs. It's called the Imperial Shield, and it was commissioned and owned by Tsarina Alexandra. It was lost during the revolution that claimed her and her family's lives. It belonged to my father," he adds with a venomous hiss in his tone.

My stomach drops straight to the floor. I blink as my eyes go as dry as my mouth.

"I—"

"I would say," Gavan rasps, leaning forward and steepling his fingers on the table between us, "that the truce between our families is a *tenuous* one at best. One hundred and twenty-four million dollars is certainly more than enough to go to war over. Wouldn't you agree?"

I stare at the piercing gunmetal gray eyes in horror.

He sighs, settling back in his chair again as he rubs his jaw thoughtfully.

"But I think we're fixating on the wrong thing here. This isn't about the egg. This is about me knowing *what you did*."

My pulse jumps again.

"What?"

"Come, come. I know you know what I'm talking about."

He stands, cracking his neck as I try to regulate my breathing.

"Look, *please*. My family doesn't know about last night. I—I can find the money somehow—"

"I'm not interested in your money, nor am I talking about your amateur burglary attempt last night."

He starts to walk around the table behind me. I twist my head, following him with my eyes, as if he's a lion or a shark who will move in for the kill if I break eye contact for a moment.

I lose him as he crosses behind me and suddenly flinch as I feel him lean down close. The heat of his breath teases the hairs on the back of my neck, and I tremble as I inhale that same bergamot, wood, wealth, and man scent that I smelled on him last night.

"I saw you that night, Eilish," he rasps darkly. *"And I know what you did."*

"I—I don't know what you're—"

His arm extends past me, a small plastic baggie dangling from his tattooed fingers.

A bag containing a bullet casing.

And suddenly, I go numb and the world flips sideways as I stare in abject horror at what's dangling in front of my face.

No...

"I was *very* curious as to why you were so eager to pick up all those spent rounds that night. Why you kept going, even after burning your finger on one that was still hot. And even more curious why those rounds in his gun were *blanks*."

Oh my God. Oh, my fucking mother of God...

"It took me some time, I'll admit. But when I pieced it together?"

He jiggles the bag right in front of my face once more before closing it in his fist. Slowly, he moves back around the table to sit in his chair again. He stares at me with hungry malevolence as my entire world starts to shatter and collapse at my feet.

"So, allow me to ask once more, Eilish." His lips curl in a devil's grin. "Does the rest of your family know that you killed your father?"

My mouth opens and then closes. It happens again, and a third time, before I realize I can't speak. I can't move. I can't even burst into tears like I want to. I'm simply too numb, and too shocked to do anything at all.

Gavan's eyes pierce into mine.

"Tomorrow morning at eight, Eilish. Come to my office." He smirks. "I'm sure you remember where that is, don't you?"

I'm still utterly silent, staring straight ahead unseeingly as he raps his tattooed knuckles on the table and stands. He buttons his jacket, levels those vicious gray eyes at me, then turns and marches out of the front door of the restaurant.

I'm fucked.

I am well and truly *fucked*.

4

GAVAN

"FUCKING *FINALLY*."

Konstantin grins, looking up as I step through the front door. He strides over and grabs me in a huge bear hug. I hug my brother back, clapping him on the back as I shove and twist the mask back into place.

The mask of normalcy. The mask of power and control, to hide the chaos and darkness roaring beneath.

"Sorry I'm late."

He grins and shakes his head. "Hey man, it's your place. Thanks for hosting tonight. Lukas and your sisters just got here."

I grin back.

It would be easy to look back on my life and focus on all the things that were taken from me: my mother, my birthright as a Reznikov for so long.

My innocence, and my ability to smile normally after the age of thirteen.

And at times, I do allow myself to wallow in the hatred that comes when I consider all that was stolen from me. But when it gets too dark inside my own head, I try to focus instead on the things I've been given.

An empire and wealth beyond comprehension, for a start. But also a family, and friends. Discovering that Konstantin was my half-brother opened a world of new faces to me: his enemies-turned-friends from the exclusive private school he'd briefly attended his senior year.

At Oxford Hills Academy, Konstantin became friends with three other Bratva heirs who were also dark shadows on the otherwise pristine, venerated, old-money school: Lukas Komarov, Misha Tsavakov, and Ilya Volkov. Through my brother, and through sitting at the head of the Reznikov empire with him, these friends became my friends as well.

But it wasn't just friends I made through discovering my past. I found that Konstantin wasn't the only half-sibling I had.

Konstantin's wife, Mara, and her twin sister Lizbet, Lukas' wife, are in fact the daughters of the man who assaulted my mother. Needless to say, the subject of fathers is pretty much not discussed within our circle.

It can get a little confusing, especially when you're trying to explain it to someone unfamiliar with the family and they've got that "what in the Jerry-fucking-Springer shit is this" look on their face. But basically, Konstantin and I share a mother, and Mara, Lizbet and I share a father.

Konstantin and Mara/Lizbet are, however, in no way blood related. I'm just the missing link between them.

"Hey, you!"

I grin, not even needing to fake it when Mara jumps out of her chair and rushes over to hug me as I step into the kitchen area. It's an impressive feat, given that she's twenty-nine weeks pregnant.

With *twins*.

"Thanks for fitting us in and having us all over!"

Konstantin and Mara do have a place here in New York. But they're mostly in London these days—in fact, Mara is flying back there tomorrow to settle in for the last stage of her pregnancy.

I roll my eyes. "Right, like I wouldn't come over to say goodbye before you jet off to England and disappear into babyville for the next who-knows-how-long."

She grins, pulling away from me to let Lizbet give me an equally rib-crushing hug. When she slips away from me, she pulls a face.

"You do know that Lukas is cooking tonight, right?"

"Oh, fuck you."

I chuckle, turning to grin at Lukas as he looks up from something he's sauteing on the stove, while simultaneously juggling my one-year-old niece, Luna, in his other arm.

"Lukas!" Lizbet hisses at him. "Really?"

He beams at her before pulling his gaze back to his daughter and kissing her tiny forehead. "It's fine. She's not picking up words yet."

"Umm, yes she is?"

Lukas just shrugs, nuzzling Luna's nose with the tip of his own and making her giggle in a way that's impossible not to smile at. Lizbet sighs with exasperation, but you can tell by the way she's looking at her husband that there's nothing but adoration there.

"When her first words are 'eat a dick' or 'fuck no', I'm going to kill you."

"Woah, Liz," Konstantin admonishes. "Let's not use the f-word in front of the kid, okay?"

He and Lukas crack up as Lizbet glares at the pair of them.

"Okay, seriously, fuck you both."

Mara laughs as she nods at me. "Can I pour you a drink?"

"Nah, I think I'm okay—"

"Uh-uh. I want one and I *can't*, so you're drinking for me tonight. Here ya go, it's a Burgundy."

I chuckle as she all but smashes a wine glass against my chest. Lukas turns off the burner and heads over, where I gladly take Luna off his hands and into my arms. I grin as I nuzzle my niece, letting her giggles melt away some of the tension throbbing in my head.

"Oh, hey, by the way," Lukas' face shadows with one of his "serious Lukas" faces, as Lizbet loves to call them teasingly.

"What's up?"

He nods his chin across my expansive downstairs area to the massive staircase that leads to the second floor. "I restocked your emergency kit. Luna's adrenaline pen has a five-month expiration date. So, you know. Since I was here anw[a]y…"

He shrugs in a way that's clearly meant to look casual, even though I can see the seriousness on his face.

I mean, I don't really blame him.

Lizbet was born with a heart condition that has since been fixed. It's *rarely* hereditary, and so far, not a single doctor has found anything that would suggest Luna has it as well.

But Lukas saw my sister almost die once. Suffice to say, "over-prepared" doesn't begin to describe his mindset when it comes to his daughter. The "emergency kit" is a worst-case scenario safety net against the *extremely* unlikely, almost non-existent chance that Luna has some sort of heart episode while they're at my place. It's basically a baby-sized defibrillator, an oxygen mask and tank, and an epi-pen loaded with adrenaline.

I smile as I lean in to kiss my niece's cheek. She's completely healthy. But fuck it, if it makes Lukas breathe easier having one of these emergency kits basically everywhere he'd ever take her, so be it.

"You ready for the big day, Gavan?"

I roll my eyes at my brother as Lizbet scoops Luna out of my arms. "Why does everyone keep acting like I'm heading off to my first day of fucking kindergarten?"

Konstantin grins as he clinks a wine glass to mine. "Come on, man. It's a bit of a big deal. I'm psyched for you."

"I think I'm the most psyched of anyone," Mara adds, sliding against Konstantin's side as he wraps a muscled, inked arm around her. "Having you all to myself and such."

"See, you say that now," my brother snickers. "But I don't think you're *actually* ready to have me around full-time. I give it a month before you're begging me to pick up a hobby or something."

"Diapers and midnight feeds. That can be your hobby!" Lizbet crows as she and our other sister crack up.

Konstantin groans, shooting me a pleading look. "You know what? Maybe let's rethink this whole temporary transition of—"

"I will cut you in your sleep," Mara mutters through a sarcastic grin. "*Cut. You.*"

I shrug at my brother. "Looks like the plan's locked in, man, sorry. Don't worry, I'll keep the chair warm for you."

"Yeah, just don't fucking fart in it, prick."

"No promises."

It is and at the same time it isn't a big deal. Currently, Konstantin and I rule the Reznikov empire as equals. But there's also the Bratva High Council—seven seats, one for each of the major Bratva families worldwide. It's sort of like a criminal United Nations. It doesn't mean any of us have an official truce or anything. But there's an agreed-upon pact of non-aggression, let's call it that.

War, at least between Bratva families, is, generally speaking, *terrible* for business.

But even though Konstantin and I rule our own empire together, the High Council rules allow for only *one* vote and one chair per family. Since he's the oldest, and the late Antin's son, my brother currently has that chair and vote. That's about to change.

At the Council meeting this week, Konstantin will officially announce his temporary departure from his role as co-head of the Reznikov family. He's taking a year off—or at least mostly off—to be with Mara as she gives birth to their twin daughters. Bratva paternity leave, basically.

And along with that departure from our own organization, he'll be passing on the vote and the chair at the Council table to me.

Like I said, it's not a big deal, but it also *is*. Because for the next year, the weight of the crown is *just* on me.

No pressure, right?

But for now, I shrug that off, intent on savoring this moment. I don't deserve any of this—this life, this family, these friends. And I will *not* let them down.

Even though trouble is already knocking. Hard.

Lizbet juggles a giggling Luna as she pouts at Mara. "You're *sure* I can't convince you to stay in New York? I mean, c'mon. I'll baby-proof the hell out of your place *for you* if that seals the deal."

Her—our—sister grins. "I know, I know. But I *love* my OBGYN in London. And I kind of have this fantasy of bringing the girls to Regent's Park, letting them see all the street musicians, and chalk artists, and—"

"Chimney sweeps in magical animated fantasy lands?"

Mara turns to arch a brow at Konstantin, as he grins at her.

"Mary Poppins. You're literally describing Mary Poppins."

"Oh, we've got jokes for the pregnant lady, have we?" She glares at him. "Keep it up, mister funnyman, and you'll go so long without a spoonful of sugar you'll be begging for it."

"Are we talking about the same 'sugar' that helps a certain pregnant lady with her backaches and pelvic floor stretches? *That* sugar? Cause, I feel like she's the one asking for that on a twice-daily basis—"

"*Kon!*"

Mara turns bright scarlet as Lizbet cracks up.

I make a face. "Dude, lest we forget, that's my *sister?*"

"Sorry I knocked up your sister, man."

I shake my head, chuckling as Mara jabs Konstantin in the ribs. "You are *so* gross."

"Yeah, but you love me anyway."

"Unfortunately, yes. Hopelessly."

I can't help but smile when he leans down to kiss her.

Yeah, I don't deserve any of this. But I'll fight to my dying breath to protect it.

AFTER A DELICIOUS DINNER, with the entertainment courtesy of our niece and her fantastic pitching arm when it comes to the food on her plate, Mara and Lizbet take Luna upstairs for a much-needed bath. Lukas, Konstantin and I clean up dinner and Luna's mess before moving out to the outdoor patio with a round of whiskey.

Konstantin clears his throat after clinking his glass to mine.

"I wanted to ask you about something."

"Shoot."

He makes a face, glancing at Lukas. "You're not gonna like it…"

Fuck.

I know what he's going to ask me about. And he's right, I fucking hate it.

"The Svetlana situation?"

He nods. "Look, I wouldn't pry, except—"

"Except for the fact that her fucking vendetta has the potential to fuck all of us over?"

Lukas and Konstantin glance at each other again unhappily before nodding.

"Pretty much," Lukas growls quietly. "Look, I know you fucking hate her—"

"It's all good," I shrug. "We've come to an agreement on assets, and she'll drop the rest of her goddamn crusade."

Svetlana, otherwise known as "the devil-cunt herself", is Vadim's sister.

My nemesis.

My hatred.

My pain.

She's the reason I'm the way I am. The one who broke me when I was thirteen.

Vadim never had much love for his sister. But he trusted her enough to send me to live with her here in New York when I was in my early teens and he was traveling a lot for Antin Reznikov. And he liked her well enough to leave her a sizable amount in his will when he passed.

A sizable amount that I promptly did everything I could to cheat her out of. Not because I needed the extra money. But because *fuck her*, that's why.

Because we're talking about a woman who *destroyed* me when I was barely more than a child. She didn't have an ounce of respect or love for the man I called father, and she took out her rage at her brother on me.

But since then, Svetlana has lawyered the fuck up. And she wants back what I took from her. The scary thing is, she's actually got a chance at getting it. She's managed to hire one of the most fuck-you estate law firms in the world—not sure how, since she's basically broke at this point—to come after me. And because they can prove malfeasance on my part, they're trying to leverage that to get not just what I denied her in the will, but a *lot* more of my assets.

Assets like Ironclad Capital. More specifically, the ninety percent controlling interest Ironclad Capital has in Koikov Bank in Russia.

Koikov Bank is where and how Konstantin and I, Lukas' family, the Volkov Bratva, and the Tsavakov organization clean their dirty money. If my aunt were to get her hands on Koikov, it would be catastrophic.

Luckily, after a few months of legal battles to the near-death, we've worked out a deal. Devil Cunt will forever back the fuck off from my company in exchange for the one thing of Vadim's she's always coveted. One little thing—which seems like a bad deal for her, but what do I care—and this whole fucking thing is over.

It's a simple deal, the easiest one I've ever made in my life. Except it became very much *less* simple and easy last night, when Eilish Kildare smashed that one thing that Svet wants so much into about forty pieces on my office floor.

The egg. Svetlana wants the fucking Imperial Shield Fabergé egg.

So, yeah…that's how *that's* going.

Konstantin's eyes go up. "Drop the crusade? Seriously?"

I nod. "Yeah."

"Just like that? She's dropping all of her bullshit? In exchange for what?"

"Just something of Vadim's she always wanted. It's all good."

It's not good at all. In fact, it's the very, very opposite of good. Because when she finds out the egg is off the table…so to speak…this shit is going to go nuclear.

I need to figure out how to stop that.

Konstantin shakes his head in admiration. "Well fuck, man. This is why I'm not at all worried about screwing off for a year. See? You've got this handled."

Yeah, totally handled.

Right.

Lukas shakes his head. "I've only met Svetlana once, but Jesus fucking Christ. I can't imagine what it was like growing up with her around, never mind *living* with her for all those years."

No, you can't.

Nobody can.

No one can, or *should*, imagine the horror show I went through for almost four years. Before I found out who I really was and suddenly was on my way to Oxford Hills Academy on Konstantin's dime for my last year of high school—a year I spent purging the nightmare of my teen years by throwing myself into normalcy. Or, at least, trying to.

I went to student parties. Met girls. Made friends. I played on the school's *rugby* team, for fuck's sake.

But there's not enough "normal" in the world to cover the scars and traumas of some pasts.

Konstantin rips me from my spiraling thoughts as he raises his glass.

"Well, fuck Svetlana. To Vadim. To a father I would gladly have killed for."

"Me too," Lukas growls quietly with a levity I understand. While he's now the adoptive son of the incredibly loving Viktor Komarov, head of the Kashenko Bratva that Lukas himself will one day lead, Lukas was an orphan on the streets of Montenegro before that.

Actually, if there's anyone who can understand the hell I went thought with Svetlana, there's a very good chance it's Lukas. The maze of scars on his arms—arms he usually keeps covered—are a testament to that.

The three of us clink our glasses together as I nod. "To you, Dad," I say quietly as we all drink. Then I shake off the melancholy and grin at the other two. "And to other fathers. To you, Lukas," I grin, nodding at him. "And to my brother, who's about to become a father twice over and *buried* in diapers."

Lukas snickers as he claps Konstantin on the back. "I can't even imagine. *One* is a fucking gauntlet. Two? Holy *shit*."

"Yeah, fuck genetics," Konstantin mutters. "*You* knock up a twin and you get one baby. I do it, and I get a two-for-one deal."

I laugh as I pat him on the shoulder. "Yeah, but you know what?"

He lifts a brow at me.

"You're going to be amazing at it. You know that, right?"

He grins wryly at me. "Not really. But if you say so, I'll believe you against my better judgement."

We all take another drink before Konstantin sighs. "Well, getting back to the business side of things, thanks for taking care of that Svetlana shit. Glad to hear we can all breathe a little easier concerning Koikov."

The smile stays on my face. Behind it, blackness swirls as I try to keep my gut from churning.

Even now, I'm not thinking about the evil bitch trying to destroy everything I have, after already destroying so much of me. I *should* be. I should be figuring out ways to circumvent the massive security Svetlana's got protecting her in that huge, tacky mansion she has across the river in New Jersey so I can kill her with my bare hands and be done with this fucking nightmare.

But I'm not. I'm not thinking of Svet at all.

I'm thinking of a certain blonde haired, green-eyed Irish princess.

The goody-two-shoes little ray of sunshine with an inky black secret.

A woman I should hate—for what her family did to mine. For Vadim. For the vengeance that she stole out from under me, and the shitstorm that's about to rain down on my head because she broke that fucking egg.

Well, fuck. Maybe I do hate her. But maybe it's possible to hate someone even when you desire them with every fucking fiber of your being.

Maybe it's possible to spend a year stalking someone, and learning their every secret, and destroying every possible possibility of a relationship they might have—telling yourself it's her punishment but knowing it's really because you cannot and *will* not stand to see another man touch her.

Therein lies my problem concerning Eilish Kildare.

I hate her.

And I want her.

And now that I *have* her, I'm honestly not sure which of those desires will win.

But tomorrow morning, we're going to find out together.

5

EILISH

I WASN'T A "SNEAK out at night" kind of teenager. I mean, it's not like I was a total square, or didn't have any friends. But sneaking out of the house to go hang out with friends was more Neve's thing, not mine.

So it's Neve I'm channeling when I come home after hiding in one of the academic buildings on campus for the rest of the afternoon.

After my meeting with the devil himself. The one where he smiled while telling me he basically owns me now. I shiver at the thought. But I still manage a smile at Barry and Jon—the two guards on front entrance duty tonight at the Kildare family home—before I unlock the door and quietly slip inside.

These days, the huge, rambling Upper East Side brownstone I grew up in is a bit quiet. It's just Castle and me left now, and while he'd never openly admit it, I know even he's just here because *I'm* still here.

Castle isn't officially my or Neve's bodyguard anymore. He's basically Cillian's number two for the whole organization. But, try telling *him* that he doesn't have to look after me anymore.

Neve lives with Ares now, obviously. And I guess even overly protective Castle has conceded that she's more than safe over there, with an army of Drakos guards watching over her, not to mention Ares himself. But me? I have a feeling I could move into Fort flipping Knox and Castle would be setting up a sleeping bag outside my room "just to be sure".

It's a good thing I love him like the big brother Neve and I never had.

So, yeah, Neve's gone. And Cillian's moved into his place with Una in Brooklyn full time. Which leaves just Castle and me here. And the reason I'm using Neve-inspired sneak tactics tonight is that Castle is the last person I want to face right now.

The man is a freaking bloodhound when it comes to picking up on things that might be bothering or worrying you. There's no way I could be in a room with him right now without him knowing in a nanosecond that something's amiss.

Well, "amiss" is putting it lightly.

"Defcon one" would be more apt.

Gavan knows.

A cold, cruel shiver curls its way up my spine as I tiptoe through the front entryway and toward the grand staircase that leads up to the sanctuary of my room. My memory flashes to the growled voice in my ear, to the raw, dark power emanating off his sculpted, imposing body.

To the baggie he dangled in front of my face containing a single spent bullet casing.

He fucking KNOWS.

He knows what I did that night. Which means he saw me. Fuck me, he might have even filmed—

I cringe as my weight sinks onto the foot I've just placed on the first step of the staircase, causing the old wood to whine like a screaming baby.

"Eilish?"

Shitshitshit.

I swallow back the groan, pulling a smile out of my ass just as Neve pokes her head around the corner from the direction of the kitchen. She beams when she sees me.

"Hey hey! I was wondering when you'd be home from class."

"Surprise?" I shrug with an awkward smile.

My sister smirks. "Were you just trying to sneak upstairs?"

"Not at all."

She snorts. "Yeah, sure. For future reference, steps one, six, eleven, and eighteen—but just the right side—squawk like motherfuckers. Not that you were trying to go unnoticed, but *if* you were—"

"I wasn't!"

She rolls her eyes with a grin and nods her chin at the kitchen. "Well, since you're *not* avoiding humans, come have a drink."

Crap. I can't say no without raising serious suspicion flags with her. So I shrug and start to follow her back, steeling myself as I hear the sound of Ares and Castle laughing it up about something in the kitchen.

"I didn't know you guys were coming over."

"Yeah, it was just a spur of the moment thing…" She frowns, pausing in the hallway before turning to me. "Okay, that's a lie. I wanted to talk to you."

Dread pools in my stomach.

"About?" I wheeze.

She sighs. "I…might have heard about the McKinnley thing."

My insides relax. "Oh, that."

"Yeah, that." She makes a face. "You know it's seriously just an idea, right? Like, there's no real reason for Cillian to push for that, and he's not—"

"It would be a smart play, linking the family with a potential future President."

Neve's gingery-auburn brows knit above her eyes that are as green as mine and Cillian's.

"Okay, business-nerd, turn off the strategy brain for once. I know you don't want to marry Brooks."

I shrug.

Neve doesn't know about what happened to me in my senior year of high school.

Nobody does.

The weird thing is, of all people I could talk to about it, Neve would be the most understanding. She went through something similar, when two assholes she went to school with

57

took a bunch of gross pictures of her when she was blacked out at a party—like, up her skirt and stuff. Really horrible, disgusting shit.

But I can't talk to her about it. Partly, that's because that's who I am. I internalize everything, and file it all away in color coded folders.

But the other thing is, I literally cannot talk about it to *anyone*. Because if he finds out…

"Hey, you okay?"

I blink, focusing again on Neve. "Oh, yeah, fine. Sorry, weird day."

She frowns. "Just say no. To the Brooks thing, I mean. He was a douchebag, Eilish. I never understood why you dated him."

Because I was young, inexperienced, and desperate for the cool kids to like me.

"I'll probably say no," I shrug. "It's just smart to at least consider the potential—"

"Okay, okay, I get it, Ms. Analytical. C'mon. Wine beckons."

Neve and Ares don't end up staying long. After they leave, Castle convinces me to hang out in the upstairs living room with him, where we watch *Say Anything* on the huge projector screen for the eleven millionth time.

"You know this is just how I'm guaranteeing your loyalty for life, right, big guy?"

Castle glances over at me from the couch he's sprawled across. His hand absently strokes the furry black and white ball curled up on his chest—Una's cat Bones, who's staying here while she and Cillian are in Ireland.

Castle arches a brow. "Huh?"

"If you ever try and cross me, I mean. You know that *I know* that you fucking *love* cheesy 80's teen comedies."

He snorts. "*Say Anything* is a classic. There's nothing embarrassing about that."

"Yeah? There's a *lot* embarrassing about the number of times you've watched *Dirty Dancing*."

"Whatever. Jennifer Grey was, and is, a babe. And Swayze was a god in that movie."

"*Nobody puts Castle in the corner,*" I grunt in a truly terrible Patrick Swayze impression.

Castle rolls his eyes and tosses a throw pillow at me as I crack up.

"Hey, before you try and sneak upstairs again..."

I swallow. "I wasn't trying to sn—"

"You do realize it's impossible to tiptoe past an Army Ranger, right?"

I make a face. "I just wasn't feeling social."

The smile fades from his face. "The Brooks thing, huh?"

I look back to the credits of *Say Anything* scrolling across the screen, my teeth clenching a little tighter as I nod.

"It's a no," Castle grunts. "I mean, it's an *easy* no. Like, fuck that little douchebag. I didn't like him when you guys went out, and I can't imagine he's done anything but become an even *more* insufferable piece of shit since then."

For a second, I try to imagine how Castle would react if he knew the depths of my hatred for Brooks, and the reasons for it.

Yikes.

I shrug, the "good, loyal Eilish" mask slipping easily back into place, like a bad habit I can't break.

"I don't know. It could be hugely beneficial to us. To the family, I mean."

When he doesn't say anything, I glance over to see a dark look etched across Castle's face.

"What is it?"

He sighs. "I just…" he shakes his head. "I just feel like I'm letting you down. Like I've *already* let you down. You and Neve both. I mean I was supposed to protect you guys. And first she goes off and gets herself arrange-married to our enemy, and now you're seriously considering marrying some snotty little douchebag for the political clout it would give our family."

I grin. "I thought you liked Ares now."

"Oh, I do. Obviously."

"Is it the fact that he saved Neve's life, or that he hooks you up with Dimitra Drakos' baklava on a weekly basis? Be honest."

Castle snorts and rolls his eyes before frowning. "Seriously, this Brooks situation—"

"You're not my protector anymore, Castle," I say quietly.

He glances back to me. "I'll always be your protector, Blondie."

I grin.

"Hey, we don't have to talk about it if you don't want to. But..." he frowns. "Why *did* you and Brooks split up? I mean, don't get me wrong, I hated the little shit. But you two seemed pretty serious for a month or—"

"It just didn't work out," I say quickly. I don't know if Castle buys it or not, but he lets it go with a nod.

"All right," I yawn as I stand. "I'm going up to bed. Night, love ya."

"Love ya too, kid."

As much as I wanted to disappear and avoid people when I first got home, it was a nice reprieve from my thoughts to hang with Neve and Ares, and then have movie time with Castle.

But the minute I'm upstairs in my room, alone, the darkness and the dread swirls back in from every side. Like it's been just lurking there, waiting to consume me again.

He knows what I did.

I shudder as I try to shower away the day. Dread fills my heart as I slip into pajamas and crawl into bed.

Gavan *knows*.

He knows that a year and a half ago, Neve's and my father, Declan, was going to a sit-down with Vasilis Drakos, Ares' uncle. Things were tense between the Kildare and Drakos families, and even though they were meeting to discuss a possible truce, I knew my father would still bring his gun.

His gun that I *loaded with blanks* an hour before he went to that meeting.

When I think back on it, it's almost surreal how calm I was. I mean, yes, I was livid, and in so much pain after I'd discovered the truth about our mother, and what that bastard did to her. But when I was in his study—in this very house, actually—and silently loading his gun with bullets that wouldn't protect him if things went south, I was totally calm.

I was *praying* for things to go south, to be honest.

I didn't learn until later that neither Vasilis Drakos nor my father started the shooting that got them both killed that night. But from the spent rounds I picked up after the carnage was over, I knew my prayers had been answered.

My dad did try to defend himself. The blanks I loaded his gun with made sure he couldn't.

I might not have pulled the trigger myself, or fired the bullets that ended his life. But I *did* kill my own father that night.

I'm a murderer.

And now, the devil himself knows it.

In the darkness of my room, my eyes squeeze shut miserably. We *finally* have peace. After all the drama between our family and the Drakoses. After all the ghosts of the past. After all the enemies that have tried to hurt us time and time again, it feels like we've *finally* hit a place where there's not a threat of violence always lurking around the next corner.

And now I've gone and welcomed that violence back into our lives by crossing Gavan.

I swallow as I replay our meeting: the vicious, lethal and yet at the same time sinfully smoldering look in his gray eyes. The malevolence and raw sexuality oozing from his very pores.

A shiver ripples through my core.

Whatever he wants, I can do it. I can face Gavan Tsarenko.

I won't let my family down.

6

EILISH

There's no blindfold involved the second time I step off the elevators into the offices of Ironclad Capital. This time, I can truly stare in awe at the sheer opulence of the place.

Holy crap.

The main offices are decorated in a similar fashion to Gavan's personal one, all slate gray and dark wood tones. The far wall—the height of two floors—is all glass, with a view similar to the one from Gavan's office. It smells like it did the other night: clean, cool, and *rich*.

Even though it's only seven-fifty in the morning, the place is already teeming with activity. In the main area, sitting at small clusters of desks boasting top-of-the-line curved, widescreen monitors, financial analysts and traders stare intently at margin lines and stock tickers as they bark buy and sell orders into phones.

A pretty brunette looks up from the very on-brand slate and dark wood reception desk and gives me a tight, professional smile. "Yes?"

"Hi, I'm…" I swallow. "I'm here to see Gavan."

Her brow furrows a touch.

"Mr. Tsarenko, I mean. He's expecting me."

She eyes me cooly. "And you are…?"

"Uh, Eilish. Kildare."

She glances at something on her screen and purses her lips. "Of course." She stands, smoothing down a chic dress as she steps out from behind her desk. "If you'd like to follow me."

As we walk across to the sweeping staircase that I remember Britney leading me up, the receptionist glances back at me.

"I love your dress, by the way."

I already can tell "cold bitch" is clearly her default setting, and knowing Gavan, it's probably the reason he picked her to be the unfriendly but attractive face people first see when they walk into his company offices. I can also tell that she clearly *enjoys* having that frosty attitude, and that mentioning my dress isn't just her "being nice".

"Dior?"

I nod, glancing down at the sleeveless peachy-pink belted mid-length dress. I might have plenty of flaws and faults—okay, I *do* have plenty of flaws and faults—but one thing I've got down to an art form is dressing stylishly for a business meeting. "Yeah. Is it a bit much?"

She eyes me up and down. "Oh my God, *no*. I'm just jealous. It's gorgeous."

I smile. "Thank you."

At the top of the staircase, a balcony wraps around the perimeter of the main floor below. She leads me to an imposing dark wood door, and I realize with a nervous clench of my stomach that we're here already.

Gavan's office.

The scene of the crime. *My crime.*

Or of one of them, at least.

"I'm Rachel, by the way."

"Eilish, hi."

She smiles a much less frosty smile than she first did downstairs before turning and knocking lightly on the door.

"Send her in."

After she leaves with a nod I turn back to the door and, taking a shaky breath, open it to step inside.

Instantly, and I mean *instantly*, I'm nailed to the spot when those piercing, gunmetal gray eyes stab into me from across the room. I swallow, my pulse hammering in my ears and my mouth going dry as I stare across the office at him.

Gavan's sitting at his desk, leaning back in his chair, both causally and stiffly at the same time, if that's possible. He's wearing another impeccable three-piece suit—this one a dark navy blue with a crisp white dress shirt with French cuffs. His longish hair is shoved back from his face—somehow cavalier and yet perfectly styled.

The dark scruff on his razor-sharp jaw ripples as he grinds his teeth and eviscerates me with those eyes.

Whatever this is, whatever he wants, I can do this.

"Uh, hi," I mumble, feeling lightheaded and awkward as I shut the door behind me. Shit. I should have had a bigger breakfast. Or, you know, *slept* a little last night.

Or not broken in here and smashed the hundred-million-dollar gift from his dead father in the first place, you absolute moron.

Gavan doesn't say a word. He just raises a hand, and I *hate* that something disturbing in me twists heatedly when he crooks two fingers, beckoning me to him in the same way he did before. I obey him, clicking across the room in my heels until I'm standing in front of his desk.

"I...I just wanted to say again how sorry I am for—"

"Coffee."

I stumble over my words, frowning at him. "Pardon me?"

"*Coffee*," he repeats, a glint in his eyes and a note of annoyance in his voice. He nods his chin across the room. Next to an elegant brass and glass bar cart, there's an alcove built into the wall that houses a sink and a super fancy and complicated-looking espresso machine, with what appears to be a polished metal mini-fridge beneath it.

"Specifically, a cappuccino. Two-percent milk, no sugar, with a sprinkle of cinnamon on top."

I blink, staring at him.

"I—I'm not sure I under—"

"I was under the impression that you spoke English."

My lips thin. "Obviously, I do."

"Well then, *obviously*, lose the fucking attitude."

I chew on my lip as my fingers twist together in front of me.

"Do I need to repeat myself?"

"I think I'm just confused as to what it is I'm doing here."

"Currently?" he growls. "Currently you're *not* getting me that fucking cappuccino. But I think there's an easy solution to that dilemma. Can you guess what it might be?" There's pure venom in his tone, and malice in his eyes.

I clear my throat. "Um, making you a cappuccino?"

"Ahh. I knew there was a reason Columbia University let you in."

My eyes drop. "Look, again, I am *so* very sorry about what happened—"

"Is continuing to ignore my request humorous to you?" The pure ice in his voice chills me to the bone and my eyes snap back to his. "Like, is this a *bit* of some kind? Part of a weak standup comedy routine?"

I shake my head. "No," I mumble.

"Well?"

Okay, he's pissed. He's more than pissed, but I guess I deserve that. "Is...that what I'm here to do?"

Gavan snorts and his eyes rake me up and down. "You're here to do whatever I goddamn tell you to do. Whenever I tell you to do it. Without question."

He suddenly stands, towering over me. He steps out from behind the desk, moving slowly but deliberately, like a jaguar stalking prey he's already mauled half to death.

"And to be clear, Eilish," he growls, brushing my shoulder as he circles me. "I mean *anything* I tell you to do."

I gasp sharply as he moves my ponytail away from my neck and leans down. His hot breath teases over my skin as my own catches.

"*Anything,*" he rasps darkly and sensually.

Raw energy, fear, and adrenaline explode in my core.

"You…" I shake my head, still looking forward. "You don't *own* me—"

"Oh, but that's where you're wrong. I *do*, Eilish," Gavan growls as he prowls around me in lazy circles, moving in for the kill. "If I tell you to get me that goddamn cappuccino, you *get it*. If I tell you to do it in the next thirty fucking seconds, you *will*."

He pauses behind me, and my breath hitches as I feel his lips millimeters from my ear.

"And if I tell you to get that goddamn cappuccino in the next thirty seconds wearing nothing but your bra and panties…"

My eyes stare, and heat explodes in my face.

"I will *not* be—"

"I wasn't asking the first time, and I certainly won't be the second."

The room goes still, humming and crackling with a dark malevolence. My pulse pounds in my ears and the hollow of my throat as Gavan slowly finishes circling me, until he's standing right over me again, glaring down into my eyes.

"Now, are you going to be a good girl and get me that coffee?"

It's like the flick of a lighter sparking in the darkness when he says it. A lick of flame igniting where it shouldn't.

Are you going to be a good girl?

My jaw tightens. Gavan's flinty eyes gleam as his lips curl, spotting the defiance in my silence.

"The clock is ticking," he growls. "Tick-fucking-tock, Eilish. Lest you forget, one hundred and twenty-four million, five hundred thousand dollars is more than enough money to go to war over."

I swallow. "So that extra five hundred thousand is back on the ticket?"

He smiles coldly. "My charity has run dry. War looms. Your family finding out *exactly* the murderous type of girl that you are also looms—"

"Fuck you—"

I gasp, choking as his arm shoots out and his thick, tattooed fingers grip my jaw tightly, tilting my head up to his gaze.

"Speak to me like that again, *solnishka*, and I'll find another use for that mouth."

Sweet fucking Jesus.

Just like a moment ago when he said "good girl", a spark inside of me flickers and licks at the darkness.

"Ten. Nine. Eight—"

"Okay!" I blurt. "Okay! I'll get you your freaking cappuccino, okay?!"

Gavan smiles ruthlessly, saying nothing as he lets his veined hand drop from my jaw. He turns and casually strolls over to the dark leather tufted couch by the windows and sinks into it before crossing his legs, his arms draped across the back casually. He lifts a brow as I stand there, my face burning.

"I'm waiting."

A lump lodges in my throat as I slowly turn away from him. I wet my lips, shaking as I reach around to find the zipper at the back of the dress. I can feel the fabric peel away from my skin, from my nape down to the middle of my back, exposing the clasp of my bra.

Shivering, I pull my arms free and push the dress down over my chest, still facing away from him, but feeling his smoldering gaze tracing over my bare skin.

I twist my hips as I slide the dress further down, pausing for a moment.

"Seven. Six—"

"I'm doing it, okay?" I hiss quietly, my face throbbing with shame and something else. I slip the dress the rest of the way down, blushing furiously when I have to bend at the waist, feeling his eyes on my ass as I start to remove my heels.

"Leave them on."

My core clenches as I nod quietly, slipping the dress over the shoes. I stand, awkwardly holding the dress I was so pleased with myself for choosing for today's meeting. I fold it in half and numbly place it on his immaculate desk.

I am now standing—for the first time ever, I might add—in front of a man in nothing but my underwear.

"Two percent milk. No sugar. Dusting of cinnamon."

I nod and start to walk over to the espresso machine.

"I prefer verbal answers, Eilish."

I grit my teeth, my jaw tensing. "Okay."

"Not 'okay'. Yes."

"Excuse me?" I mutter, turning to glare at him over my shoulder.

Gavan smiles smugly at me. "When I ask you for something, you will say *yes*, not *okay*. Let's try that again. I'll have my cappuccino now."

My lips purse. "Yes."

"Yes what."

You're fucking kidding me.

"I'm not joking," he growls quietly, reading my mind. "Say it correctly. I'll have my cappuccino now."

My eyes turn to green slits. "Yes, *Sir*."

"Good girl."

My cheeks flame as I turn, acutely aware of the way the heels make my hips sway—in my fucking *underwear*—as I walk to the machine. Luckily, I'm not a total cliche mafia princess who's never worked a day in her life. I had a job at a café in undergrad when I was at NYU, and mercifully it all comes back to me in an instant.

I grind the espresso beans and tamp them down in the little metal filter before securing it into the elegant, Italian machine. While the shot dribbles out, I steam the milk—two percent, as requested—until it's topped with a nice foamy froth before adding it to the espresso when it's done. No sugar, and I end with a dusting of cinnamon. I learned how to make a heart in the foam at the café, but I do *not* do that this time.

When I turn back to him, my face heats when I realize he's been staring at me, basically naked, the whole time. Again, he raises his hand to crook two fingers at me. And again, it has a physical effect on me I *truly* wish it didn't, but it does.

My jaw is tight as I march back over to the couch and hand Gavan the cappuccino without a word.

"And my tablet. On my desk. *If* you would be so kind."

I glare at him. Gavan just smiles a tight smile right back at me. I turn again, all too aware of his eyes still on my ass as I walk over to his desk and grab the tablet. When I hand it to him, he just looks at me cooly with those flinty eyes and sips his coffee.

The second tick by. I squirm under his gaze as it traces down my body, zeroing in on my sex as my legs shift. Then they slowly drag to my pink scars—the ones from the explosion—on my thigh and my shoulder. I squirm again, the muscles under my skin twisting as if to hide these imperfections from him.

But there's no escaping that steely gaze. His eyes pierce into my scars, narrowing for a moment as if angry before dragging back up to my face.

"Well, what am I doing now?"

He lifts a brow, saying nothing but everything, and smiles that thin smile. "Ask the right way."

"You're joking."

Gavan's lips curl. "I'm not."

"What am I doing now, *Sir*," I mutter.

"That'll be all for today."

73

I blink.

"Excuse me?"

"I don't believe I mis-spoke, and we've established that you're fluent in English."

Seriously? I came all the way here at eight in the morning to make him a fucking coffee in my goddamn underwear?

"That's it?"

"You're welcome to sit on the edge of my desk with your legs spread so that I can fuck you while I go through my morning notes if you'd prefer."

Holy. Fucking. GOD.

My face explodes with heat, and my eyes go wide.

Gavan just smiles.

"If not, then that will be *all*, Eilish."

He picks up his tablet, thumbing it on and sipping his coffee, pointedly ignoring me.

Okay...?

Turning, I march over to the desk, my face throbbing as I yank my dress back on. Gavan still says nothing as I walk to the door, furiously avoiding looking at the now-empty glass case that once contained a hundred-and-twenty-four-million-dollar Fabergé egg.

"To clear up any confusion, Eilish..."

I pause, still facing the door, when he speaks.

"When I say that will be all, I mean that will be all for *today*. We aren't done by a fucking mile, in case you were feeling hopeful that making me an average at best cappuccino was anywhere close to paying back what you destroyed."

My brows knit as I turn to glance at him. "I didn't think—"

"Monday. Same time."

"I have class."

"I really don't give a fuck. Monday, eight o'clock."

Tyrant.

I turn to the door again.

"And Eilish?"

I pause again, my hand on the knob.

"Wear some nicer fucking panties next time."

My lips curl into a snarl. "*Asshole.*"

I've barely started to twist the doorknob when I hear and feel the thunder of his approach. I whirl, gasping, and my face goes chalk-white when he surges right into me. I choke and sputter as he grabs me hard by the throat and the hip, slamming me against the door. His huge, powerful frame pins me to it, sending alarm bells and forbidden heat exploding through my core.

"I did mention what would happen if you spoke to me like that again."

My eyes bulge. "I—"

One second, I've gone twenty-one years without being kissed by a man like Gavan. The next second, it's a sensation I could never forget in a million lifetimes as his lips slam into mine.

It's a kiss like the invasion of Normandy was a trip to the beach. A kiss like the Sistine Chapel has paint on the ceiling. It's not even really a kiss.

It's a declaration of war.

It's subjugation.

Annihilation.

And yet, at the same time, the single hottest moment of my life.

He kisses me viciously, and when his teeth sink into my bottom lip so hard that a coppery taste spills across both of our tongues, I cry out into his mouth. It's only then that he draws back, leaving me stunned, swimming, and breathless, the taste of blood on my lips.

"Consider that a warning shot," he growls quietly. "Monday. Same time."

Everything's a blur as I turn, dazed and stunned, and open the door. When it shuts behind me, I have to actually lean against it for a moment, lest I have a heart attack while I'm trying to walk down the stairs.

When I've collected myself, I make a beeline down the stairs, across the main area, and past the receptionist desk toward the elevators.

"Nice meeting you, Eilish."

I jolt, whirling to see Rachel smiling at me from behind her desk.

"Uh, yeah, same," I stammer, frowning. "You too. See you Monday."

She nods, but then her brow furrows. "Oh, and hon?" She frowns, touching the corner of her own mouth delicately with a knowing smile. "Yeah... The liquid gloss always drips for me, too."

It takes a moment before it clicks.

Blood.

There's a drop of *blood* at the corner of my mouth.

I reach up and hastily thumb it away.

"See you Monday!"

I'm not going to survive this.

How the *fuck* am I going to survive this?

And why the hell am I so fucking wet right now...

7

GAVAN

I GROAN as my cock pulses like velvet steel in my hand. The release draws a snarl from my lips as ropes of hot, white cum spray against the tiled wall of the shower before dripping heavily to the floor. I lean an arm against the tile and rest my forehead on it. My chest heaves as I watch the last of my fantasy swirl down the drain.

It's the fourth time I've done this since Eilish walked out of my office, after that kiss.

That was eleven fucking hours ago.

Since then, since that first taste of her swollen, full, defiant lips, I've pictured her in a dozen different fantasies. Stretched out on my desk, holding her knees up against her magnificent tits as I drive my cock into her. Bent over, whining for more as I pump gallons of hot cum up her ass.

On her knees in my shower, swallowing every drop from my swollen cock head like a good little girl.

I knew bringing her further into my world would be problematic. I knew it would throw me, given the confusing swirl of hatred and lust I have for her. But I'm not sure I was adequately prepared for the hurricane of destruction she's already bringing into my head and my thoughts.

As I shower off, my dick still throbbing hard and needy against my thigh, unsatisfied, my mind replays the morning. I *like* that under that gorgeous dress, she was wearing plain, boring underwear—a very utilitarian, probably-laundry-day blue bra with mismatched off-white full-coverage panties with little red roses on them.

Clearly, she wasn't expecting to undress for me.

In that case, she'll never expect what I have in store for her next.

I towel off after the shower before heading into my walk-in closet to dress for the hugely important High Council meeting I'm on my way to. Even so, my mind is not on the meeting, and what it means for my immediate future. I'm still just thinking about Eilish, and earlier today.

The defiance in her green eyes, that still didn't mask the dark need in them. She looked at me with pure venom, but also like she hated the fact that she craved that control. Craved it even more than she wanted to hate it.

She *does* crave that control. I know she does. Because I know everything about Eilish. Every dark secret. Every fantasy. Every twisted need.

I've spent a year and a half learning more about Eilish than she knows about herself. Noting it. Categorizing it. *Weaponizing* it.

I'm going to use it to bring her to her *knees*.

"You ready for this, Boss-man?"

I roll my eyes at Korol, and his favorite dumb-ass nickname for me.

"Look, if you're insisting on it, how about just 'boss'?"

He grins. "I think Boss-man has some swagger to it."

"It doesn't if you've ever seen *Cool Hand Luke*."

"What hand what now?"

"Jesus, Korol. I'm not sure I can have a second in command who's so abysmally uncultured."

"Hey, I've got plenty of culture right here," he smirks, cupping his crotch.

"Sometimes I'm amazed you even put pants on in the morning, you fuckin' caveman."

He chuckles. "Well, if you'd actually come *out* with me some night, you'd see why pants aren't exactly a priority at my present stage in life. I mean seriously, the girls in this city? I should be wearing a kilt for easier access. They're fucking *aggressive* in this town, man. A kilt would save on broken zippers and lost belts, I swear to God."

I roll my eyes again at my new top *avtoritet*, on his way to being my official number two. Hopefully, he works out. I lost my former top captain and second-in-command about two years ago when we were at war with the Albanians. Volodymyr was also a good friend of mine, so that one really burned.

After that, I promoted Leo Stavrin to the position, even though he'd once worked for Konstantin's shithead of a father, Antin. Leo had the experience I needed, though.

But then it transpired that Leo *also* had aspirations of murdering me in my sleep, burning my empire to the ground, and pawing through the ashes. My only regret about the fact that he's dead now is that I didn't get to do it myself, very slowly.

Korol might be young and somewhat inexperienced with leadership. But he's loyal, fiercely so. Experience is learned, and leadership can be taught. But loyalty is priceless, and that's either in you or not in you.

I also grew up with Korol. His father was a good friend of Vadim's, and before it was revealed that I was actually the crown prince, Korol and I used to joke about running things ourselves one day.

Well, now, I'm here. And I'm bringing him with me. I could, and do, give him a hard time about his current fondness for going out just about every single night and the endless string of women he's been taking home. But I also can't really blame him. His new position as my top *avtoritet* comes with some *major* swagger, not to mention a seven-figure salary plus perks.

He's young, rich, and handsome, in *New York City*. Of course he's out there going fucking nuts.

I chuckle. "Just do us both a favor and try not to *catch* anything. I have no use for a second-in-command whose dick is rotting off from a new form of syphilis."

"I'll do my best."

"Not very encouraging."

He laughs as I mess up his hair, just as the guards at the front of the office building nod and let us in. Immediately, I grin at some familiar faces.

"Well well well," Ilya Volkov ducks his chin at me before turning to smirk at Konstantin, who he's been talking to. "The king is dead," he says before glancing back at me. "Long live the king."

"Who's dead?"

Viktor Komarov, Lukas' father, smiles widely as he walks over and claps me firmly on the shoulder.

"Konstantin," Ilya shrugs. "Or at least his sex life is."

My brother glares at him. "My sex life is just fine, motherfucker."

Viktor chuckles. "Yeah, well, talk to us again when you're knee-deep in diapers and spilled breastmilk, and neither you or your wife has showered or slept more than an hour at a time in over a month, Romeo."

Konstantin scowls. Ilya laughs as he pats his cheek. "Cheer up. You'll get back in the saddle. In, like, a year."

My brother's face falls. "A *year*?"

"Sorry, my man. Voice of experience," Ilya smirks. He and his wife Tenley have a son, Asher, who's about three weeks older than my niece Luna. "And then just as sex gets back on the menu, she'll start back at work pulling crazy hours to catch up, and it all goes right out the window again."

I grin. "Voice of experience again?"

His face sours. "Sadly, yes."

Tenley took about nine months off work when Asher was born. But I know she's recently back at the prestigious Blomkvist and Shier law firm here in New York where she's a partner.

"It gets better," Viktor smirks at the two of them. "Trust me." In addition to adopting Lukas, Viktor and his wife Fiona have a nine-year-old son, Sasha, who already looks like he's going to be as tall and broad-shouldered as his dad.

"What's going on over here?"

Viktor turns to grin as Yuri Volkov, Ilya's uncle, walks over. Yuri's based out of Chicago alongside Viktor, though he's been visiting New York a lot recently—in fact, he owns the building we're meeting in tonight. Again, the Council isn't a treaty or partnership between all seven families. But the Volkovs and the Komarovs have been close for a long time. Their unofficial partnership now includes the Reznikov empire as well, much to the chagrin of other members of the Council at times.

"The young'uns are complaining about not getting laid while their wives are going through pregnancy, childbirth, and everything that comes after."

Yuri, himself now the father of two-year-old Adrik with his wife River, roars with laughter.

Ilya frowns. "That is *not* what—"

"You want some advice, Konstantin?" Yuri grins at my brother who is starting to look more than a little forlorn. "Jerk off like a grownup and don't even think about trying to pressure Mara into shit until *she* comes to *you*. Pregnancy and birth is a goddamn mind-fuck for a woman. She'll tell you when she's—"

"Hey, Yuri?" There's a sharp glint in Konstantin's eyes as they narrow at the older Bratva king. "I'm taking a year off to treat my wife like the queen she is. Do me a favor and don't ever fucking presume shit about her and me again, yeah?"

We're all friendly here. And his tone is light enough. But Mara is Konstantin's pressure point, and I know everyone here fully understands that.

Yuri grins as he claps Konstantin on the shoulder. "Atta boy." Then he clears his throat.

"Well, I think the other members are already all upstairs. Shall we?" He turns to arch a brow at me. "You ready for the full weight?"

"Please. He was born ready," my brother smirks, punching me in the arm.

"Okay then," Yuri nods. "Let's do this."

"I HEREBY WILLINGLY RELINQUISH MY vote and my chair, passing both in complete confidence to my brother and co-king, Gavan, who will be voting in my place, with my blessing."

In the softly-lit conference room, there are nods from all those seated around the table.

"Are there any objections?"

Yuri, the Council chairman, drags his gaze around the room before he turns back to Konstantin and me.

"We respect and approve of this exchange. Gavan Tsarenko will henceforth be the voting voice and High Council chair for the Reznikov family."

Konstantin turns to me as we both stand, a grin on his face as he clasps my hand in his.

"You've fucking got this, brother," he murmurs as he gives me a big bear hug. "You were born for it."

He pulls away, turning to glance around the rest of the table. "Thank you, everyone. And now, if you'll all excuse me, I have a plane to catch."

Mara already flew back to London this morning, and now Konstantin will be joining her as he kicks off his year off from all things Bratva-related. With a final nod to the table, and one last firm shake of my hand, he turns and walks out of the room.

Yuri nods. "Okay, item one on our list is concluded. Next, I believe Abram wanted to—"

"Yeah, if we're done with the theatrics, can we please get down to actual business?"

My jaw ticks as my eyes swivel across the table to Abram Diduch. Until just a couple of years ago, Abram's uncle, Olek Domitrovich, had been the head of the Diduch Bratva family for close to forty years. Olek was calm, honorable, and magnanimous—in fact, he was a firm ally of Lizbet's when she was trying to wrest control of her inheritance after the death of her piece of shit father Semyon Belsky, the man whose rape of my mother resulted in me.

Olek, however, stepped down three years ago for health reasons, and passed less than six months later. Unfortunately, his nephew seems to be cut from the exact opposite cloth.

Abram is only a year or so older than me. He's a hothead, power-hungry, impulsive, and quite vocal about his dislike that the High Council even exists. Ironically, it's because of temperaments like his that the Council was formed in the first place.

Next to me, Viktor and Lukas scowl at the same time—and, amusingly, in the same *way*, despite not being biologically related.

"How about we keep this civil, Abram," Ilya snarls from behind Yuri.

Abram looks like he's about to do anything but when Yuri holds up a hand.

"Simmer down, both of you. Yes, Abram, we can now address the issue you wished to bring up at this meeting. Unless anyone else has anything else to add concerning the change in Reznikov leadership?"

Viktor and Yuri are both silent. Going around the circle, Marko Kalishnik, the head of the Kalishnik Bratva, is next, and he shakes his head no.

"*Nyet.* Welcome to the table, Gavan." Anastasia Javanović, the head of the Javanović family, which is a relatively new addition to the Bratva High Council, nods cooly at me.

Anastasia's just a few years older than me. She's also the first female head of a High Council family since its inception fifty years ago. The Javanović family is also on decently good terms with the Kashenko, Volkov, and my own organization. Which is good, because Anastasia is a person I would *not* wish to be enemies with.

I mean the woman killed her own father—who was a shit-head on par with Semyon Belsky—by disemboweling him and *hanging him by his own fucking guts* from the walls of the actual Tower of fucking London.

I've got family issues myself, but *Christ*.

Next to her, Abram drums his fingers on the table impatiently, glancing to his left at the last of the family heads around the table. Demyan Ozerov is another newly-elected High Council member—a gruff, scowly former soldier who now leads the Ozerov family. He also happens to be Abram's cousin.

"Could we just stop wasting time and proceed with my cousin's concerns, please."

Yuri nods. "Very well. Abram, the floor is yours."

The young king takes a second to level a hard, steely glare around the table before he clears his throat.

"We've been putting this off for much too long." His eyes narrow. "We need to address the Drazen situation."

A dark cloud instantly forms over the whole table. The "Drazen situation" refers to Drazen Krylov, a Serbian-Russian warlord of sorts who now fancies himself a rising Bratva power. I've never met him—in fact, nobody here has. No one even knows what the guy looks like. But his reputation as a bloodthirsty psychopath is more than well known.

Normally, I and everyone here would be supremely happy to leave Drazen the fuck alone. Except, he's been making that an impossibility lately. In the last few months, there've been attacks made on foreign assets belonging to just about every family at this table.

One of Yuri's warehouses in Moscow was burned to the ground. A Javanović freighter ship was blown up in port in Greece. Hell, there was even a weapons shipment belonging to *my* organization worth somewhere north of a hundred million dollars that was suddenly seized by Interpol in Austria, despite us having paid off all the appropriate bureaucrats.

So yes, someone is definitely stirring shit up. Drazen Krylov hasn't made any official statement claiming responsibility. But he *has* made it more than a little well known that he would like to be voted onto the High Council.

"This is only a 'situation,'" Viktor grunts, "because you're making it one, Abram. We don't actually know that Drazen has anything to do with the attacks. We don't even know if they're all related."

"Of course we do!"

Yuri shakes his head. "We *don't*. Abram, I don't mean this as an insult, but you'll learn with time that there will *always* be fires starting on the edges of your empire. Where your power is weakest, that's where your enemies will always—"

"There is no *weakness* in my fucking empire, Yuri," Abram snaps. "And I am quite insulted by the insinuation."

"Take it easy, Abram," I growl. "No one's trying to insult you."

"He wants onto this table," Abram continues insistently. "It's the one thing he's reached out to this Council about."

He's not wrong. Again, no one's met Drazen, or even knows anything about him beyond his reputation. No one's ever seen him: he's notoriously secretive about his identity, and refuses to have his picture taken, I suppose for security reasons. But six months ago, he sent a simple message to this Council stating his desire to be voted onto the table.

It was a ten-word message: "Vote me to the table. Or live with the ashes."

Yeah, "diplomacy" doesn't seem to be his strong suit.

"What we need to do is make a preemptive strike," Abram barks loudly, rapping his knuckles on the tabletop. "Find this rabid dog, and put him down."

Yuri's brow furrows. "That isn't how we do things, Abram. I share your concerns. We all do. But this Council is not about going out there and preemptively starting wars. It's about keeping the peace and the status quo that benefits all of us, yourself as much as I—"

"The *point of this council,*" Abram hisses, "seems to be more about acting like soft, privileged businessmen, not the warrior kings you all once were. Or at least, the kings your *fathers* were."

"Times have changed," Viktor says quietly.

"No, it's *you* who have changed!" Abram shouts. "I say we put this to a vote."

I frown, perplexed. "Put *what* to a vote? Openly declaring war on a psycho warlord who might or might not have started some fires? Hell no. Count Reznikov out."

"Count Kashenko out too," Viktor mutters.

Yuri holds up a hand. "Hang on, we're not officially voting on anything yet—"

"Then let's vote on *this,*" Abram snarls. "I have a motion to bring before the table." His jaw tightens as his eyes dart to the side, glancing first at his cousin Demyan, then to Anastasia. He takes a slow breath as his lips curl. "I would like invoke *Okhrana Soveta.*"

What? My brow furrows, and when I glance at Korol, he looks equally confused. So do Lukas and Viktor next to me. Yuri's face, however, darkens.

"That's…a big decision to make, Abram," he says out of the side of his mouth. He clears his throat, his voice raising to address the full table. "For those who aren't aware, *Okhrana Soveta* is an archaic provision within the Bratva High Council bylaws, granting a founding table family total authority over *every* family at the table in the event of an existential threat on all." His eyes go around the table. "It can only be invoked by a founding family, so currently only the Diduch or the Kalishnik family," he growls, turning to glance at Marko. "It does require a majority vote to pass."

Yuri glances at Viktor and I before turning to Abram. "I'm only the chairman of this table. I can't stop you from invoking this, but I need to caution everyone here that this is an *extreme* measure. Abram, I'm assuming your vote is for the Diduch family and yourself to assume full control?"

"It is," Abram says tersely.

"Just to be clear," Yuri growls. "This means that if passed, every family at the table would be beholden by High Council law to give Abram full control of their security forces, without question. I hope everyone is aware of the full implications of that."

"You're being overly diplomatic, Yuri," Viktor hisses through his teeth, glaring at Abram. "It means he gets to play dictator with *our* men."

"Yes," Abram sneers back. "To stop Drazen from—"

"To do *whatever you want*, once you're in control," Viktor fires back. "I'm almost twice your age, Abram. Don't think for a second that I'm unaware of the concept of leveraging fear for power."

Abram shrugs as he turns to Yuri. "Start the vote."

Yuri's mouth tightens, but he nods. "So be it. I vote no."

"*No*," Viktor mutters.

I shake my head. "Until we have even a shred of evidence that Drazen is behind any of these attacks, this is impulsive at best. It's a no from Reznikov."

Abram glares at me but then turns to smirk at Demyan, who smiles.

"The Ozerov family votes yes to my cousin's generous offer to save this Council."

"*Well there's a shocker*," Lukas mutters next to me. "*Sanctimonious little boot licker.*"

"Obviously, I vote yes as well," Abram tosses out.

My gaze swivels to Anastasia. Well, this should be a fast vote. It's currently three no to two yes. Marko Kalishnik is old school. And while he and Olek were friends, it's pretty clear that friendship hasn't extended to the nephew with the Napoleon complex. And Anastasia? I bite back a grin. She's no idiot, and Abram's attempt at making himself emperor of this table is so nakedly obvious—

"Javanović votes yes to the measure."

You can almost hear the record scratch. I stare at Anastasia, but she carefully avoids all eye contact.

"These are dangerous times, and they require a firm response. My vote is yes."

What the fuck?

It's clear Yuri, Ilya, Viktor, and Lukas are all as confused as I am as the attention shifts to Marko—who is suddenly the tiebreaker, and after being so wrong about Anastasia, I'm suddenly not so sure about this vote being such a slam dunk.

Marko frowns, staring at the table in front of him as his fingers drum the surface.

"Marko," Yuri says gently. "You have the deciding vote."

"*Vote*," Abram hisses.

The silver haired Bratva king takes a deep breath, the lines on his face deepening heavily before he finally clears his throat.

"I am afraid…"

Oh shit.

"No."

The word blurts from his mouth as he shakes his head.

"The Kalishnik family votes no to *Okhrana Soveta*."

"You *motherfucker—*"

"*Until*," Marko adds, shooting a cold look at Abram, "such time that it can be proven that Drazen is behind these attacks, or that we need to invoke this to defeat him, my answer is *no*."

Viktor exhales slowly, shaking his head. Yuri nods. "Well then, the vote is done. The motion is not passed."

"*Cowards!*" Abram snarls.

"That's enough," Yuri mutters back.

"Grow some fucking balls and—"

"I said *ENOUGH.*"

I almost grin at the way the room goes silent. Yuri's a master at diplomacy. He can be cool and collected…until he isn't. And then, when he lets loose, shit gets real *really* fast.

His eyes narrow at Abram. "It's over, Abram. The vote is done. There will be no infighting between members of this table over the result of that vote. We can revisit the question in a month. Now, are there any more items to discuss this evening?"

The table is silent.

"Then we're done here. Meeting adjourned."

Abram and his second-in-command, Hadeon, storm angrily from the room with Demyan Ozerov close behind. I stand and make a move toward Anastasia, because I've got some serious questions about the way she voted. But she avoids me and slips from the room with her imposing number two, Danylo.

Marko at least has the decency to bid goodnight to everyone who is still there before he himself leaves, though he makes no move to speak about what just transpired.

"That was much closer than it should have been," Ilya growls, leaning against the table and flicking his Zippo open and closed meditatively. He quit cigarettes years ago. The Zippo thing is a lingering stress reliever.

"*Way* too close," Lukas murmurs.

"Anastasia's vote was…surprising," I say.

Yuri nods. "I agree. That was very odd. Demyan is obviously in Abram's pocket, but I wouldn't have pegged her to side with those two."

"I'll reach out to Misha," Lukas frowns. As in Misha Tsavakov, another friend from Oxford Hills. While not officially Bratva, the Tsavakov empire is firmly in bed with families like mine, Ilya's, and Lukas'. "Kristoff, Misha's number two, was once somewhat close to Anastasia. He might be a better choice to get answers out of her."

Viktor nods. "Solid idea, asking him."

"Until then," Yuri says quietly, even though we're the only ones left in the room, "I say we make an effort to look into the Drazen situation. And I think it goes without saying, let's all keep a close eye on Abram. His ambition might be venturing into dangerous territory."

When we leave, I end up tagging along with Ilya and Lukas to go grab a drink.

"Welcome to the fucking table, huh?" Ilya smirks, clinking his glass to mine as he rolls his eyes. "Nothing like hitting the ground fucking running."

Lukas chuckles. "It'll get sorted out. Abram's just a hothead. He'll simmer down." He glances at me. "Don't let tonight shake you, man. Everyone's got the fullest confidence in your ability to wear that crown solo."

I nod and smile my thanks, and I drink with my friends as we discuss the table business, and other business, and the two of them being fathers now. And I do that all well, because I'm very, very good at wearing this mask.

But on the inside, I have my doubts about exactly how well I'll be wearing the full weight of the crown. Not just because of the events at the table tonight, or because of anything to do with the possibility that Drazen is basically advancing like he's Hannibal marching on Rome.

Not even because of the ticking time bomb Svetlana poses to all of us, given that the one bargaining chip I had just got destroyed in dramatic fashion.

No, I'm worried about my ability to wear the crown because even right now, smack dab in the middle of it, I'm not thinking of *any* of that shit. Not Abram. Not Drazen. Not Svetlana.

I'm only thinking of her, *still*.

Even when I smile and nod, or scowl if that seems indicated, or shake my head when Ilya and Lukas do, my thoughts are firmly and squarely on Eilish and that kiss I stole from her.

It wasn't what I expected.

It was *more*.

Now, we'll see how far I can push her before she breaks.

Or—let's be honest—before I do.

8

EILISH

I SHIVER as my dress drops to the floor and Gavan's eyes sweep viciously and hungrily over me.

"Better. Much better."

My pulse races, my blood boiling.

He means my underwear.

It's Monday morning, and I've been in Gavan's office for less than sixty seconds before being ordered to strip down to my bra, panties, and heels.

I *hate* that I feel a flutter of pride and elation at the praise in his voice. I hate that I literally went out this weekend and bought new matching bra and panties, entirely because of his comment last week about wearing something nicer.

I hate what it says about me that I carefully shaved my legs, my bikini line—and more—and my armpits this morning. That I did my makeup with more than my usual attention. That I selected my outfit, did my hair, and all the rest of it— in preparation to disrobe for him again.

"Turn around," Gavan growls. He twirls his finger in the air, as if I need a demonstration of what that means. I glare at him, but keep silent as I slowly turn. I can feel his eyes sliding over my skin. And my face flames when I feel his gaze glued to my ass that is barely covered by the tiny black lace thong that matches my bra.

I've never really felt "sexy" before. I mean, I know I'm conventionally attractive enough. I have good skin, and I really like my mouth and the rest of my face. I keep in pretty okay shape, I guess. But I'm not, and never have been, one of those girls on social media posing in bikinis with the "ass-back, tits-forward, duck-lips" look.

Neve loves to say that while most girls are out there trying to be Marilyn, I'm content being Jackie O. Honestly, I take pride in that assessment.

All this is to say, my current situation, twirling around in a skimpy lace thong in front of one of the most—if not *the* most—dangerous and ridiculously good-looking men in New York is pretty much the definition of "outside my comfort zone".

"Well?"

I shiver when I turn back around, facing him. My eyes instinctively drop to his lips, and I flush.

I flush because I know how those lips taste. I know the sinfully exiting punishment they can bring. I know the way they almost brought me to my knees.

I shake myself, pulling myself from my reverie and focusing on what he just said.

"Well…what?"

He cocks a brow, his jawline grinding.

"Do you really need a reminder?"

I resist the urge to roll my eyes, which is not an easy thing to do right now.

"Cappuccino again?" I mutter.

Gavan's eyes flash, cold and metallic. My face heats.

"Would you like a cappuccino, *Sir*?" I mumble.

He smiles thinly.

"Good girl."

I shiver.

Fuck you, body.

When I'm done fumbling my way through making his goddamn coffee, feeling his eyes on every inch of my backside while I'm doing it, he sips it slowly while I stand there like an idiot. When he drops his gaze back to the laptop in front of him, I frown.

"Is…there something else I should be doing?"

His eyes raise, his brow arching expectantly.

Goddammit.

"Is there something else I should be doing, *Sir*?"

Gavan smiles savagely. "The shelves over there haven't been dusted in far too long."

I stare at him.

"There's a duster in the closet of the private bathroom." He turns and nods with his chin at the door next to the coffee station alcove. When I glance down uncertainly at my dress pooled on the ground, he smirks and shakes his head. "Current dress code applies."

Asshole.

Gavan's office ensuite is, of course, ridiculously gorgeous. I mean, I've grown up with plenty of wealth and privilege. And I've seen even more of it now that the Drakos family are my in-laws. But holy fucking hell. There's an air and a gleam to Gavan's—well, *everything*—that makes me feel like I'm dealing with a monarch or something.

Back in the office holding what might actually be the fanciest feather duster ever created by humankind, I teeter over to the shelves on my heels.

"Don't forget the middle section, right over there."

I don't even need to see where those lethal eyes are aimed to know he's talking about the now-empty glass case.

He's rubbing my face in my crime, and we both know it.

I work my way left to right across the first two levels of shelves before my brows knit, my eyes rising to the two shelves that are too high for me to reach.

"Use this."

I gasp, jumping at the sound of his voice right behind me. When I whirl, he's looming right there, effortlessly holding one of the two guest chairs usually situated in front of his desk in one hand. He sets it down and nods at it.

"Stand on that."

In heels. Yeah, sure. No problem.

Gavan stands right where he is, making zero offers of help as I awkwardly step up onto the chair. I wobble, then catch myself.

"Don't fall," he mutters dryly.

My mouth thins as I start to dust. When I glance down, I flush when I realize he's still standing there—like *right* there behind me, with my ass now at his eye level. My skin tingles as I start dusting again, feeling his heated gaze on me while my legs shake.

"Perhaps you should wear something more office-appropriate, Eilish. I'm not sure heels and lingerie is either suitable or helpful for something like this."

My face burns.

You motherfucker.

I turn, glaring down at his smug face. "You—"

"*Careful.*"

My mouth snaps shut. Gavan grins.

"Good girl."

He boldly stares at my ass again, mere inches in front of him, before he turns and casually strolls back to his desk.

Fifteen *long* minutes later, I'm finishing up the final section of the built-in shelves when I hear him talking loudly. I whirl, confused, until I realize he's on some video conference call on his laptop, listening through an earpiece.

"One moment," he growls, tapping a button and taking the earpiece out as his eyes raise to mine. "This cappuccino got cold. I'll have another."

My jaw grinds, my nostrils flaring. Gavan just smiles at me, the corners of his lips curled up, daring me to say something.

"Of course, *Sir*," I hiss quietly.

I'm at the coffee machine when he gets back to his meeting.

"Apologies for the delay. My new assistant needs her hand held for even the simplest task."

My fury goes through the roof. I turn, looking at him just sitting there at his desk, wearing another ridiculously expensive looking charcoal gray suit—three piece, again, with another French cuffed dress shirt underneath.

"You know the type," he continues, smiling magnanimously into the camera. "The kind who gets by on her looks but has no brains. Wears revealing things to the office in an effort to get my attention."

You. Mother. Fucking. Asshole.

I turn back to the milk, steaming almost as much as it is. My lips purse tightly, my jaw grinding as I keep the steamer going. And going. And *going*, until the milk is bubbling like lava. I spoon it into the cup and dust it with his goddamn cinnamon. I almost spit in it, too, except that won't matter with what I'm about to do.

I turn, smiling benignly as I slowly walk over to Gavan's desk. I'm halfway there when he hits a button and turns to me.

"After this, do the windows. Then the bathroom. Silently. This is an important call."

He hits the button again and returns to his meeting. I keep smiling as I walk the rest of the way, pause just out of sight of the camera…

And promptly dump the scalding contents of the cappuccino mug directly into his lap.

Gavan's eyes flame. His jaw clenches so tightly that veins pop out on his neck.

He does *nothing*. He doesn't even turn to look at me, or swivel his gaze. He just clears his throat, smiles into the camera, and keeps talking.

Shit.

That didn't go as planned.

I pale, turning as if to leave. But Gavan raises one finger, still not looking at me, waving it back and forth in a "no-no" motion.

Seconds tick by. Then minutes. Every time I go to move in the slightest from where I'm standing, he holds his finger up in admonishment and shakes it again. And that one motion keeps me stuck right here, unable to move, unable to run away.

For some reason, it's even more terrifying than him yelling at me, or blowing up. It's like part of my punishment is to wait and see what my fate is.

"That'll be all, then," he growls into the camera. "Korol, I want you leading the team on Drazen. If you find anything, call me immediately."

Suddenly, the long wait is over as he slowly closes the laptop. His gunmetal eyes raise to mine, narrowing dangerously.

"That was incredibly stupid."

"Well, if you're going to be an insulting asshole—"

"Come here."

I swallow, rooted in place, unable to move. Gavan's eyes blaze.

"*Come. Here.*"

Fear explodes through my system. Not just fear. Excitement comes along with it. And a tingling shiver follows. Slowly, I walk over and around his desk until I'm standing right next to where he's sitting.

"That *stung*," he growls.

I arch a brow at him. "Oh, really? Which did I hurt more? Your fragile ego, or your poor balls—"

"Are you familiar with the term *free use*."

My pulse skips. Something wicked explodes in my core as my face turns a shade of crimson that I'm pretty sure gives my answer away.

I am.

"Free use" is a kink wherein one partner is "free to use" the other however, and almost more importantly *whenever,* they choose to. I know this because there's a small chance that it's become my biggest secret fantasy over the last couple of years.

I don't need a shrink to know that it's probably at least partially due in part to what happened to me my senior year of high school. I probably *do* need a shrink to unpack the why of that whole trauma-kink connection, but I digress.

Suffice to say, it's my darkest, most visited yet also most resisted fantasy. I don't exactly watch a *lot* of porn online or anything. But when I do?

It's free use. Like, exclusively.

Dominant men coming up to their partners while they're on the phone, or washing dishes, and just…doing whatever they want to that partner. Lifting her skirt and just going right into fucking her. Or using her mouth while he's watching a movie. Or coming all over her face while she's talking to a friend on the phone.

Yeah, it's fucked up. It's probably indicative of trauma running way deeper than I'm prepared to consider.

It's also outrageously hot, at least to me.

Gavan's eyes glint as the corners of his lips curve dangerously.

"*Bad girl*," he growls quietly, which makes my core throb. "You do know, don't you?"

I swallow, nodding my pulsing hot face so subtly it almost doesn't move.

"That's going to be our arrangement."

My eyes bulge.

"*What?*"

"You, Eilish," he murmurs darkly, "will be my free use little plaything. I'll do whatever I wish to you, whenever I wish, and you'll allow it without question."

My jaw drops.

"*No—*"

"Alternatively, you can find me another one-of-a-kind, historically significant, one-hundred-and-twenty-four-million-dollar Fabergé egg commissioned by Tsarina Alexandra. Your pick."

My entire body shivers. My pulse throbs heavily as my face heats.

"If…"

I can't believe I'm even asking this.

I take a shaky breath and start again. "If I *were* to say yes, how long—"

"Six months."

My core clenches.

"You'll be my willing little fuck-toy for six months."

My thighs squeeze the second he says it.

Fuck-toy.

It's crude. It's demeaning.

It's also ridiculously hot, in a very confusing and fucked up way.

"For six months, I do whatever I want to you, whenever I want. And you don't say no."

A tingle traces down my spine.

"I—I have a…"

"A *what*," he smirks. "A boyfriend?"

"A fiancé," I lie, thinking about Brooks, as revolting as that is.

Gavan rolls his eyes. "No, you don't."

"I—"

"And even if you *did*," he hisses. "I wouldn't fucking give a shit, nor would it change a thing about this arrangement."

My face throbs.

"Tick-tock, Eilish," he rasps darkly. "Do we or do we not have a deal? Six months, and when we're done, I forget all about it. You have my word on that."

"And what good is your—"

"*Very*," he growls. "My word is *very* good. And I *know* that you know that."

I hate that I do. But—yeah. Everyone who's ever heard of him knows three things about Gavan: that he's ruthless; that you *do not* cross him; and that he is an absolute man of his word, for better or worse, come Hell or high water.

"And if I don't agree?" I choke in a very small voice.

He shrugs. "War, hardship, lots of money being owed to me, your family finding out that you're a killer. For a start."

"You're a bastard—"

I choke, gasping as he raises a hand and traces one fingertip up my thigh, which instantly has the effect of making my skin tingle and my core turn into a molten puddle.

"Correct on a technicality. I am a bastard," he growls. "And you're *wet*."

My mouth falls open, my eyes widening at his words.

"Do we," he murmurs, "or do we *not* have a deal. Five. Four. Three—"

"*Okay*."

The word whispers from my lips like a secret as my eyes close.

"Louder. Properly. And I want you to fucking look at me when you say it."

I force my eyes open, my face pulsing as his gaze rips into mine.

"Well?"

My heart skips.

"*Yes, Sir.*"

His lips curl triumphantly, raw power surging in his eyes.

"*Good girl.*"

I flush bright red.

"When…when do we—"

We start? Immediately." He raises a hand, crooking two fingers and then pointing to his lap. "Lie down right here."

My jaw drops. Gavan smiles dangerously.

"You did, in fact, hurt me, Eilish," he growls. "Now you will be punished for it."

9

EILISH

IT HAPPENS SO FAST, I'm barely even aware of it. One second, I'm standing there gawking at him, trying to get my brain to function properly. The next, he's grabbing me and yanking me across his lap.

And suddenly, that's exactly where I find myself: in freaking black lace lingerie and heels, face down across Gavan Tsarenko's muscled thighs. I gasp, shivering when I feel the expensive linen of his suit pants against my naked torso.

Shivering too at the realization that my bare ass is up in the air, only covered—barely—by a thong.

"Wait! What the—"

And that's when it happens. With one motion, his broad, powerful hand comes down with a hard smack against my ass. Heat blossoms out from the place of impact, chasing across my skin like electric currents from a live wire.

Then he spanks my other butt cheek, and I choke back a gasp as I squirm against him.

"What the *fuck!*" I blurt. I try and twist either toward him, or *off* him. But one of his hands grabs my ponytail firmly. The other one, the one that's just spanked me, grips my throbbing, smarting ass tightly. Between the two, I'm not going anywhere.

"What the fuck do you think you're doing!?"

"*Punishing you,*" he growls, making me shiver as the hand on my ass lightly strokes the stinging skin.

"This is *not* part of our—"

"Did you or did you *not* agree to be my willing little free use toy, Eilish," he rasps darkly.

A tremble ripples through my core. Visions of the darkly sexy fantasies and the filthy videos I've watched online start dancing teasingly through my mind.

"Answer me."

"*Yes,*" I choke.

He's silent, but when his grip tightens on my ass and my ponytail, I know what he's thinking.

"*Yes, Sir,*" I whisper.

"Good girl. Now—count."

My eyes widen and I gasp sharply as his hand leaves my ass and then comes crashing back down. Heat explodes across my skin once again.

"*One!*" I whimper, my head spinning as I try to process the idea that this is actually happening.

Gavan's powerful, tattooed hand spanks my ass again.

"Two!"

JAGGER COLE

Three and four follow quickly, then five. There's a long, tortuously drawn-out second before the sixth spank rips a squeal from my throat and makes my toes curl.

When he's done, his hand lingers on my tender, tingling ass. My face is throbbing, partially from being face down like this, but mostly from what just happened.

…That, and the fact that I am horribly, mortifyingly, *soaking wet*.

Suddenly, his hand moves, his fingers slipping into the waistband of my panties. Swiftly he yanks them down, peeling them off me, away from my pussy and leaving them tangled at my knees. My throat closes off, my breath choked with shame and horrible desire as I feel his eyes center between my slightly spread thighs on his lap.

And the bastard *chuckles*.

"My my *my*, Miss Kildare," Gavan murmurs, making a tsking sound with his teeth. "What do we have here?"

My eyes squeeze shut as my face throbs.

"Open your mouth."

I barely have time to do so before suddenly his fingers are slipping between my lips. My eyes fly open.

"*Suck.*"

Heat fills my face. I awkwardly hollow my cheeks, trying to actually suck on his fingers. My tongue tentatively swipes over them, wetting them. When I hear him groan, I keep doing it.

Then I feel something.

Something hard. Something big. Something I thought was his thigh until it pulses and jumps against my stomach, and I realize it's not his leg. It's his cock.

He's *hard*.

I did that.

Heat pools in my core as Gavan suddenly slips his fingers from my mouth. Without hesitation, he brings the hand back to my ass, and moves his fingers down between my spread legs.

He didn't have to make me suck on them. I'm already *dripping*. And when he drags his fingers along my wet lips, there's no stopping the choked whimper that catches in my throat.

"Now, what is it that got this little pussy so messy for me, *solnishka?*" he growls, making me gasp as he suddenly sinks two fingers deep inside me. My head spins with a mix of fear, desire, uncertainty and *need* exploding through me all at the same time.

"Was it getting your ass spanked like the bad girl you are? Sucking my fingers while wishing it was my cock? Or are you just a brat who gets excited knowing you're ruining my suit pants with that sopping wet pussy dripping all over them? Because you've. Left. A. Fucking. Puddle. On. Me."

There's no stopping the cry that tears from my lips as he punctuates each word with a deep, firm stroke of his finger-tips against my g-spot. My eyes roll back in my head, and I moan through grit teeth as Gavan starts to finger me harder and deeper.

His thumb rolls my clit at the same time, and the waves of pleasure begin to pulse and throb through my core like a heartbeat. He slips two fingers of his other hand into my mouth, and he doesn't even ask or tell me before I start to suck on them like I did a minute ago.

He's not pinning me down anymore. But I don't try to escape. All I can do is writhe and whimper across his lap as Gavan fingers my pussy and my mouth, sending me spiraling upward with desire. The lewd, mortifyingly wet sounds of my pussy dripping all over his plunging fingers fill the room along with my muffled moans as I suck on his fingers like a porn star. His thumb rolls my clit over and over, until all at once it hits without warning.

Suddenly, for the very first time, I'm coming from someone's touch other than my own.

Hard.

I spasm, my legs flailing and kicking, my panties still around my knees. My body twitches and writhes as I feel my pussy clamp down tight around his fingers while wave after wave of my arousal floods his hand and his slacks.

Slowly, he slides his hands from my mouth and from between my thighs. I'm still shaking when I feel the sudden heat of his lips right by my ear as he bends over me.

"Get on your knees, solnishka."

It's all a hazy blur. Slowly, my heartbeat pounding in my ears, I slide from his lap onto the floor. I don't do it because I feel threatened, though there's a part of me that's still sitting with that fear and *feasting* on it.

I don't do it because I'm worried about the consequences if I don't do as he says, or because I feel like he owns me.

I drop to my knees on the floor in front of Gavan Tsarenko, my thighs still wet and my panties tangled around my legs, because *I want to.*

I stare with wide, eager eyes as he slides his hand to the belt of his tailored pants—which do, in fact, have a large wet spot on them. Two wet spots, actually. One is from the cappuccino I dumped in his lap.

The other is from *me.*

"You were right," he growls quietly as his steely gray eyes slice into me. He smiles thinly. "Not about my ego. But you did hurt my balls."

His belt opens. His zipper tugs down over the massive bulge beneath it. Then he slips his hand into his boxers.

"Maybe you should kiss them all better."

Gaven lifts his hips and pulls his cock free.

My jaw drops.

What. The. Actual. Fuck.

He's fucking *huge.* I mean like *huge*-huge. Long, veined, and literally as thick as my wrist, with a swollen crown already leaking precum.

My throat bobs as my eyes widen, shamefully staring at his monster dick.

What the fuck...

HOW the fuck...

"Eilish."

I shiver, my eyes dragging from his enormous cock up to his smoldering eyes.

"Open your mouth."

I flush as my gaze drops back to his hand wrapped around his huge dick.

"*Yes, Sir.*"

I say it unprompted. And when I do, a flicker of something wicked sparks in my core. The flicker burns hotter and stronger when I hear him groan.

"*Good girl.* Now take my cock in your mouth and show me just how good a girl you can be."

My lips part. Slowly, I lower my face down to the swollen head. My lips brush the tip, and I shiver at the salty-sweet taste and the scent of desire mixed with that same bergamot, wood, and *wealth* scent that always seems to come with him.

I pucker my lips, kissing his crown once, twice, and then a third time. Then I shiver as I feel him wrap my ponytail around his hand before he clenches it in a tight fist.

"*Open.*"

I've never given a blowjob before. When we dated in high school, Brooks would whine and beg for one, and even occasionally made threats that if I didn't, he'd find another girl to "take care of him". I hate so much that that revolting tactic almost worked, but I was so caught up with wanting to be liked by his crowd. Luckily, we never actually got to that part before…well, before it blew up.

Before *that* night.

And after that? Well, I went on dates for the first two years of undergrad. But I wasn't interested in casual hookups, unlike most of the guys I met, who very much *were*. And I didn't really have time to date anyway, because I was so busy trying to grind my way to the top of my class.

Then, when I *did* finally try to start dating a year or two ago, it just never happened. To the point where I'm truly convinced that I'm cursed when it comes to meeting guys.

They'd never call me back. Or they'd stand me up. Or we'd have a great time getting a drink or a bite to eat and then they'd inexplicably ghost me forever.

Which is how I've gotten to the age of twenty-one, and only now am finding myself on my knees about to give my first blowjob.

And Jesus Christ, look at him. It's like learning to ride a bike on a Grand Prix motorcycle.

But I'm determined to do this. I also, much as I hate to admit it, *want* to do this. So I open my jaw as wide as I possibly can, shivering at the delicious feel of his hand gripping my hair tightly. He's not shoving me down. He's not forcing me. But the pressure and the control are there.

And they're pushing every fucking button I have.

The thick, velvety head slips into my mouth. I moan, feeling him stretch my lips wide as my tongue drags over the underside.

"Close your mouth around it," he growls. "And *suck*."

When he groans after I start, an emboldened feeling throbs in my core. So I carry on doing it, thrilled at the way he hisses in pleasure, and at the way his hips rise and fall.

"Use your tongue more. Against the underside. *Fuck yes*, just like that…" he growls.

He must know I've never done this before. Or at least, that I'm not very experienced. Because he's giving me all this direction. But he's not belittling me about it. He's not mocking me or anything.

And the directions are...*hot*. It's also hot, ridiculously so, when his fist tightens at the back of my head and his hips start to thrust. He's not choking me or anything, but he's stopping just short of that as he shallowly fucks my mouth, sliding his cock over my tongue.

Using me. Using my mouth to get off. Which maybe should feel demeaning. Okay, it *definitely* should feel demeaning.

But it doesn't.

It feels amazing.

"*There's* my good little free use toy," Gavan groans. He reaches down, pushing my bra down and spilling my smallish breasts into his hand. He rolls my nipples between his thumb and his forefinger, making me whimper as his cock hits the back of my throat.

He thrusts a few more times shallowly before his fist pulls my hair back, sliding my mouth wetly from his glistening cock.

"I think you need to kiss them all better after kicking them the other night."

I shiver with heat as he pulls my mouth down his shaft, letting my lips slide across his cock before they get to his heavy, full balls.

"Kiss them."

I do, pursing my wet lips together and kissing first one and then the other.

"Now stick out your tongue."

He groans when I do, tracing over one of the orbs.

"Lick them like a good girl."

Gavan hisses again in pleasure. It only fuels me on as I start to lick and suck gently on his balls, alternating between them. His fist tightens in my hair again, pulling my mouth right against them with his pulsing cock draped hot against my face.

"Harder."

I moan, sucking and slurping on his balls and kind of making a mess with my spit. He's not angry. If anything, it's turning him on even more.

Honestly? It's turning *me on* even more.

It's somehow even dirtier than a blowjob, sucking on his balls like this. It feels even more erotic, more intimate in a weird way.

"Give me your hand."

He takes it and wraps my fingers around his shaft, pumping it once to show me the rhythm.

"Now jerk me off against that pretty face while you slobber on my balls like the greedy little cum slut that you are."

Jesus. Fucking. Christ.

Obviously, nobody has ever spoken to me like this before. In fact, I couldn't have imagined *anyone* talking like this, outside of the kind of porn that I've watched online.

Apparently, Gavan does.

And apparently, that sort of talk makes me wetter than rain.

My thighs squeeze together, my core aching with need. I'm desperate to touch myself, or to be touched. Or to do literally *anything* he wants right now, I'm so outrageously turned on.

I moan and whimper into his balls as I stroke his cock harder and faster, feeling him tense and, unbelievably, swell even *bigger* in my hand.

He suddenly groans. And in one motion, he's pulling me up, pushing his cock back into my mouth, and then moaning in pleasure.

Then Gavan starts to come. Or rather, he starts to *explode* down my throat.

My eyes almost start from my head, and I choke a little as jet after jet of hot, salty-sweet cum blasts across my tongue. I try and swallow it all, but a ton of it slips out from my lips and dribbles down his length. He twitches in my mouth over and over, his head thrown back in ecstasy before he finally groans and drags his gaze back to mine.

And when our eyes lock...*fuck.*

The look in his eyes is...intense. As intense as the kiss from the other day.

A declaration of war.

Subjugation.

Annihilation.

His hand drops from my hair. Slowly, blushing fiercely, I slip my mouth from his cock.

"*Good girl,*" he murmurs.

Heat tingles through my core.

"But...you made a mess," he growls quietly, his eyes blazing into mine. "Time for you to clean me up."

Sweet. Jesus.

I lean back down, my eyes still utterly captivated by his as my tongue darts out to lick his cock clean of all the cum that spilled from my mouth. I tongue every inch of him, licking from his balls back up to his head until it's all gone.

"Such a good girl."

I bite my lip.

"That will be all for today, Eilish. You can get dressed and go."

I nod, not quite sure if I'm relieved or disappointed that this is over.

What is wrong with you? You're relieved. Obviously you're relieved.

Yeah, obviously...

I'm shaking as I stand on wobbly feet, pull my panties back up, and adjust my bra back into place. I walk over to my dress, still pooled on the ground. My face is throbbing so hard I have to face away from him as I slip it on and reach back to zip it up. I take a shaky breath and have just started to walk for the door when he stops me.

"Wait."

I pause, taking a halting breath before I turn around. I shiver when he stands, crooking two fingers at me.

His cock is still out.

And very, very hard.

I walk back to him, my face crimson, my entire body tingling and on fire, until I'm standing right in front of him.

"Lift up your dress," he grunts with a fierceness in his eyes.

I do, and then I gasp as he reaches out, slips his fingers into the top of my panties, and pulls them away from my body. I stare, my mouth in an O-shape as he pushes his swollen cockhead against my pussy and strokes it. A thick bead of white cum drips out of his head, followed by another two, a thick, sticky rivulet slowly dripping down my pussy lips.

With a smirk, Gavan slips my panties back into place. I gulp as I feel his cum seeping into the lace against my sex. He lowers his face to my side, making my breath catch as his lips brush my ear.

"I want you to feel me there later when you touch yourself. And when you do, know just how fucking *mine* you are."

"Later" ends up being precisely twenty-seven minutes later, which is *exactly* how long it takes for me to leave the building, jump into a cab going uptown, and rush up to my bedroom, locking the door before I replay every single filthy detail of what just happened.

10

GAVAN

I HAVE A PROBLEM.

My utter control over Eilish was supposed to subjugate her. Humble and humiliate her. *Break her.* Because as much as I've craved and desired her over the last year of prying into her every secret and stalking her like an obsession, I've always had to remind myself who she really is:

The enemy. A Kildare. A member of the family who killed mine. A weak pressure point for me to press and squeeze to destroy their empire.

Except my plans have gone askew. My plot has gone astray. And there's a good chance it all started to go wrong with that single brutal kiss against my office door.

Since then, my master plan to destroy Eilish before casting her back to her family just in time for her to watch me dismantle their kingdom has started to unravel. Having her around is…a distraction. It's consuming, and it's addictive.

Part of the rush comes from the power I hold over her, of course. But even more of a thrill is the way she so eagerly submits.

It's not overt. And she tries to hide it—both from me and from herself. But it's there.

It's been three days now of having her in my immediate vicinity, in my office.

In her bra and panties, or more recently naked, submitting to my every demand and desire. I've fucked her mouth three more times since that first one, and fingered her greedy pussy to orgasm twice as many times as that.

The thing is, it's not a pathetic or resentful submission. I doubt that would turn me on so much. It's the fact that she fights me, even when she submits. It's the defiant fire in her eyes mixed with her eagerness to obey me.

It's that deep down she *wants* to. She just doesn't know how to make peace with that.

The elephant looming in the room is why I haven't fucked her yet. I've come down her throat four times. I've even had her grind on my lap, rubbing her needy little cunt all over the underside of my cock until she soaks me with her release.

But I haven't fucked her.

Part of it is my assumption that she's a virgin. Which is honestly *not* something I signed up for or wanted with this. I've never wished to be anyone's first.

There's too much of my own baggage wrapped up in that concept.

But the other reason I haven't slept with Eilish yet is purely that I want to deny myself the pleasure until I can't stand it anymore. I want to ride that dual rush of want and desire until I can't possibly hold back anymore.

Because when I do dive in and finally have her, I'm not sure I'll ever be able to come back up for air. Before all of this fell into place, yes—I'd have had no problem sullying Eilish, making her my whore, and absolutely *ruining* her for any other man before casting her away.

But that was before that fucking kiss. Before the rush of adrenaline and roar of something I can't quite place the first time I tasted the defiance and sweetness on her lips.

Now, I'm not so sure I'll ever be able to "cast her away" once I've had her like that. It's the same reason I haven't feasted on her pussy yet.

Just her *mouth* is already a drug I'm spiraling into addiction with. So are her whimpered little moans and the way she chokes out a gasp when she comes.

Any deeper down the rabbit hole with my little *solnishka*, and —truthfully—I'm not so sure I'll ever be able to climb back out again.

But for the time being, I make a valiant attempt to shake Eilish out of my head as I wrap a towel around my waist and step into the warm, steamy fog of the bathhouse on 78th. I hear Korol flush the toilet after taking a piss in the changing room behind me. Soon, he joins me in the steam, also clad in a towel as we move through the empty, tiled rooms toward the back of the place.

Which I own. That's why it's empty today.

I like having meetings here with those I trust. It's secluded, private, and it's pretty much impossible to bug or otherwise eavesdrop, what with all the steam and humidity dripping down the tiled walls, white with blue Imperialist Russian designs.

Also, having a meeting soaking in a steam room while wrapped in a towel is fucking *fantastic*. I'm honestly not sure why corporate America hasn't caught on to this yet.

"Hey, Boss-man," Korol's dark brow furrows when I turn to him. "I just got a message from my buddy Pytor. You know, Yuri's guy."

I frown. "And?"

"One of Yuri's shipping tankers just caught fire docked in port, in France. Suspected arson."

My jaw grits.

Fuck.

"Let me guess…"

Korol nods darkly. "Yeah. The rumor mill says it's Drazen again."

Goddammit.

Here we are trying to stop a psycho warmonger like Abram from using *Okhrana Soveta* to basically turn the High Council into his own personal fucking army. And now the temperature just went up even more.

Fucking great.

I'm still scowling as Korol and I step into the last steam room. From the looks on their faces, I can tell that Ilya and Misha have already heard this little tidbit.

"How bad?" I growl at Ilya.

His eyes flicker with the venomous, brooding edge he's known for. "The fire? Not totally terrible, as in no loss of life or merchandise, and the ship itself isn't even that damaged. But bad, because it's thrown a giant spotlight on our operations out of the port of Marseille. Local authorities that we've never even had to pay off because they're coasting at the job anyway are suddenly swarming all over our shit like flies."

Next to him, Misha nods slowly. "I've got some connections in the French government. I'll reach out after we finish up here, see if I can pull some strings and get the rug smoothed back down over all this."

"Much appreciated," Ilya sighs.

At well over six feet tall and built like a rugby player, Misha Tsavakov cuts an imposing figure. The ink covering something like ninety percent of his body certainly doesn't hurt, either. I mean, we're all tattooed—Ilya and Lukas a bit, and Konstantin and I both fairly heavily. But Misha's in another league with his body art.

His ink goes from his sharp jawline down to cover every finger and every toe. And yes, I've changed with the guy. That ink *really does* go *all* the way down.

While not technically from a Bratva family, Misha's massive empire is firmly entwined with Bratva business. He's also got legitimate connections that the rest of us could only dream of. Misha's wife, Charlotte Bergdendem, is the crown princess of the small European kingdom of Luxlordia. This makes our cocky, tattooed friend a literal prince who will one day be an actual King Consort of a nation. Ink and all.

Misha lifts his eyes to me and grins. "Shitty news aside, it's good to see you, brother. It's been a while. How's that crown sitting on your head?"

I roll my eyes as I walk over and shake his hand and then Ilya's before Korol and I sit down on the slick tile benches diagonally opposite the other guys.

"It's fine. Easy transition."

He snickers. "Man, Konstantin's in for it. I'd take helming the entire Reznikov empire solo any day over wrangling fucking *twins*. Jesus Christ."

I grin. "Any second-borns on the horizon for you and Char?"

They've got a son, Damien, who's the same age as Ilya's son Asher and my niece Luna. Misha's trademark cocky grin widens and he laughs.

"I mean, we're practicing a lot…"

I chuckle as Ilya rolls his eyes.

"And yeah, maybe one day. But two at the same time? Sounds like a goddamn nightmare." He arches a brow at me. "How about you, King Tsarenko. When are you going to settle down with some nice or not-so-nice girl and sow your seed?"

I make a face. Misha chuckles. "What about you, Korol? Any babies on the way?"

"Better fuckin' not be," Korol mutters, his face paling a little.

Misha roars with laughter before he sighs heavily, raising his eyes back to me. "As much as I'm loving this conversation, you probably want to talk business."

"I want both," I shrug. "Which is why I have business meetings in a bathhouse."

"You might be on to something," Ilya smirks.

Misha clears his throat as he sprawls back against the heated tile wall, a heavy cloud of steam swirling around his grooved, inked muscles.

"So… I talked to Kristoff last night about your concerns with Anastasia Javanović. They're not close or anything, but he knows her slightly, and he knew her father as well. According to Kristoff, there's not a lot of love lost between the Javanović and Diduch families. Some bad blood from way back or something, I guess. When he was still running the Diduch family, Olek Domitrovich heavily lobbied against Anastasia's father, Branko, joining the High Council at all. His nephew voting in favor of Ana joining once she was running things apparently came out of left field."

My brow furrows. "Are either of you aware of any dealings between Diduch and Javanović?"

"Nope." Ilya shakes his head. I know for a fact that his uncle Yuri takes *meticulous* note of who in our world does business with whom. So if Ilya says no, it's probably accurate.

"I'm not gonna lie," Misha says. "I've occasionally done some clandestine stuff to stay off Yuri's radar," he grins a lopsided grin at Ilya. "No offense."

"None taken. He knows about those 'clandestine' deals anyway, for what it's worth."

Misha scowls. "Really?"

"Really."

I suck on my teeth, eager to steer the subject back to the Javanović question. "So why the fuck is Anastasia siding with a family she doesn't do business with, and even has a bad family history with?"

Misha shrugs. "Maybe they're fucking."

I make a face. "Doubt it. Ana's a badass. Abram's a—"

"Whiny little douchebag?" Ilya breaks in. "Yeah, I don't see that either. Could be she's in bed with Demyan Ozerov? Literally or otherwise?"

I shake my head. "Also seriously doubtful."

"Still," Ilya frowns. "I'll have some of our top spies tail them both for a while, see if there's any overlap. I doubt it too, but can't think what else would make sense."

"I'll ask Kristoff to reach out to Anastasia. Nothing overt or obvious, of course. But just to see if he can pry anything out of her," Misha adds.

THE BATHHOUSE MEETING was very early. But I've got a few other things to tie up still, so I end up calling Rachel at the office to have her tell Eilish to come in later.

The evil part of me loves the idea of Eilish just sitting in my office for a few hours waiting for me, wondering what the fuck she's supposed to do and why she's there wasting her time.

But the careful motherfucker in me who's made it through a few years as a Bratva king *without* getting assassinated thinks of her sitting alone in my office for a few hours and *ransacking it* just to stick it to me. No. Too risky.

With that scheduling change taken care of, Korol and I step into Crudo, the Michelin-rated Italian place in midtown that I own. For the next hour, I preside over four different rapid-fire meetings with a few of my top *avtoritets* on random issues. Then it's a slightly more leisurely meeting with Jayden Robinson, head of the Jamaican mafia, with whom I've recently begun doing some business.

One, because I like doing business with him, and it's profitable. But also perhaps more importantly two, because I know Jayden and I working together pisses the absolute *fuck* out of Hades Drakos and the rest of his family—which means it probably pisses off the Kildares, too.

Petty? Yes. Amusing to me? What can I say. Also yes.

When Jayden and I shake on a win-win deal that'll both open up some new shipping avenues for me and keep the Haitians off his back, I'm finally alone with my espresso.

"Mr. Tsarenko?"

Dammit. I glance up as one of my men clears his throat.

"Mr. Kalishnik is here to see you."

My brows knit as I glance at Korol. Then I sigh. "Send him in."

Crudo is closed, obviously, which is why I'm able to have meetings in the middle of the dining room. But Marko and I don't have anything planned today, which has me very, very curious as to why he's randomly showing up right now.

I nod, standing as the head of the Kalishnik family steps through the front door. Marko's in his late forties, though if he cared enough to dye the silver out of his temples he could probably pass for fifteen years younger than that. He's a handsome if grim-looking guy who clearly still works out a lot, and he has good taste in suits.

We don't interact much outside the High Council, but I like him. His close number two, Vlad, follows him inside.

"Gavan," Marko rumbles in a deep, time-roughened baritone. "I hope I'm not overstepping."

I shake my head as he walks over, putting my hand out to clasp his firmly. "Not at all. Please, sit."

He nods, both of us sitting across the white linen-covered table from each other.

"Can I get you anything to drink? Espresso? Or the wine cellar here is one of the best in the city."

He smiles, shaking his head. "Thank you, but no, nothing. I'm fine." Marko clears his throat. "I was only hoping for a moment of your time regarding the events of the Council meeting the other night."

My jaw grinds. "Abram?"

He nods. "Indeed."

"The Kalishnik family is the only other founding family currently at the table aside from the Diduchs." I arch a significant brow at him. "If you're also of the opinion that Abram invoking *Okhrana Soveta* to make himself emperor is a bad thing, you could always invoke it yourself. I'm sure Yuri and Viktor would be happy to vote for you if we all privately agreed that it was a measure meant to take the wind out of Abram's and Demyan's sails."

Marko smirks. "Don't think I haven't considered it. But while I care for the table deeply, I need to think of my own family's interests as well. I believe that crossing and making an enemy of Abram Diduch is...*unwise*."

I frown. "C'mon, Marko. You're not scared of that little prick, are you?"

He chuckles a rumbling laugh. "Scared? No. But I am...*cautious*...of him. He's unpredictable, he craves power, and he's openly hostile to the very idea of the table. It's a bad combination."

"So declare *Okhrana Soveta* yourself and beat him at his own game," I mutter.

Marko just sighs, leaning back in his chair and glancing at the guards posted at both the front door and the back of the restaurant.

"Might we have some privacy?"

I glance at Korol, who nods and stands. "Everybody out," he grunts sharply at my men. The guards at the front door step outside. The rest of them follow Korol out through the kitchen. Vlad does the same with the two men he and Marko arrived with. Then we're alone.

"I can father no more children, Gavan," Marko says quietly. "I would appreciate that staying between us: I'm choosing to share it with you as a sign of respect."

I nod, puzzled where this is going.

"Cancer, four years ago," he mutters. "I had a tumor in my lungs. Chemo beat it, but..." He lifts a shoulder. "At my age, it meant game over for having any more children. Which means even if I was lucky enough to meet another woman, I'll never have any sons." He clears his throat before lifting his eyes to mine. "You've met my Milena, yes?"

"Once, I think."

Milena Kalishnik is Marko's eighteen-year-old daughter. I've heard she's smart. But I know the Kalishnik family is old school, and very, *very* patriarchal. Him not having any sons doesn't bode very well for the future of his organization, to be honest. And even if he could sway his top captains to be on board with it, I don't get the impression that Milena Kalishnik has any interest whatsoever in becoming a Bratva queen or leading a criminal empire.

His eyes pierce mine. "What do you think of her?"

My jaw tightens. *Fuck.* Now I have an idea where this is going.

"She's very beautiful, no?"

I exhale slowly. "Marko…"

"I wouldn't suggest this to just any man, Gavan. But I like and respect you, and your brother as well. I liked you father, Vadim, very much, too." He steeples his hands, leaning closer to me over the table. "If you were to marry Milena, I believe we could come to some…arrangement. An arrangement such as what you're suggesting, namely that the Kalishnik family declare *Okhrana Soveta* in order to stop Abram."

I can't quite believe what I'm hearing. "Declaring that to stop Abram is in your own interests as well, Marko," I growl. "In case that needs saying."

He shrugs. "Perhaps. Or perhaps I understand that my family's reign is reaching its end. Perhaps I see no need to continue participating in the High Council with all its drama and infighting."

My lips thin. "If Drazen really is behind these attacks, Marko, I very much doubt he'll care if you're sitting at the table or not. Your family is *still* one of the largest, most powerful Bratva families out there. And he seems to view that as an affront or a threat for some reason."

"*If* he's the one behind the attacks," Marko grunts, frowning. "If the man even *exists*, for that matter. No one's ever even seen him, Gavan. He might be no more than a figure in a bedtime story you tell naughty children to keep them in line."

"Marko—"

"I'm not doing any of this to cause trouble, Gavan," he growls. "But I do need to think of my family and its future. Please at least consider the idea of you and Milana marrying. It would make you and I family. When I die, the Reznikov organization would absorb mine, making it the most powerful Bratva family on Earth by a landslide."

I look away, my jaw tight.

This should be an easy decision. Bratva families marry for power and to solidify business agreements all the goddamn time. And Milena Kalishnik *is* beautiful. She's cultured, and quintessentially Russian, and she understands this game. Marko's not wrong. It would be a *very* strong match, and it would crown the Reznikov Bratva as king above any and all criminal organizations on the planet.

It's a tempting offer.

It should be a no-brainer.

So why isn't it? That's easy, though I fucking *hate* to admit it.

Eilish.

That is what's giving me pause in thinking through this idea of marrying Milena Kalishnik. *That* is the cause of my reluctance.

It's more than slightly confusing.

And concerning.

"This isn't a decision I can make today, Marko."

He smiles. "Of course not. And I thank you for giving the question the weight it deserves. I'm not suggesting the idea of you marrying my daughter lightly, you know. She's my world."

"She's your daughter. Of course she is. I'm honored that you'd even consider me. We'll speak more of this soon?"

"Excellent."

We both stand and shake hands firmly across the table. Marko grins. "Imagine the two of us, family," he chuckles as he turns to head for the door.

I follow him outside, signaling to my men as Marko's black chauffeured Escalade pulls up to the curb a few spots down.

"We'll talk soon, Gavan. Thank you for hearing me out."

I nod, waiting by the glass door to the restaurant as Marko walks over to his waiting vehicle, where Ivan is holding the door open for him.

He's almost there when thunder and liquid fire split the earth open with the punching force of a nuclear explosion.

My world goes sideways as I'm slammed backward. The door and the windows of the restaurant behind me shatter from the force of the blast, showering me with beads of glass along with flaming bits of Escalade as they rain down like fiery, lethal hail.

I hear shouting. I feel arms yanking me to my feet. I'm dimly aware of Korol screaming in my face through the ringing in my ears.

Marko's SUV is a roaring pyre of flame. Vlad simply doesn't exist anymore.

Marko himself is slumped against the side of the building next to the restaurant, smoke curling from his suit jacket and blood leaking from an ugly wound to his head as his men frantically start to perform CPR.

The sound of approaching sirens fills the air.

11

EILISH

This is fucking ridiculous.

I already had to reschedule an advisor meeting I had booked this morning because of Gavan's stupid demand to be here at eight. Then I had to beg that same advisor to *actually* meet with me after all, after Gavan's assistant Rachel called to tell me her boss wanted me to come in later instead.

Now it's four in the afternoon and I've been sitting in his goddamn office doing *nothing* for three fucking hours.

I won't lie: part of me has thought about messing up his office in some way. Not trashing it or anything crazy like that, and *certainly* not stealing anything like last time. Dear *God*, no. But just screwing with him a little, like messing up his perfectly ordered shelves. Making the pens on his desk *not* in perfect parallel alignment.

Except that would drive me, with my neat-freak tendencies, about as nuts as it would him. And *I'm* the one sitting in the office right now who'd have to actually look at those messed-up shelves and askew pens.

I'm also probably the one who'd have to fix them all later.

I blow air out through my lips and try and go back to the schoolwork I've been puttering away at. I'm sitting on Gavan's luxurious leather couch with my laptop. I mean I might as well get something done while I'm...

I blush.

While I'm...what? *Not* parading around Gavan's office in front of him, wearing nothing but lingerie? Lingerie I'm mortified at myself for having specifically gone out and bought to wear for him? Pearl-white, lacy bra and matching thong panties that I purposefully made sure coordinated with the French mani-pedi I got yesterday? Again, for *him*?

I was *eager* for him to see all this. I mean seriously, what the fuck is wrong with me.

And it's not just the prancing around doing odd tasks in my underwear, or the French tips that have me—horrifyingly —*excited* to show up at Gavan's office every morning.

It's what comes *after*. No pun intended.

After the hungry, wolfish looks and feel of his eyes on me reaches a breaking point. When his gaze latches onto mine, and he crooks his fingers.

When my pulse skips when I go to where he's sitting at his desk, or on this very couch. When my skin tingles and my core melts when I drop to my knees for him.

When I swallow his thick cock, leaking my need for him into my panties.

Or when he rips them off me and fingers me to an earth-shattering orgasm. Or spanks me over his lap. Or *all three*.

None of this should be turning me on. I shouldn't hunger for Gavan's touch. I shouldn't be so eager when I walk into his office. Yet I do, and I am.

I should be sick at the fact that he's blackmailing me into this. That I've been roped into this devil's deal with him. That he's forcing me to be his…his *plaything*.

Right. Forcing you.

Sure.

You keep telling yourself that.

It would be bad, but I really could stop this if I wanted to. I honestly don't know how my family would react if I were to come clean about what I did, in order to break Gavan's hold over me. I mean neither Neve nor I was close with our dad. Neither of us, frankly, shed a tear at his funeral. And if I were to explain why I did what I did that ended up causing his death, I can't imagine Neve, Cillian, or Castle would even bat an eye.

But what if they did? What if telling them changed the way they saw me forever? The way they thought about me? Cillian didn't have much love for Declan, but they *were* half-brothers.

I love my uncle, and I know he loves me. But does he love me enough not to snap if I told him I was at least partially responsible for Declan's death?

I shudder.

Just the same, it's a chance I *could* take. And it would put a stop to all this. Because at the end of the day, it's what I did concerning my father that Gavan has hanging over my head.

Sure, the egg I broke is wildly expensive. But Gavan's worth *billions*. Would he really go to war over a hundred million dollars?

The short version is, I know I could end all this with a hard conversation with my family.

The complicated and much longer version is, I'm not sure if I *want* to.

I exhale again, forcing myself to try and concentrate on the work on my laptop. When suddenly, the door to the office slams open. I gasp, startled and jumping quickly to my feet as the man himself comes surging into the room like a furious black cloud.

And I do mean *furious*.

There's rage burning on his face, and darkness pooling in his eyes. I frown as I stop and take him in.

What the fuck?

His hair is a mess. His neck and his face are streaked with soot, and his expensive suit is ripped, even *singed* in a few places. He kicks the door shut behind him and storms over to the bar cart, positively seething with dark, swirling energy as he pours a heavy splash of vodka into a glass and knocks it back in one swift gulp.

"Are you…" My brows knit as I take a tentative step toward him. "Gavan, are you okay…?"

He whirls savagely on me, his eyes blazing, his lips curled.

"*You*," he rasps with a snarl. "On my desk. *Now*."

I frown. "*On* your—?"

Nothing could prepare me for the way he crosses the distance between us in seconds, or for the feeling that courses through my body as he suddenly scoops me up and tosses me over his shoulder like a sack of laundry.

I squirm, gasping as I feel the rock-hard muscles of his shoulder ripple against my stomach. He marches us over to his desk, and my head reels as he suddenly plants me down on my ass on the edge of it.

"Gavan—"

The world goes blank as his lips crush to mine in a fierce, feral kiss. My pulse roars, and my inhibitions melt as he devours me, his tongue conquering mine in seconds as one hand wraps around my throat.

His tongue delves deeper, invading my mouth as his other hand drops to my blouse. I jolt, protesting weakly with muffled, moaning sounds as he rips it open, scattering the buttons all over the floor. He yanks my bra down, and I whimper into his mouth as he roughly cups my breasts and pinches my nipples until electricity sparks in my core.

I gasp loudly as his mouth drops to my neck—biting and sucking and mauling me as my eyes roll back in sweet agony. He groans, moving lower to do the same all the way down to my breasts until he takes one pink nipple into his mouth.

Then he bites down.

Hard.

I shriek, shuddering as a vicious pleasure I've never known before explodes through my system. I hiss, my hand involuntarily sliding into his hair and gripping it as he moves from one nipple to the other, turning my core to molten fire.

Then suddenly, he's pushing me down onto my back across his desk. Shoving my knees apart.

And dropping down between them.

My mouth falls open with a gasp as Gavan's hands slide up my thighs to hook into my panties. In one motion, he yanks them down to my knees and then literally tears them off my legs before tossing the shreds away. He roughly pushes my legs wider, and before I can even comprehend what's happening, his tongue is buried in my pussy.

Oh. Holy. Fucking. Shit.

Fireworks and explosions rip through my head as Gavan's mouth hums against me. His powerful tongue parts my lips, dragging up and down between them before centering on my clit.

It's the first time I've felt this. The first time anyone's ever licked me there.

My eyes roll back in my head and my back arches as I slam a hand over my mouth to muffle my screams. Because Gavan isn't just going down on me. He's not just eating me.

He's doing it the same way he kisses: as a declaration of war. As a conquering hero, bringing the total annihilation of my reality and inhibitions.

He's not merely eating me out. He's eating me *alive*.

I moan into my hand, writhing and twisting under his ferocious, insanely hot oral assault on my pussy. His tongue pushes deep—so fucking deep that it feels like I'm getting fucked for the first time. He swirls it around my clit, sucking the aching nub between his lips as he sinks two thick fingers into me and curls them deep.

My world begins to come apart. My thoughts scatter. My heartbeat goes through the roof as he loudly and wetly growls into my pussy as he drives me higher and higher. His tongue darts back and forth and around and around my throbbing clit. His fingers stroke at my g-spot, demanding my release.

Owning my body.

In full control of my pleasure, and my sanity.

His other hand slides up my body, pinching and assaulting first one nipple and then the other before it moves higher to wrap around my throat. I can feel the squeeze. I can feel the way every nerve in my body erupts into tiny little explosions as every inch of my skin ripples with pleasure.

And then suddenly, the whole world crushes in around me as my head drops back against his desk. My hand clamps down over my mouth as I scream through the most intense, the wildest, the most earth-shattering release of my entire life.

Gavan sucks on my clit one last time before sliding up between my spread thighs. His eyes lock with mine, his lips curling as he yanks his zipper down and pulls out his cock. My eyes bulge, my pulse starting to quicken all over again as I stare at his sheer size.

He wraps a fist around it, pumping himself slowly as he drags the silky head over my thigh. I bite my lip, transfixed, unable to look away as he pushes the swollen tip over my clit, making my throat seize up as my body shivers.

With excitement. With nervousness. With pure, unadulterated need.

He groans quietly, pushing his cock up over my stomach and letting a drop of precum drip onto my skin before he grits his teeth.

When suddenly, he's pulling away.

My brows knit, a flush coming to my cheeks.

"Why—"

I stop myself quickly, biting down on my lip.

What the fuck is wrong with you?

What am I, *disappointed* that the Bratva king blackmailing me isn't taking my freaking virginity across his office desk?

With a shake of his head, Gavan tucks his swollen cock back into his pants and zips them up.

"This arrangement doesn't work if you're a virgin, Eilish."

My face explodes with heat.

"I…" I swallow, closing my legs and pushing my bunched-up skirt back down. "Why would you think I'm—"

"Because you obviously are," he growls, his eyes flashing like cold steel as they lock with mine. "Please don't embarrass yourself trying to convince me otherwise."

Without another word, he turns, buttoning up his jacket and walking over to the door of his office. He opens it and gestures with his chin.

Guess that's my cue to leave.

I awkwardly slide off his desk, my legs still shaking as I smooth down my clothes and hair, gather my things, and put the jacket I—mercifully—brought today over my ripped blouse. I avoid his eyes as I walk to the door. Suddenly, he moves in front of me, blocking my exit.

"Tonight, be at my home at nine o'clock sharp. I'll text you the address. Don't be late."

I shiver, my eyes finally meeting his.

"Why am I coming to your house?"

Gavan's lips curl darkly at the corners.

"So that I can take your virginity, Eilish."

12

EILISH

WHAT THE FUCK am I doing here?

I stare up at the building looming over Central Park as the Uber I took over here peels away. Swallowing, I glance down at my phone, at the single text from Gavan that had this address.

I know damn well *why* I'm here. What I'm trying to wrap my head around is why I still *came.*

So that I can take your virginity, Eilish.

Like literally everything else where it concerns Gavan, I'm trapped at the crossroads of fear, apprehension, and excitement at the dark, beckoning unknown. It's a twisting, electrifying struggle, one that I've been dealing with ever since the night he grabbed me, when I shattered the egg.

It's a battle that was raging inside of me when I left his office today, after he put his mouth on me and made me explode. It was still raging when I got home and somehow got a through a conversation with Castle—about motorcycles, I think. Maybe.

And now here I am, hours later: showered clean, my body meticulously shaved bare all over, wearing *another* new lingerie set—this one dark green lace, and fairly transparent—under a simple green wraparound dress, with black heels.

Eager. Nervous.

Sinfully excited.

Is this the new me? The "I've looked death in the face after being blown up by a bomb", devil-may-care Eilish? Do I really *want* this?

I know I do. Because again, I could so easily stop this. I could turn around, hail another taxi, and go straight back home, where I could immediately 'fess up to my crimes and shatter Gavan's hold on me.

But I'm not going to. And it's not because of the fear of what my family will say or think.

It's because I don't *want* to turn around and walk away right now, knowing what's in store for me up there in Gavan's penthouse apartment.

Or, at least, having an *idea of* what's in store for me.

I take one last deep breath, smile weakly at the doorman, and step inside.

A huge guard inside who clearly works for Gavan checks my bag and waves a wand over my body, like he's looking for a weapon. He takes care not to actually touch me, though. A dark elevator with sultry light brings us up to the top floor. There, the guard uses a thumbprint reader to open the double doors. Wordlessly, he nods, and I step into a dimly lit room.

The door shut behind me. Gradually, my eyes adjust to the dark.

Whoa.

Gavan's apartment is...*vast*. Ridiculously so. Like, it takes up the entire top floor of the building. The whole place is decorated not dissimilarly from his office, but here, in his lair, it's as if someone turned that "dark and masculine" dial up to eleven.

Soft floor lights dramatically illuminate the slate-gray stone walls. I step across polished, dark hardwood floors toward a living room area with an enormous wall of windows looking east over Central Park.

The furniture is all dark brown leather and deep wood tones, with brass and slate accents. Soft, thumping, sexy music murmurs from hidden speakers as my pulse begins to quicken.

"I was wondering if you'd show up, *solnishka.*"

My heart jumps into my throat at the sound of his dark, purring voice. I turn to see him walking down a dark wood and steel floating staircase.

So, not just the entire top floor of the building. The entire top *two floors* of the building.

As always, Gavan somehow manages to look both feral and immaculately put together at the same time. His longish hair is shoved back from his face. His stubbled jaw and regal cheekbones are as razor sharp as always. He's wearing a simple but elegant dark gray suit—no vest this time, or tie—

with his customary French style dress shirt open at the neck, revealing a maze of tattoo ink across his chest.

My skin heats as his eyes sweep over me.

Hungrily. Darkly. Promising a night of sin and damnation.

"Would you like a drink?"

I nod. *"Yes,"* I choke out. "Please."

A hint of a smirk teases his lips as he moves closer, reaching up to cup my jaw and my face.

"I'm not going to hurt you, *solnishka,*" he growls quietly before lowering his lips to my ear in a way that makes my chest squeeze tighter. *"Unless you ask me to."*

Heat explodes in my core, my face throbbing.

"I like your dress."

I flush. "Thank—"

"Take it off."

Desire pools between my thighs. A shiver tickles down my spine. Nodding, I set my bag down on the edge of a couch and undo the tie at my waist. The dress falls open, and with a burst of bravery, I shrug it off my shoulders to let it drop to my feet.

Gavan growls deeply in his chest, his jaw clenching as his eyes sweep over me. And again, as it frequently does when I disrobe in front of him, his gaze seems to linger on the scars on my thigh and shoulder. His eyes narrow, and a flicker of something I can't read sparks behind them.

I can never tell if that anger I see in him when he sees my scars are because he views them as blemishes on what's "his".

Or if it's because they remind him of Leo, his former captain who ordered the bombing that gave these to me, who was also plotting to take Gavan himself out, too.

Gavan swirls his finger in the air. "Turn around for me."

My face throbs as I do as he asks, turning slowly and feeling his eyes drag hotly over my skin. When I'm back around facing him, my belly ties in knots at the fierceness in his gaze.

"Come."

He takes my hand and leads me to the staircase. He has me walk up ahead of him, and I swear I can feel the physical heat of his eyes on my ass as he follows behind me.

At the end of a dark, moodily-lit hall, we come to a stop at a door. Gavan opens it, leading me through, and my eyes widen.

Holy shit.

It's a bedroom, obviously. But it's also pretty clear it's not *his* bedroom. Not the one he usually sleeps in, at least.

Virgin or not, I'm pretty sure this particular bedroom isn't for sleeping in at all.

There's no windows. At all. The walls are a deep stone color, and the only light comes from long strips of warm-toned but dim LED lights by the floor around the perimeter of the room. It has the effect of giving the whole place an almost sinister erotic feel.

A bed takes up most of the far wall—a massive four-poster made of more dark wood, with the posts and frame around the top all done in black metal.

Like a cage.

My eyes widen and my throat tightens as my gaze drifts around the room—to the small leather couch against the wall opposite the bed, next to the door I've just walked through. Then to the table full of...*toys* against another wall.

Whips and floggers. Handcuffs. Chains and ropes. Plugs of several different sizes.

Raw, sensual desire mixed with a heady nervousness floods my system as the door shuts behind me with a soft click. Gavan's hand brushes casually but possessively over my hip as he walks past me and sits on the sofa. He turns to me, his eyes cool and impassive as he raises a hand and curls those two fingers at me.

"Come here, *solnishka*."

My head buzzing, my breath coming shallow and fast, I walk to him.

"Stop right there," he growls when I'm standing midway between him and the bed. "Take it all off except the heels."

I've been naked in front of him before. I've had his cock in my mouth and his cum down my throat. I've had his mouth on me, making me writhe and scream.

But somehow, the stakes seem higher now. The intensity is jacked through the roof. Because, this time, he's going to fuck me.

I'm about to lose my virginity to this man.

...and it's a thought that has me *very* wet.

I unhook the bra and peel down my panties, stepping out of them to stand in front of him.

"*Good girl*," he growls thickly. "Now, go to the bed."

Oh fuck. Oh fuck.

I turn, shaking a little as I walk toward it.

"On it," he grunts. "Hands and knees, facing the headboard."

Jesus Christ.

My skin feels electrified as I obey his demand and climb onto the bed. My face burns hotly as I bend over, fully aware of his eyes on my most intimate places, completely on display for him.

I hear rustling sounds behind me and start to turn my head back.

"*Eyes forward, solnishka,*" he rasps darkly.

I shiver, whipping my gaze back forward. But I've already gotten a glimpse of him—now naked, the sultry lighting etching the grooves of his insanely chiseled body in the shadows.

Illuminating the massive cock between his thighs.

...The one he's going to fuck me with.

Nervousness and arousal sizzle through my veins as I hear him approach me. He moves into my peripheral vision, and even though I'm still looking forward, my eyes are able to drink in the sight of his lethally hard body.

"Arms out."

I shift, blushing as I lower my cheek and shoulders to the dark gray duvet and stretch my arms forward. It has the effect of arching my back and thrusting my ass up into the air. Gavan smirks as he grabs something at the head of the bed.

Before I know what's happening, leather cuffs are clamped around my wrists.

My pulse goes through the roof. But I bite down hard on my lip, shivering as I feel him pull the chain tight that attaches them to the headboard. He strolls lazily around me, and when I feel two more cuffs clamping around each ankle, keeping my legs wide and locking me in place, heat explodes again through my core.

His finger drags down my spine, teasing every vertebra until his palm slides over my ass. He gives it a swat, and I whimper.

"*Such* an eager little fuck toy," he growls, making me moan as his fingers move agonizingly close to my pussy without actually touching me there.

I shift, trying in vain to close my thighs. But there's no hiding from him with the way I'm chained up.

Gavan chuckles darkly, making a tsking sound.

"Don't even try hiding how wet you are for me, my little toy."

This time, he boldly cups my dripping wet pussy. He drags a finger up my slit, and I choke as I gasp in pleasure.

He pauses, and I hear him sigh. "Where are my manners. I offered you a drink and never got it for you."

I hear him step across the floor. Then the sound of a bottle clinking in ice water, followed by the dull pop of a cork.

"I hope you like champagne."

I swallow, nodding.

"*Good*."

Suddenly, my eyes fly open, a shiver ripping through my body as I feel the ice-cold bubbles of the champagne dribbling *right over my pussy*. I gasp, arching my back, but helpless to escape it as Gavan pours the cold bubbly in a small river across my ass and my sex. It's so cold as almost to burn, before suddenly, the temperature radically changes.

…When his *mouth* drags up my slit.

I cry out, moaning as he tongues my pussy deeply, his lips and tongue warming the places where the champagne was ice cold. He pours more wine over me, growling as he sucks and licks, dragging his tongue up to my asshole, making me squeal.

Then he moves back to my clit, dribbling even more champagne over my pussy as he sucks on the throbbing nub between his lips. My eyes squeeze shut, my toes curling as my arms and legs strain at the binds holding me firm, as the pleasure swarms inside of me.

Just as I think he's going to make me come, he stops.

I groan in audible frustration when he pulls away before realizing what I've done. I wince, blushing furiously when I hear Gavan chuckle darkly.

"Such a greedy little girl."

His hands skim my ass, giving each cheek a deft smack, which pulls another whimper from my throat. He moves behind me, and suddenly, I feel it.

His cock.

My eyes fly open, my breath coming faster and faster as his hot, swollen cock head drags up and down my slick, eager lips.

"Now be a good girl," Gavan growls quietly. "And *fuck my cock like a good little toy.*"

The huge head pushes into me. I gasp, wincing a little at the initial sensation of penetration. But even as big as he is, and as tight as I am, I'm also fucking *soaked*. Quickly, the initial discomfort melts into something needy. Something thrilling.

Something that makes my eyes roll back in pleasure and my toes curl.

Oh fuck…

He groans, his big dick pulsing, just the head inside me. His hands grip my hips, and when he starts to push further into me, a cry of pleasure erupts from my mouth.

"There's a good girl."

He pushes in deeper, his huge cock stretching me wide open to what feels like my absolute limit. The sensation is *insane*.

Gavan isn't just fucking me.

He's *consuming* me.

Controlling me, owning me, and conquering me. And the swirling mix of all that has me choking into to the sheets as pleasure ripples through my body.

He keeps going. Just when I think I must have all of him inside of me, he *keeps going*. Inch after thick inch sinks into my swollen pussy, until finally I can feel his abs against my ass and his heavy, swollen balls against my clit.

Holy fucking shit.

He's deep.

And very, very big.

His fingers dig into my skin, and I gasp as he starts to slide out of me. Pleasure blurs the edges of my vision as I feel my slick lips cling to every inch of him as he withdraws, only to slam right back inside me again. I moan loudly, my hands twisting to grip handfuls of the sheets beneath me as Gavan begins to fuck me.

Not "make love to".

Not "have sex with".

Fuck.

And Gavan fucks like he kisses. Like he doles out orders. Like he conquers his enemies and controls his empire.

Brutally. Unmercifully. And with a savageness that turns me into a fucking *puddle*. I scream in pleasure, my back arching and my eyes squeezing shut as he grips me possessively and fucks me like I belong to him. His thick cock sinks deep, hitting pleasure spots I wasn't even aware I had. His hands are everywhere: gripping my hips and spanking my ass, reaching under me to rub and pinch my clit, dragging up my spine, tangling my hair in a fist and pulling tight as he fucks me to within an inch of my life.

I start to come around his cock, my pussy squeezing tight as I scream into the sheets. Gavan just keeps going, never slowing for a moment as he drives me from one orgasm to the next. At one point, he makes me whine like a desperate little sub when he slips out of me, only taking a moment to chuckle before his mouth covers my pussy.

I explode on his tongue twice before he buries his thick cock in me again. This time, he goes even harder.

Faster.

Fucking me with deep, powerful thrusts as his abs slap my ass and my cum covers his swollen cock.

Something starts to build inside me. And build. And *build*, until the wave that's coming is so big, nothing on earth could possibly stop it. I scream when it crashes over me, and when Gavan groans and buries his enormous cock to the hilt in me, it only makes me twist and writhe even harder.

I can feel him coming, the hot bursting spurts of his release spilling into me as I bite down on the sheets with my face scrunched all the way up.

My entire world goes blurry and fuzzy. I can't move. I can barely even force myself to breathe. But I can feel him stirring around me, slowly unclasping the leather cuffs from my wrists and ankles. I collapse onto the bed. Then I'm vaguely aware of him picking me up in his arms and carrying me away.

We move to another room that I eventually realize is the bathroom—still dim, but slightly brighter. I blink as he sets me down on wobbly feet, leading us into a glass-walled shower and turning on the rain nozzle above. I glance down at his sweat-glistened, chiseled body.

My face heats when I see the blood on his cock. But he doesn't seem to notice or care as he reaches out and takes my hand.

"Come here, *solnishka*."

He wraps me in his arms, pulling me under the warm spray of the water as it cascades over us. His lips find mine, hungrily kissing and biting and assaulting my mouth as it willingly opens for him.

His cock rises thickly between my legs.

Oh fuck...

Before I know what's happening, he's lifting me up, my legs wrapping around his grooved hips as he presses my back against the glass wall. The swollen head of his cock slips between my lips, and I cry out as he drives all the way up into me.

Yessss...

I'm sore. Everything hurts. And yet, I want more. I *need* more, like a drug I'm addicted to already. Like a rush I'm going to keep chasing. I cling to him, moaning into his mouth and then biting down on his shoulder to stop from screaming as he fucks me hard against the shower wall, until we explode together again.

After the shower, we're back in the windowless bedroom, which the bathroom we were just in is attached to. Gavan scowls as I drop my towel and start to put my lingerie back on.

"What the fuck are you doing?"

My brow furrows, my face blushing as I turn to him.

"Did...umm...you want to go again?"

He scowls deeper. "Of course."

"Oh." I swallow, shivering as I start to take my bra off again.

Gavan shakes his head. "No, I mean..." His frown deepens. "What *were* you doing?"

Now I'm confused.

I peer at him, smiling awkwardly. "Going home?"

He frowns. "No. You're staying the night."

Something electric spikes through my core.

It's tempting. Very, very tempting. Even if this whole thing is a devil's deal, and even if Gavan is, well, *him*, he *is* still the man who just took my virginity. Purely sexual arrangement rooted in blackmail or not, staying here, and like...I don't know, cuddling? Being close to him?

It sounds...nice.

It also sounds like an impossibility with a man as cold, dark, and brutal as Gavan Tsarenko. That's not what this is. That's not what *we* are.

It can't ever be that.

"If you want to have sex again..." I blush at how boldly I say it. "Then, okay. If not, I'm going to go home."

His eyes narrow at me. "I said, you're staying—"

"I'm not," I say quietly.

Gavan's jaw grinds.

"I don't think you heard—"

"You said you wouldn't force me to do anything."

He glares at me. "I know what I said."

"Well then?"

He goes silent for a moment.

"Fine," he finally mutters. Without another word, he turns and strides out through the door, towel-clad, bristling.

Okay?

I follow him back along the hall and down the stairs. I pick my dress up from where I left it, wrapping it back around myself, feeling his eyes on me.

This is very confusing.

So far as I've been able to tell, Gavan's interest in me, and in this whole arrangement, is purely sexual—mixed with a touch of humiliation when he has me clean his office in my underwear. But now he wants me to sleep over?

It feels like it has to be a trick or a mind game. But if it's not?

Well then, that's alarming for a whole load of other reasons.

Because this—this whatever-it-is between us—can't be *that*. Not given who I am, and who he is.

I'm already sleeping with the enemy. I don't need to *sleep over* with him, as well.

"My people will take you home."

I shiver as I feel his warm breath on the back of my neck. Turning, I flush when I see him towering over me. His hand cups my jaw, a raw darkness in his eyes. And suddenly, he's kissing me, just as hard and as punishingly as ever.

When he pulls back, I'm tingling all over. And throbbing. And *wet*.

And seriously considering asking if I *can*, in fact, stay over after all.

"Gavan—"

"Eight o'clock tomorrow morning," he growls. "Don't be late."

Without another word, he turns, strides over to the front door of the penthouse, and holds it open for me.

Yep, that's my cue.

I simmer as I sit in the back seat of the black Range Rover that takes me home, luxuriating in the soreness and the flickers of heat still throbbing deep inside me.

And wondering just exactly how far down this rabbit hole I'm prepared to fall.

13

GAVAN

I WAS RIGHT: she was a virgin.

Was being the operative word there. Because after fucking Eilish that night in my playroom, and then in the shower, I've spent the last week and a half making sure her pussy doesn't go five goddamn minutes without remembering me filling her until she screams.

I've spent the last ten days making Eilish's pussy completely, unequivocally *mine*.

It started the morning after that first night at my place. She was in my office promptly at eight a.m. as instructed, and if it was a whole thirty seconds before I had her panties pulled to the side and my cock buried balls-deep in her greedy little cunt, her back pressed up against my office door with my hand over her mouth, I'd be shocked.

No foreplay needed. That girl walked in *dripping* wet for me.

She left later that afternoon even wetter, with my cum soaking her panties.

This has since turned into a daily occurrence. The only break in the schedule was on Saturday, when obviously she wasn't at the office. It was a day I spent drumming my fingers on the edge of my couch back at home, glaring out over the city and telling myself I didn't "need" Eilish at all.

That lasted about twelve and a half hours, until I called her Sunday morning and demanded she come over, where I promptly fucked her four times in a row before sending her home.

I didn't ask her to spend the night again.

That was an error in judgment that won't be repeated.

Just the same, this girl has become a fucking addiction. An obsession, even more than she was before. And as much as I'm reluctant to admit it—because I never, ever wanted to be anyone's first—the notion that I *was* that for her is…intoxicating.

Way, way too intoxicating.

It's also insane that I didn't know that before, given the time and effort I've spent learning her every secret. I know *everything* about Eilish, at least from the age of nineteen on.

Since the night I saw her picking up the spent cartridges on the ground of that fateful meeting between Declan Kildare and Vasilis Drakos—furtively looking around. Wincing when she burned her fingers on a still-hot casing.

Standing over her own father's dead body and spitting on it.

That was the moment I realized there was more to Eilish Kildare than I thought. The moment she caught my eye as anything more than revenge.

It was also the moment that dictated the *way* in which I followed her every move for the next year and a half. I wasn't just learning about her and uncovering her every secret after that. I wasn't simply looking for leverage, or ways to break her.

I became obsessed with her.

I didn't just stalk her. I deep dived into her. I hacked into her email and laptop, allowing me to see her every web search. To see every dirty video she watched involving submission and free use kinks.

It was the intimacy of that violence I saw in her, that I doubt anyone else ever had, that made me make damn sure no other man ever *would* see that part of her, or any other part of her for that matter. It's why I—even when I wasn't sure why, and even when I wanted to stop—spent a year and a half sabotaging her every attempt at a relationship before they could even be called that.

Men who got her number never called. I made sure of that. Men who managed to take her out for lunch or a drink once never asked again.

Also me.

I've spent a year and a half flipping between vengeance and desire whenever Eilish Kildare comes into my head, which is very, very frequently.

But somehow, through all of that, until I met her and finally had her in my clutches, I never knew she was a virgin. I'd just assumed she'd crossed that bridge years before I made her my obsession. I mean for fuck's sake, *look* at her. She's beautiful. Smart. Driven. Ambitious. Friendly and nice to a fault. It's *insane* that no man got his hands on her.

It's also a good thing. Because if any man had, I'd have *taken* those hands from him.

"Mr. Tsarenko?"

I frown, shaking the thoughts of Eilish from my head at the voice coming from the intercom on my desk. It's Thursday, and I'm especially broody and grouchy. For one, because devil-cunt herself, aka Svetlana, decided today was a good day to start blowing up my phone.

I've ignored every call. I know she's calling to whine about why I haven't finalized the deal we agreed upon—the one where she gets the Imperial Shield egg, and I get her off my fucking back concerning my company and its shares in Koikov bank.

Obviously, that deal is no longer on the table. But I've been too preoccupied with taking on the full empire myself to deal with it.

Well, that's not quite true. It's more that I've been preoccupied positively losing myself in my new addiction named Eilish Kildare to give a shit about the deal with Svet.

That's the other reason I'm in an especially vile, asshole mood: Eilish skipped coming to the office today. Apparently, she occasionally *does* need to actually attend class or meet with her advisors. I agreed to let her miss today, but I plan on taking out my aggression on her ass later. I grin, imagining all the ways I'll have her on her knees, or bent over the arm of my sofa back home, when Rachel interrupts my thoughts yet again.

"Sir?"

I scowl at the intercom. "Yes?" I mutter.

"Sorry, but you have a phone call."

My brow furrows. "Who is it?"

"It's Ms. Crown's office."

Shit. Ms. Crown as in Taylor Crown, the partner at Crown and Black who's my personal attorney. She's also helping with the deal with Svetlana and the whole situation of me having, you know, stolen her inheritance from Vadim.

Because—and I can't stress this enough—*fuck* Svetlana.

"I'll take it."

I pick up, waiting for the click as Rachel transfers the call before I sigh.

"I know, I've owed you a call for like a week."

"Longer than that."

I stiffen, my eyes drawing to slits and my lips curling at the sound of the voice on the other end.

Mother. *Fuck.*

"You know, your secretary really ought to not take what people tell her at face value."

It's not Taylor. It's fucking *her*.

Svetlana laughs coldly. "Don't you dare even think about hanging up on me."

My jaw grinds.

"What the fuck do you want, you miserable bitch," I snarl.

Svet makes a tsk-tsk sound.

"I want to know why our deal has stalled. Unless, of course, you're having second thoughts. In which case, my attorney and I are happy to move forward with taking you to court for *everything*—"

"You'll get your fucking egg," I hiss. "It needs to be authenticated and appraised before—"

"I'm well aware of that," she fires back. "But I also don't trust you, Gavan," she purrs in a silky voice that makes my skin crawl. "Not after you tried to cheat me before."

"Die in a fire that could have been prevented, you hag."

"*Careful*, you little shit," she hisses. "As I was saying, *I don't trust you*. Which is why I've hired my own independent appraiser to come see the egg and verify everything. Then we can move forward."

My stomach lurches.

"He's *very* good, Gavan," she drawls on, as if we're suddenly talking tennis instructors over white wine spritzers at her fucking country club. "Simply the best in his field. And he specializes in Russian Imperialist—"

"Is there anything *else*, Svet," I snap coldly.

She's silent for a moment.

"Seeing anyone?"

My eyes close. A wave of dizziness and nausea spins through my head.

No one except me. No one will ever love you. Not like I do. No one will understand you, my baby boy.

I don't realize how hard I'm squeezing the phone until I hear the plastic almost crack.

I slam down the phone and then glare at it, my pulse roaring in my ears and a cold, clammy sensation settling over my skin.

Fuck you.

Still throbbing with hatred, I snatch up my cell to text Eilish. When I do, I notice the time, and I groan.

Shit. I'm going to be late.

THE MOOD IS DECIDEDLY SOMBER when I walk into the High Council meeting this time. Ilya and Lukas shake my hand firmly but grimly. Yuri and Viktor do the same, the former shaking his head.

"Dark times, my friend," Yuri mutters. "Dark fucking times."

He's not wrong.

Marko Kalishnik is in hospital, still in a medically-induced coma in the wake of the car-bombing outside Crudo. This is an unprecedented attack on a head of High Council family. A *founding* family, no less. Vlad, his number two, is dead.

"Have you seen him?"

Yuri nods. "I went yesterday. No change in his prognosis. But, he's alive. Technically."

Lukas folds his arms over his chest. "So, what exactly is the protocol here? I mean, if a council member is unexpectedly unable to sit at the table. It must have come up before…"

Yuri and Viktor glance at each other uneasily before Viktor clears his throat.

"The last time we had anything like this was *years* ago, when..." His face darkens as he glances at me.

"When Semyon was killed?" I finish for him.

The man who raped my mother and sired me in the process. The man who also fathered my half-sisters Lizbet and Mara.

May he burn in hell.

Viktor nods. "After that, there were simply fewer chairs at the table. Until we voted in Ozerov, and then Anastasia."

"This vote is going to be impossible," Ilya mutters. "It's dead-locked without Marko."

"Or an opportunity," Lukas murmurs, looking over at the door to the conference room just as Anastasia Javanović walks in. "She might be able to be swayed."

"I've had some of our people working on what we spoke about before," Ilya mutters quietly. "So far, nothing."

"Are we starting this party or not?"

The five of us turn together to glare at Abram, sprawled in his chair tapping his fingers on the armrest impatiently.

"In a minute," Yuri growls at him before turning to me. "Can I speak to you privately for a second?"

I nod, following him to a corner of the room, where he leans close.

"I heard that Marko spoke to you about...well, you know... right before the attack."

He means the arranged marriage to Milena.

"*If* it's something you were considering," Yuri murmurs quietly, "now might be a good time to put it in writing. As much as I'm hoping for his recovery, and as much as I consider Marko a friend, if he dies, there's going to be an ugly power grab for his empire. Both from outside and from within, given that he has no male heir. If there was a marriage on the table, though—"

"Hey, Yuri?" I interrupt him.

He shrugs. "Forgive me. I'm not trying to meddle. I just try and think long term as much as possible."

"No offense taken, and I understand perfectly." I clap him on the shoulder. "It's not something I've completely written off. I'm considering it."

No I'm not.

After we all sit, Yuri glances at me and then clears his throat. "One of our own has been attacked. The reason I've called this impromptu meeting is to—"

"Fuck this."

I glare at Abram as he stands, pounding a fist on the table.

"Sit *down*, Abram," I hiss. "Yuri was—"

"Talking, yes, I know," Abram spits. "Because that's all this table of soft financiers and investors want to do. *Talk*. Not take action. Not go to war, as their own fathers would have, as is the way of the Bratva!"

I glance next to me at Lukas, who is shaking his head.

"And exactly who should we be going to war *with*, Abram," he sighs.

The head of the Diduch family scoffs. "We all know who. This was all Drazen's doing, and he's going to *keep* doing it until you all find your balls and vote to allow me and my cousin to defend this council as we—"

"For the *last fucking time*," Viktor snaps. "We are not declaring war on a fucking fairytale! Who's next, Abram?" He snarls. "The goddamn Tooth Fairy? Are we going to pool our resources to hunt the fucking Easter Bunny?! Maybe you'd like to order a hit on fucking Santa Claus while you're at it."

Abram's lips curl, his teeth flashing dangerously. But Viktor keeps going.

"Giving *you* of all fucking people control of all of our forces in order to go after a Boogeyman is absurd. You need to understand: it's not going to happen."

"And I wonder how this grand opinion of yours will change, *Viktor*," Abram yells as he gets to his feet. "When Drazen comes for *you* next—"

"WE DON'T KNOW IT WAS DRAZEN!" Viktor bellows. "For fuck's sake, Abram, what do you not understand about this? There's literally not even concrete proof Drazen Krylov is a real person!"

The room goes quiet. Even Abram shuts up and then sits. Then, slowly, his lips curl.

"No? Well then, I wonder what the fuck this is supposed to mean."

He slips a hand inside his suit jacket. When he pulls it out, he's holding a plastic baggie with "New York Police Department Evidence Locker" stamped on it. "I got this from one of my connections on the force," he sneers. "I wonder what it could be?"

He tosses the baggie on the table.

"Go ahead," he jeers. "Take a look."

Viktor glances first at Yuri, then at me, before he reaches over and plucks up the bag. I lean close, frowning as I try to figure out what I'm looking at.

The evidence bag has "Kalishnik, Marco" printed on it, together with the date and location of the bombing the other day, along with "Attention: Organized Crime Division". Inside is a playing card—the King of Diamonds. But the head has been burned out with what looks like a cigarette, and there's burn marks around the edges.

There's writing on it, too—words scrawled in fine-tipped black marker. And when I lean closer, my body stiffens when I read it:

Now there is a seat at the table for me.

I am coming.

-Drazen Krylov

The room is silent. Abram's eyes land on each of us in turn.

"I don't know, Viktor," he snarls. "Maybe he's not real. But he did just *literally leave a calling card* with his fucking signature on it. So you tell me."

Viktor's jaw is clenched tight as he glares at the card before he turns to eye Yuri and me.

"I call for a vote—"

"And we will have one, Abram," Yuri growls. "But not today. We've already agreed on a second vote a few weeks from now."

The younger Diduch looks like he wants to start shit again, but then just glares at Yuri and settles back in his seat.

"Now," Yuri sighs. "In line with the Council code, we need to figure out how to work with Marko's people to ensure the whole Kalishnik empire doesn't implode. One, because Marko's our friend. But also, purely from a business perspective, if his organization goes up in flames, we're all going to get burned."

IT's hours later when we finally adjourn the meeting. On the plus side, it was productive. Yuri reached out to Anatoli, one of Marko's most trusted captains and the obvious person to make decisions within the Kalishnik ranks, and we hammered out some assurances to make sure the Kalishnik organization doesn't go up like the fucking Hindenburg. Luckily, Anatoli is fiercely loyal to his boss.

When we're done, Ilya and Lukas invite me out for a drink, but I shake my head and mutter something vague about needing to catch up on some work shit.

The truth is, what I really need to "catch up on" is hearing Eilish's moans in my ear as her pussy milks the cum from my balls.

I texted her hours ago, during the meeting. Twice.

She hasn't responded, not to the "Be available to come over tonight" first one nor the "Answer me" second one.

And now I'm pissed.

I want to punch myself in the face for calling her. But I do it anyway, as soon as I get into the back of my Range Rover. It goes to voicemail.

Both times.

Goddammit.

I'm stressed, and I'm pissed. Which means I'm pent up. Which means I want release. And the only release I seem to be able to get—or even want—these days is from *her*.

I glare at the screen as I hammer out another text.

> ME
>
> Where the fuck are you

If she's trying to ignore me, she's just slipped up. Because I see the three telltale dots appear to indicate she's typing before they disappear again.

> ME
>
> I saw that.

> EILISH
>
> And?

> ME
>
> Come to my place. Now.

> EILISH
>
> lol
>
> No.

My lips curl into a snarl.

> ME
>
> Excuse me?

EILISH

Sorry.

ME

That's better.

EILISH

Did that text not come through before? I said "no".

Then she sends me a fucking *winky face* with its mother-fucking tongue poking out. I glare at the little yellow emoji and imagine ripping that fucking tongue right out of its mouth.

ME

I think you might have forgotten the nature of our arrangement. I want you at my house, naked, on all fours on my living room floor, in twenty minutes.

EILISH

I can't tonight.

What the fuck.

ME

Once again, I'm not sure if you're remembering our arrangement. Be there in twenty or there will be consequences.

EILISH

LOL. Liek what?

Ruh-row. The tyrant is madddd! Watch out, wrld!

I frown. Her spelling is off. And she's never "goofy" like this, either in person or over text. Suddenly, it clicks.

> **ME**
> Are you drunk?

> **EILISH**
> None of ur beeswax. I'm not a surgeon and I'm not on call.

I glare at the screen.

> **ME**
> Where are you.

> **EILISH**
> night night mister grumpy pants

> **ME**
> Get your ass to my goddamn house right now or else.

> **EILISH**
> lol this is getting pathetic. Go jerk off if you're that hard up. Byyeee

Thunder rolls in my head. I thumb away from my texting app and call Korol.

"What's up?"

"That phone I asked you to geo-trace."

It's not exactly ethical. Then again, I do run a worldwide criminal organization.

"I need to know precisely where it is. Now."

"You got it, Boss-man," he mutters, clicking away at something on his end. "Okay, it's at a bar called Angel's Share. Texting you a map pin of it now."

I hang up and relay where we're going to my driver.

Eilish just made her bed.

Now, she's going to get fucked in it. Hard.

14

EILISH

"Who's that?"

My eyes snap from my phone to Callie.

"What?" I all-but-yell. I have to: it's loud as absolute shit in here with the rock music thudding over the loudspeakers and so many people that the place is almost certainly over legal capacity.

Callie rolls her eyes. "Who's the guy you're texting?"

I swallow, my heart skipping as I put down my phone.

"No one. There's no guy."

Next to Callie, Dahlia smirks at me.

"I call bullshit."

Callie snorts, turning to clink her margarita against Dahlia's. "Right?"

I glare at the pair of them. "Okay, first of all, I feel set up."

Callie snickers. "How so?"

"You told me we were going out for research purposes."

She shrugs, gesturing around the crowded bar with her brows. "I mean, it is, isn't it?"

I roll my eyes. "No. This place is nothing like our plan for The Banshee when it reopens, and you know it."

Callie grins as she takes a sip of margarita. "Yeah, well, it's a fun vibe, the margaritas are strong, and they have a conveniently loose stance on checking IDs at the door."

I sigh and shake my head as she giggles. Callie's not quite twenty-one yet. On the plus side, it means she still doesn't have to deal with the whole bullshit arranged marriage thing she's got with that creep Luca Carveli. On the downside...well, Callie likes a good cocktail, but she doesn't have a good fake ID.

"Secondly, I feel ganged up on."

Dahlia lifts a shoulder. "It's two on one, love. You *are* being ganged up on. Spill. Who's the guy?"

"There is no guy!"

Such a lie.

I've been staring at Gavan's texts for almost two hours.

GAVAN

Be available to come over tonight.

Answer me.

That should be off-putting, right? I mean, rude? I'm not at his beck and call.

Except you sort of totally are.

And you kinda totally like it.

178

I probably need to set some boundaries with him. I *definitely* need to set some boundaries with him.

Dahlia gives me a look. "No one checks their phone that much without it being a somebody."

I wrinkle my nose. "What?"

"It's a fact," Callie shrugs. "So… Who is it?"

Oh, just the man who I lost my virginity to. Which I haven't mentioned to you, even though you're my best friend. Or even mentioned it to my sister, for that matter.

Because the man I lost my virginity to is the enemy. A man who almost went to war with both my family and Callie's. A man who maybe didn't give the actual order, but whose wrath lit the fuse which blew up the Banshee, almost killing Callie, her grandmother, and me.

Which *did* kill Sean Farrell.

But when I'm with Gavan, it doesn't feel like he's the enemy at all. When I'm with him, it's more like for the first time in my life, something feels completely right. Which is maybe a bit of a problem. Or a lot of one.

I might need psychiatric help.

Because I can't stop what I feel when I'm near him. It's a seductive, magnetic pull that I'm helpless to resist. The anxious neediness when I'm waiting for his next touch. The throb of nervous energy and the sharp inhale of breath when I defy him, which is like taunting an angry lion.

And *God* do I love it when he finally snaps and mauls me.

There was that one time he didn't, which would be that first night at his home when I told him defiantly I wouldn't be staying over, though he clearly wanted me to.

We've never circled back to that, and it's never come up again. But it hasn't gone unnoticed to me that he's slightly more standoffish now, even though we've been having sex just about every single day *since* that night. It's almost as if we got too close to a line, and then both backed off.

But I do stand by my decision not to stay over. That would have been...too much. Especially on the night I lost my virginity. Too intimate, maybe, like crossing a line from being just his fuck toy, which is fun and amazing, to...something more, which I'm not prepared to be.

But as for the sex part?

Um, *yeah.*

It's otherworldly. Like, I didn't know the human body could orgasm like that. And even though the first time was rough, and aggressive and wild, and I was tied up, it was also perfect. And hot, and not at all triggering, which is always good.

"Oh my God, why are you being so weird about this?" Callie sighs, ripping me from my x-rated thoughts.

I cover the blush on my face by slugging back half of my—admittedly delicious—margarita.

Callie makes a face and holds up her finger. "Wait, it's not that Brooks douchebag, is it?"

I stiffen, my eyes snapping to hers. I've only briefly mentioned Brooks to her in passing, just in reference to high school. I haven't mentioned his ridiculous "joining of the families" suggestion.

Nor have I told her what happened back in high school. I haven't told anyone that, actually.

I can't.

"How did you know about that?"

She lifts a shoulder. "Ares."

Instantly, her face twists when my eyebrows fly up and I stare at her, open-mouthed.

"Okay, before you blow up, he didn't knowingly tell me anything. I was over at his and Neve's place and heard them talking about it when they thought I was in the other room."

"Who's Brooks?"

I ignore Dahlia's question and look into my margarita, something cold and sharp twisting inside of me. Callie answers for me.

"Old high school boyfriend. He's a douche. Dad's a congressman or something."

"He's a senator," I say coldly. My eyes raise to Dahlia's. "It… didn't end well. His father recently reached out to my uncle about Brooks and I marrying as some sort of political move."

She makes a face. "*Wow*. Medieval much? Who the fuck even still gets arranged—"

She winces, whipping her gaze around to a glowering Callie.

"Shit. Sorry."

Callie shrugs as she polishes off her drink. "Don't be. That is *not* happening, anyway. I'll flee the country and buy a new face and change my identity before I marry Luca fucking Carveli. Gross." She shivers. "But we're getting off topic. We're supposed to be ganging up on Eilish about the identity of her mysterious text-messager."

"True." Dahlia swivels back to me. "Well? It's *not* this Brooks wanker, is it?"

I groan, rolling my yes. "*No*! It's *not* Brooks, okay?"

Shit. I realize I've slipped when I see the Cheshire Cat grin spread across Callie's face.

"Aha! So you *are* chatting with someone!"

"*No*! C'mon, you know me. When would I have the time or interest for anything like that?"

Dahlia grins. "I mean, you could make time. You've got someone staring holes in the back of your head right now."

I frown, turning to see a dark-haired, built, somewhat swarthy guy in an out-of-place suit leaning against the bar. Staring at me. He immediately glances away when I spot him, but I shiver.

I don't think he's an admirer.

There's a good chance he's one of Gavan's men. Which is both an alarming and electrifying thought.

"Yeah, pass," I mutter. When I turn back and see the insistent looks on their faces, I know this isn't going away.

I sigh. Fuck it.

"Ugh, okay. *Yes*. Maybe I've been...seeing someone."

That's one word for it.

The two of them squeal.

"*Oooo*," Callie giggles. "Tell all. Now."

My face heats.

Not a fucking chance.

"It's…just a guy. It's nothing, really."

Callie glances at Dahlia before smirking at me. "Nothing like *nothing*, or nothing like you're just casually banging?"

My face goes crimson. Callie's eyes instantly bulge.

"*Hold up*," she breathes, staring at me. "I was kidding, but… Oh my God, are you seriously sleeping with someone?!"

My throat bobs up and down. "No."

"Because if you went out and had sex for the first time and *didn't* tell me, that's fucked up."

I frown. "Or, that's private?"

"Dude, have you *met me*?"

I snort.

"Yeah, I'm going to need to see your phone."

"Not happening."

"C'mon!!"

"No!" I laugh nervously.

"My brother saved your sister's life."

I stare at her flatly. "Okay, that's cheating."

"Don't worry," Dahlia grins. "We won't snoop. Just show us what's had you staring at your phone like you don't know what to say back."

Jesus, these two are fucking relentless.

"Hang on."

They both grin as I pick up the phone and click on my text exchange with Gavan. There's nothing really *that* bad in the text history. Mostly just demands like "Be here at 8, sharp", or "My place, right now. Do not wear panties."

I flush, mortified at the idea of these two seeing those. But they already basically know I'm seeing someone. And I mean, I'm twenty-one. I'm allowed to have sex.

Quickly, I delete any older texts where I mention his name, and then change his contact name to "Tyrant". Then, I take a shaky breath, slug back the rest of my margarita, and slide the phone toward my gleeful friends.

"*No* snooping. Seriously. Please."

"Cross my heart," Callie chirps before catching the attention of our waiter. "Hi, yeah, we're going to need two more of these, please. Each."

I groan. "You're trouble."

"Guilty as charged. Okay, let's do this."

I tense as she and Dahlia pick up my phone and focus their attention on the screen. Callie instantly explodes into fits of giggles.

"'*Be available to come over tonight?*' '*Answer me*'?" she blurts. "Is this guy fucking for real?"

I groan. This was a horrible idea.

"No, it's…it's not like that. It's like a joke—"

"I'm going to tell him to chill the fuck out."

"CALLIE!"

I grab the phone out of her hands, deleting "be polite, douchebag" before she can send it.

Except another message instantly pops up.

TYRANT
I saw that.

Crap, he saw her typing.

ME
And?

TYRANT
Come to my place. Now.

The phone is suddenly gone from my hand again. I pale as my eyes snap to a grinning Callie, who is now in possession of it.

"*Callie—*"

"I'm not going to be a bitch about it. But seriously, this dude needs to calm down with the possessive macho shit. What are you, his slave?"

I blush fiercely.

"Can you just give it—"

"Hang on."

I groan when I see her typing and then sending something.

"No stress," Dahlia giggles. "She just told him 'no', and then 'lol'."

I cringe.

Yeah, to a normal person, that's a simple response. To Gavan, it's an act of rebellion that needs to be crushed.

I grab the phone back.

TYRANT

Excuse me?

ME

Sorry.

The phone is snatched from my hand again.

"Callie!"

I grab it back, paling as I read what she wrote.

ME

Did that text not come through before? I said "no".

After that, there's a freaking winky face.

He's going to lose it.

TYRANT

I think you might have forgotten the nature of our arrangement. I want you at my house, naked, on all fours on my living room floor, in twenty minutes.

My thumbs dance across the screen.

ME

I can't tonight.

Boundaries. We seriously *need* boundaries.

TYRANT

Once again, I'm not sure if you're remembering our arrangement. Be at my place in twenty or there will be consequences.

"Mother*fuck*! Callie!"

I lunge for my phone again after she grabs it. But she's faster.

"Oh my fucking *God*!" she blurts, giggling as her face goes red. "Eilish Kildare! Who the *fuck* is this guy?!" She laughs, with Dahlia staring at the screen in shock. *'I want you at my house, naked, on all fours on my living room floor'*?! Who even talks like that?!"

Dahlia flushes and grins. "I mean, *I* wouldn't be mad if someone talked to me like that—well, depending on the someone, of course."

Callie cracks up. "*Yeah*, same. Now I'm super curious who the hell 'Tyrant' is."

"He's *nobody*," I mumble through a throbbing face.

She stares at me. "Wait. You're totally fucking this guy, aren't you?"

I swallow thickly but don't answer, chewing on my lip.

"What the *fuck*, Eilish!?" She glares at me. "You don't keep something like that from your best friend!"

You do when it's a man who almost went to war with both our families.

"I…" I look away just as the waiter arrives with our obscene number of margaritas. Which we all instantly dip into.

"Look, I was going to tell you, I swear. I'm just…" I shrug. "Figuring it out, I guess? It's not anything serious. Really."

She glares at me before sighing. *"Fine.* I forgive you." She waits a beat for emphasis. "Dick."

"Thank you."

Callie gives me a look before giggling again. "But seriously. *'Or there will be consequences'?"* She shakes her head. And before I can stop her, she's typing rapid fire responses, mumbling them out loud as she does.

"El-oh-e*lll,"* she giggles. "Like what?"

I groan. He's going to make me pay so hard for this.

Except you're not super upset about that, are you?

Callie keeps going. "Ruh-row. The tyrant is mad! Watch. Out," she types, "World!" She instantly laughs. "He just asked if you're drunk."

"Not nearly drunk enough for this," I mutter, slamming back three large gulps of my margarita.

"I told him it was none of his beeswax, and that you weren't an on-call surgeon."

I groan. "Will you *please* give me back my phone?"

"Not until you tell me who I'm texting on your behalf."

"Not happening."

"Well then, I guess this is my plane to pilot then, huh?"

I lunge again, but she pulls back, typing away.

"Night night, mister grumpy pants," she giggles, sending a text. Her eyes bulge when she reads his response. "Dude, this guy is insane. '*Get your ass to my goddamn house right now or else*'?!" She glances up at me. "Okay, seriously. Should I be worried? Honestly?"

Maybe.

"Just about me killing you to get my fucking phone back!"

"Okay, okay. Hang on. One more." She sends something and then slides the phone across the table to me with a flourish. "I hope the sex is fantastic, 'cause this guy seems like a complete psycho."

"At least he's not a phone thief," I mutter darkly, picking up my phone and glancing at what she said.

Jesus. Christ.

ME

lol this is getting pathetic. Go jerk off if you're that hard up. Byyeee.

My head jerks around, my eyes searching for the guy who was at the bar before, who I'm still convinced was one of Gavan's guys, spying on me, ready to pass along exactly where I am. When I don't see him anymore, my core clenches.

Yeah, I'm fucking screwed.

15

EILISH

THIS HAS GONE from bad to worse.

After half an hour of anxiously waiting for Gavan to somehow magically find me and exact his punishment on me for saying no to him, I'm at the bar getting another round of drinks none of us need in the slightest when a hand lands heavily on my arm.

When I turn, I physically recoil. My stomach knots, and my entire body goes numb.

"Been a while, Eilish."

No. *No.*

I haven't actually talked to or even seen Brooks since our high school graduation, which he absolutely ruined for me.

When he cornered me, after I'd managed to avoid him for a week, and snarled his threats at me. Dangled what he had on me over my head as a way to keep me quiet about what had happened.

What he'd done.

I've spent years trying to pretend that what he has that could destroy me doesn't, in fact, exist; that the events of that night never actually happened.

Coming face to face with him has it all rushing back at once.

When I don't respond, he smirks. "Damn, Eilish. You're looking gorgeous."

I want to throw up. Or fade away into dust. Or scream. Or possibly all three.

"You know, I've been meaning to reach out personally after my father and your uncle touched base."

He shrugs, grinning at me like we're old pals. Like he's only my ex-boyfriend and not the face of my nightmares.

I flinch as he moves closer to me.

"Look, Eilish…" he shakes his head. "What happened before…I mean, we were kids, yeah? Just stupid kids fucking around. You know how it is. Awkward teenage years, amirite?"

He flashes me a thousand-watt JFK smile.

I suddenly very much wish I was Lee Harvey Oswald.

"Just kids fucking around…?" I echo numbly, staring at him.

A shadow flickers behind his all-American bright blue eyes.

"Exaaactly," he says slowly and quietly, a hint of warning in his voice. "It's easy to look back at something like that and cast blame. But who can say who did what? You know?"

I'm going to be sick. I can say exactly "who did what". My body goes cold and numb, my pulse thudding in my ears.

"What *I* think, Eilish," he growls, moving closer, "is that what's best here is to look to the future. Don't let what you think happened in the past govern you. The two of us, going forward? I mean, the power of our families combined, we're talking a *dynasty* here…"

I flinch when his hand lands on mine as it clings to the bar. The room spins and blurs as he leans close.

"*And of course, Eilish,*" he growls quietly. "Don't forget about, well…you know."

His leverage. His hold on me. The nightmare I've tried to erase from my mind and push down in the hopes I can forget about it.

But I can't.

It's always there.

He *still* has the means to destroy me.

"Good," Brooks mutters. "I feel we're on the same page. Now, I'm thinking next week we should set up a meeting with my father and his people, and we can go over—"

Brooks squeals like a stuck pig as he's suddenly ripped away from me. A dark, malevolent shape hurls him away into the crowd, which scatters to let him crash to the floor.

Then, the dark, hulking shape whirls on me with violence and fire brimming in his gunmetal gray eyes, and my heart stops for a second.

Gavan.

Part of me wants to hug him for shattering that horrible moment with Brooks. But another part of me has me squinting at him, my lips curled in a sneer.

"How the hell did you find me?"

It's hardly the right response right now, given how furious he looks. But fuck that.

His eyes narrow. "Excuse me?"

"Were you spying on me?" I snap. "Was that your guy before at the bar?"

Gavan's jaw clenches. "I can and always *will* find you," he says icily. "Especially when you're ignoring my simple—"

"*Demands?*" I blurt. "When I'm ignoring your irrational, tyrannical *demands*?!"

"If you're still unclear on the nature of our particular arrangement," he hisses, "I would be happy to—"

"Oh, *fuck off!* You don't *own me*, Gavan!"

"Like hell I—"

He snarls as a hand grabs him by the shoulder and yanks him back. My face pales as he whirls on Brooks, who looks sputteringly mad.

"Just who the fuck do you think you are, buddy?" Brooks sneers at Gavan, completely unaware that he's basically sticking his hand into a hungry lion's mouth. "Do you have any idea who *I* am?" he continues. "Do you have any idea who my fucking *father* is!?"

Gavan smiles dangerously at him.

"Listen, pal," Brooks blunders on. "She's with me. So why don't you go find a nice corner you can go fuck yourself in—"

He screams when Gavan's forearm smashes into his nose with a horrible crunching sound. Blood spurts down his face as tears bead in his eyes.

"You fucking *hit* me?" he chokes, stumbling backward before falling unceremoniously on his ass. He looks up at Gavan in pure shock, then flinches when the Bratva king stoops down, grabbing a handful of his collar in his fist.

"The only reason I'm not doing more than hit you, little boy, is that I have more important things to do tonight beside washing your pathetic blood off my shoes."

Brooks turns white, his eyes bulging.

"I don't give a fuck who you are, and I certainly don't give a fuck who your daddy is. But if you touch what's mine again, I swear by whatever you hold holy that I will *remove* your hand from the rest of your arm with a rusty fucking soup spoon. Do we understand each other?"

Brooks stares, then swallows, nodding quickly.

"*Say it*," Gavan hisses.

"I…!" He shudders. "I understand!"

"Now fuck off back to your playpen."

Brooks scrambles to his feet, whirls, and makes a beeline for the exit. I shiver as Gavan slowly turns back to me.

"Are you fucking *insane*?!" I hiss. "Do you have any idea who that—"

"Nope. And I don't care."

I gasp as he moves into me, grabbing me possessively with one arm around my waist as his other hand slides up to fist the back of my hair. Gavan tugs my head back, tilting my face up to his.

"But when I come for what's mine after she refuses to do as I say, and I find someone else touching—"

"Oh my *God*!" I blurt, well past tipsy from all the cocktails as I roll my eyes and pull away from him. "You *do not*. Fucking. *Own. Me*!"

His eyes blaze. "Like fuck I don't—"

I can't do this right now.

Without another word, before he's even done speaking, I whirl and shove my way through the crowd. I zig and zag through the mass of hipsters drinking craft beers before I find myself at the back of the bar, at the hallway down to the restrooms. Stumbling, I bolt into the women's single occupancy one and slam the door shut.

My fingers are literally still on the lock when the door kicks back open. I gasp, stumbling back with wide eyes as Gavan spills into the room like a puddle of black ink—like a dark storm cloud brimming with thunder and lightning.

I shudder as he moves into me, pressing me back until I can feel the edge of the sink at the small of my back.

"*We need boundaries*," I blurt, shivering as heat teases through my core. I *want* to be mad at him, even if he did just save me from Brooks. I want to throw his possessive "I own you" shit right back in his face. I want to make him understand that *nobody* "owns" me.

Except when I look at this man—when I even *think* about this man—I'm not so sure that's true anymore.

Someone *does* very much own every single part of me, as much as I might try and convince myself otherwise.

He does.

And the worst of it is, I'm not so sure I'm upset about it.

Still, my throat works as I glare at him.

"Boundaries," I hiss again. "We need fucking—"

I whimper when his hand darts out, cupping my jaw firmly. He reaches back with his other hand, and I hear the lock click shut on the door.

"You want boundaries, *solnishka?*"

I shiver, my breath coming fast and shallow as his strong fingers grab my jaw and throat, twisting my head to the side as his lips brush my ear.

"The only boundaries you'll have with me are the mother-fucking brick walls I put between you and any other man who even tries to touch you, look at you, or *think about you.*"

My body jolts, my breath hitching as his teeth rake down the soft skin of my neck. Then, without warning, he's spinning me around and pinning my hipbones against the sink. I whimper, my hands gripping the edge of the porcelain as he fists my hair, shoving it aside and nipping at the nape of my neck.

"*Any questions?*" he rasps darkly.

I whimper, shaking my head side to side as my body melts against the rock-hard heat of him.

"*Good girl.*"

I sputter as he suddenly yanks my dress up over my ass.

"Because you're my good little free use fuck-toy, aren't you?"

This is so fucked up. So *deranged*.

How come I can't even bring myself to say no?

How come I don't *want to* say no?

"*Yes,*" I blurt.

His powerful hand slips between us, sliding boldly between my legs to cup my pussy through my soaked panties, making me whimper eagerly.

"And this messy, greedy little pussy is *mine* to do with as I fucking please, isn't it?"

My vision blurs. Heat floods my core as I nod, dazed, my chest heaving. Then I jump again when he deftly smacks the inside of my thighs, making me shiver.

"*Answer me, Solnishka,*" he snarls.

"*Yes...*" I shudder. "Yes, *Sir...*"

I whimper when he yanks my panties aside and deftly sinks two thick fingers deep inside my aching pussy. I whine, arching my back and pushing my ass into him as he starts to finger me hard and fast.

My eyes roll back, my knees threatening to buckle as Gavan bites down on my shoulder. His other hand snakes around, yanking the straps off my shoulders and pulling down the top of my sundress. He groans, fingering me even harder as he pulls my bra down and cups one of my breasts in his powerful hand. His fingers roughly pinch the aching, eager nipple, pulling a ragged cry from my lips as his other fingers curl deep against my g-spot.

"*What are you,*" Gavan rasps.

I moan, my pussy shuddering around him.

"I—"

"*Answer me.*"

"*A good girl!*" I blurt, sobbing with pleasure as he starts to roll my clit with his thumb.

"Be more fucking specific."

Holy fucking God.

"*YOUR good girl,*" I choke.

Gavan groans, and I moan in anticipation when I hear and feel his pants coming undone. I shudder when I feel the hot, swollen head of his cock push between my thighs. I whine when his fingers slide out of me, frustrated, but when I feel that thick head tease against my lips, my breath catches.

"And who am *I*, baby girl," he hisses into my ear as his teeth drag over the lobe.

I don't even hesitate. I *can't*, not with that throbbing promise of pleasure teasing hot and hard against my pussy.

"*You're the one who owns me.*"

"*Good girl.*"

Every. Single. Inch of his thick, swollen cock rams into me with one powerful thrust. My eyes fly wide and my mouth goes slack as I cry out in ecstasy. The force of his thrust has me up on the balls of my feet, my toes curling as my hands go flat to the tiled wall on either side of the mirror in front of us.

In it, I lock eyes with him, my face caving in pleasure as his tenses. His hands tighten on my flesh as he rams in and out, fucking me hard against the sink with deep, powerful thrusts that have me climbing the goddamn walls.

His hand cups my breast, pinching my nipple hard as the other hand wraps around my throat. His teeth bite down on my neck, making me cry out as pain and pleasure blur together.

As he consumes me entirely.

His thick, swollen cock drives in and out of my slickness, coating my thighs with my own arousal as my hips pound against the sink. His tongue drags up my neck over the bite marks he's left, all the way up to my ear, which he sucks between his lips.

"You. Are. Fucking. *MINE*," he rasps savagely, punctuating each word with a brutal thrust that drives me screaming right to the brink of my sanity.

We slam together faster and harder. My world blurs, and I gasp, reaching back and up to wrap my arms around the back of his neck as he fucks into me.

"Open your fucking eyes, solnishka," he snarls into my ear as my lids flutter open. *"Look at yourself."* I whimper, my face going crimson as I see the way I'm tangled up with him—clinging to him eagerly, my hair a mess, my dress down over my bared breasts and hiked up around my waist.

The marks of his mouth and his teeth like welts down my neck. My panties shoved haphazardly to the side and my back arched. His hands on my tits and wrapped possessively around my throat.

My body shudders and bounces off him as his fat cock rams into me over and over, until my world turns blurry.

"Gavan..."

When I come, it's like a neutron bomb going off. It's like reality glitches and breaks into fragments around me. I scream, completely uncaring about anyone possibly hearing me getting fucked within an inch of my life in a bar bathroom.

My body wrenches and seizes up, the cry tearing from my lips as I feel my pussy clamp down around his cock. Gavan keeps thrusting into me as my orgasm explodes through me before suddenly he groans and buries his cock deep. My head is swimming as I feel his cock pulse and throb, his cum spilling deep into me as I cling to him for dear life.

Slowly, his grip on me releases. His lips tease over the bite marks on my neck, soothing both them and the pulse racing beneath. He gently eases out of me, pulling my panties back into place and making me blush when I feel them start to get soaked with his cum as it begins to dribble out of me.

"Turn around."

I shiver, turning just in time for him to cup my face and kiss me fiercely. His tongue snakes into my mouth, conquering it before he pulls back again.

"On your knees."

My pulse throbs. That dark part of myself he brings out in me stirs and grins.

And I do as he says, knowing exactly what he wants.

"Be a good girl and clean off my cock."

So I do.

Eagerly.

Hungrily.

My tongue snakes over his cock, still hard and swollen, tasting myself and his cum mixed together on it. I drag my tongue up and down, then dance it across the underside as my eyes lift to lock with his.

Gavan's face goes rigid, and his jaw clenches as he reaches down to tangle his hands in my hair. My mouth opens, and I moan when he groans and pushes the head past my lips and over my tongue.

His hips rock, a groan rumbling from his throat as he starts to fuck my mouth with shallow, quick thrusts.

"Touch yourself while I fuck this pretty mouth, *solnishka*," he murmurs. "Play with your messy, freshly-fucked pussy while you clean off my cock like my good little toy."

Sweet. Fucking. *Jesus*.

I should be so disturbed by all of this—him, the situation, *myself*. But I'm unable to even try to feel that way. All I can do is eagerly moan more and more loudly on his dick as my hand slips into my panties to rub my throbbing clit frantically, feeling the stickiness of his cum coating me.

Gavan groans, pumping faster as my hand keeps time between my thighs. And just as I start to explode again—whimpering around him as my thighs clamp around my twisting fingers—he starts to come, too.

My own orgasm rips through me as his spurts across my tongue and down my throat.

I stay where I am, licking and sucking until he's clean again. Then I shudder when he reaches down to pull me up and press me against the wall. His mouth crushes to mine, his tongue demanding entrance, seemingly uncaring that he's just come down my throat.

"There *are* no boundaries between us, *solnishka*," he growls quietly.

I don't respond, smoothing my dress back into place and trying to fix my hair as Gavan zips his pants back up and straightens his jacket.

"My car is waiting outside to take you home."

I bite my lip, turning to him.

"Whose home?"

His brow arches.

"Funny. Mine. Come with me."

I pull my hand back from him.

"I just…need a minute?"

He nods. "You have five. I'll be out front."

When he's gone, I turn to stare at myself in the mirror and blush.

I look like…well, like I just got the shit fucked out of me in a bar bathroom, that's what.

I fix that as much as I can before I take a deep breath and step out into the hallway. Back in the main bar area, I swallow as I arrive back at the table where Callie and Dahlia are talking.

"Dude!" Callie frowns at me. "Where the *hell* did you…" She arches a brow, and slowly starts to smirk. "Where exactly did *you* get off to?"

"And more to the point, who did you get off *with*," Dahlia adds, making the two of them crack up as they grin at me.

I desperately try to contain the heat on my face.

"*Har har har*," I sigh, trying to look amused and sarcastic and not, well, floating and well fucked. "I got to talking with someone at the bar, and—"

"Uh oh! Don't tell Mr. Tyrant," Callie teases.

"Hilarious," I roll my eyes, still trying to keep my face from heating. "It was a girl from my corporate litigation class. Relax."

She frowns. "Uh huh. How come you're all sweaty and glowing?"

I frown, shrugging. "It's hot as hell in here. And the bar is swamped. Anyway, I'm gonna take off."

"Well, yes," Callie sighs. "Wouldn't want to keep Mr. Demanding waiting. The living room floor awaits," she says with a wink.

I know she's just kidding. I know she's just joking around. I *know* she doesn't mean it maliciously or anything.

But when I hear it like that, I frown.

What the fuck am I doing?

Boundaries.

We really do need some fucking boundaries if this is going to work. And this is one of them. I'm not a puppy. I'm not his to parade around on a leash wherever and whenever he pleases. And as the mix of emotions, adrenaline, and alcohol swirl inside of me, my brow furrows.

My car is waiting outside. You have five minutes.

Yeah, no, fuck that. Controlling and dominant is hot in bed—or over his desk, or against bathroom sinks, for that matter. But the rest of the time, when we're *not* fucking?

I'm a freaking person. My *own* person. Not his. And I'm done being constantly ordered around like I am.

There are limits, and I just found mine.

"Hey, you okay?"

I blink and focus on Callie. She frowns.

"I was totally just kidding. You know that, right?"

I smile. "Yeah, of course."

She stands and takes my hand. "I love ya. I just want you to be happy and safe. And if Mr. Tyrant does that for you?" She shrugs. "Go for it, girl. And have fun," she winks.

"Thanks," I grin back as she hugs me close.

I say goodnight to Dahlia. Just as I'm leaving, Callie stops me. She smirks, lifting a brow as she pulls close.

"*Nice men's cologne,*" she snickers low in my ear, turning my face the color of red wine. "And don't think for a second I didn't see you stagger over to our table from the direction of the ladies room looking like you just got off a rollercoaster."

When she pulls back, I stare at her, not sure what to say. Callie just grins and gives me a friendly swat on the butt.

"Go have fun, lady. Call me!"

She and Dahlia head over to the bar for a last round of margaritas. I turn to glance at the front door, where I know Gavan is waiting for me.

Then I turn, smile to myself, and march out the *back* door.

Screw. Him.

The night is warm. But it's still *way* cooler out than it was in the sweltering, overly crowded bar. I shoulder my bag, grinning, a little pep in my step—partly from the mind-blowing sex I just had, and partly from my decision to create *my own* boundaries with Gavan.

The pain comes out of nowhere.

I choke out a gasp, knocked off balance by the sheer force of the blow to my head. I hear a grunt as someone hits me again, making me cry out as I fall to the ground.

The gritty pavement of the alley behind the bar bites into my palms and knees. I try to stand, when suddenly a powerful kick slams into my ribs, knocking the wind out of me and sending pain exploding all through my side.

There's another kick, and then another as I cry out again and feebly try to block it with my hands. A shadow looms over me, spiking fear through my heart before another blow slams into my head.

The world spins and blurs. Dark spots cloud my vision as the shape leans close to my ear as I lie on the ground, dazed.

"Please...don't..."

"Stay the fuck away from Gavan Tsarenko."

The voice with a thick Russian accent snarls into my ear as everything starts to fade.

"The next time you decide to be a Reznikov whore, there will be bigger consequences."

Something slams into my head one more time, and everything goes black.

16

GAVAN

I WAS angry when Vadim was taken away from me. *So* fucking angry. The kind of rage and hatred that eats its way inside you until it poisons your very soul. An anger to be drowned in chemicals and strangers and violence.

Those were dark days—even darker for anyone who had the misfortune of even looking at me the wrong way. There was a solid month where I disappeared and almost went feral. It was my sisters, Lizbet and Mara, who finally found me: half-dead, a near-lethal amount of cocaine up my nose, holed up in the Presidential Suite of The Plaza. It was them who got me cleaned up and back to society.

And still, as angry as I was back then?

It's not *touching* the rage I feel surging through my system like sizzling hot lead as I gaze at the girl sleeping in the hospital bed in front of me.

My hand reaches out, curling around Eilish's small, still one as my jaw grits so hard it hurts.

I hate that I wasn't there. I *hate* that I wasted ten long minutes pacing outside the front of that goddamn bar, dreaming up creative ways to punish her for deciding to thumb her nose at me. I walked back in expecting to see her flipping me off with another drink in her hand. Instead, I saw her friends—Calliope Drakos and that other girl, Dahlia, from school.

No Eilish.

I combed through the place. I checked both bathrooms before noticing the back door to the place was ajar. That's when I found her, bleeding and unconscious on the ground.

My body tenses up so hard I quickly snatch my hand away from hers before I accidentally crush it.

When I find those responsible for doing this to her, they'll *beg* for hell. I'll make a fucking Olympic sport of skinning them fucking alive inch by fucking inch.

I'm going to avenge her, I vow to myself as my eyes trace the softness of her cheek, marred by an ugly bruise.

Behind me, the door to the hospital room bangs open with a crash. When I whirl, I come face to face with a terrified-looking Neve Kildare. She skids to a stop as she realizes it's me, suddenly very confused, and her expression when she looks at me is dangerous.

"Neve," I growl quietly, dipping my head.

Her throat bobs heavily, her nostrils flaring before she deftly pushes past me. She takes Eilish's hand in her own, her shoulders hitching as she brings her sister's hand to her lips. After taking another shaky breath, she glances back at me.

The room is silent except for the hum of the air conditioning and the steady beeps from Eilish's heart monitor. Both of us are keenly aware the dark history between our families. Neve's clearly weighing that dark history against the current need to make sure her sister is okay.

"What happened a few months ago between our families was...regrettable," I murmur quietly. "And I hope it's been made clear how much of that was the fault of my *former* captain, Leo."

Neve's lips thin. "We don't need to talk about that right now."

She glances back at her sister, sucking in deep breaths and squeezing her hand again. Then she turns back at me with a slightly softer look.

"They told me when I arrived that you're the one who brought her in."

I nod.

"Thank you."

Before I can respond, the door bangs open again, even louder this time. I've just started to turn when what feels like a fucking *truck* slams into me, driving me right into the wall with a barely-contained roar.

"You son of a bitch," Castle snarls, his face livid with rage.

"Take your fucking hands off—"

He hauls back and punches me in the face. I grunt from the force of it, black stars dotting my vision as I try to shake off the quite honestly *monster* of a hit. Snarling back, I slam into him, catching him in the middle and using his weight against him. I wince when I take another brutal punch to the ribs.

"CASTLE!"

Neve's voice booms through the room, stopping both of us cold. She uses the pause to elbow herself between us and shove Castle back against the wall.

"*Enough!*" she yells. "He's the one who brought her in!"

"Yeah?!" Castle hisses at me. "And how is you just *happened* to be right there like a good fucking Samaritan, you moth-erfucker?!"

My eyes draw to slits. "Watch what you say next."

"Oh? What if I mention exploding fucking bars and lighting *children* on fire?!"

Anger surges inside. Both those events—the Banshee being blown to hell during its soft opening, as well as the son of one of the Kildare vassal families being jumped and lit on fire, which was truly horrific, even to me—were done on the initiative of my former number two, Leo Stavrin.

Events, I should add, I would have happily cut him into small pieces with gardening shears for having brought about, if someone else hadn't beaten me to it and killed him first.

I can't blame Castle for the accusation. But it still makes my blood turn to fire and my temper flare. I grit my teeth as I take a step toward him.

"You're going to have to let that go."

"I don't *have* to do a goddamn thing!"

Neve screams as Castle slips past her and tries to haul him back. But he ignores her and slams into me again. His huge hand goes around my throat.

My knife is up in a flash, pressing to his jugular.

Then I stiffen when I feel his gun barrel pressed to my stomach.

Castle's teeth flash dangerously. "I should blow you to hell right fucking—"

"What's going on?"

We stop the grappling and the fighting in an instant, whirling to see Eilish looking at us with a hollow, confused look on her face. Then her lids slowly close again, her head dropping back to the pillow.

Neve swallows heavily and turns to Castle.

"Please," she hisses quietly. "Let me handle this, all right? She is *okay*, Castle. I need you to step outside. *Please.*"

He turns to glare at me. Then his gaze drops back to Eilish— with a sort of fawning love in it that I'll admit makes my blood boil—before he nods.

"I'll be right outside," he growls, dragging his eyes back to me. "*Right* outside.".

When he's gone, Neve takes a deep breath as she holds her sister's hand. Then she turns back to me.

"Okay. What were you doing with my sister?"

I'm honestly not quite sure how to answer that. It's not like I thought Eilish would tell anyone about the two of us. But it's also quite clear that we've moved way past our initial black-mail situation. We've never openly talked about it, but what there is between us right now is there because we both want it, that much is clear.

"Neve?"

Neve whips her gaze back to Eilish at the sound of her soft voice. So do I, just in time to feel my heart lift a little when I see Eilish smile at her sister. Then, slowly, her eyes slip past Neve to me.

Her cheeks turn pink.

Her smile widens.

And fuck me, so does mine.

Eilish blushes as little deeper, still looking at me. "What are you doing here?"

"Gavan brought you in, Eils," Neve says gently.

"You did?"

I nod.

Neve squeezes her sister's hand and then turns to me.

"I'm not done asking what you were doing with my sister," she says quietly. "But thank you for finding her, and for bringing her here."

I nod again, my jaw clenched.

"Right now, though," Neve says tightly. "I need you to leave."

My gaze slips past her, to Eilish.

"*Thank you*," she mouths silently, smiling at me.

17

EILISH

WHEN GAVAN LEAVES, my heart clenches a little.

I liked that he was here.

A lot.

Neve frowns, and I can see the million questions swirling in her eyes. Just as she starts to open her mouth, Castle storms back in. His face crumples when he sees me, and he comes right to my side, taking my hand in both of his.

"*Fuck,* Blondie," he growls grimly, his head shaking side to side. "*Fuck.*"

I smile wryly at him. "I told you, Castle, it's not your job to protect me anymore."

"The fuck it isn't," he grunts. "It will *always* be my job to protect you."

"Well…" I wince as I try to shrug in an attempt to lighten the mood. "You can't be everywhere at once, can you?"

His face ripples with a dark shadow as he glances up at Neve.

"I just got off the phone with Cillian. He and Una are getting on a plane right—"

"No!" I blurt, shaking my head. "No. Tell them to stay on their honeymoon. I'm *fine*."

Neve and Castle both look at me with frowns on their faces. Castle shakes his head.

"C'mon, kid. the bravery is great, but—"

"I am asking you again: *please* call Cil back and tell him that I'm fine."

Stay the fuck away from Gavan Tsarenko.

The next time you decide to be a Reznikov whore, there will be bigger consequences.

This all happened because *I* got involved with "the enemy".

Me. Not Cillian. Not Una. Not anyone else in my family. They've all been through so fucking much already—all of them—before we've *finally* reached this place where no one's trying to hurt anyone, or declare war, or trying to kill each other.

I *not* going to ruin that and bring violence and that danger back into their lives. And I'm sure as *hell* not going to screw up Cillian and Una's much-deserved, long overdue honeymoon because I chose to get in bed…literally…with Gavan.

No.

Neve's brow furrows. "Eilish—"

"Look, some asshole tried to grab my purse and I was an *idiot* because I was drunk and tried to fight him off. He hit me, I blacked out, the end. *That's it*! I am *fine*, you guys. It's fucking New York, okay? This shit happens."

There's a cold, white look on Neve's face as she glances away, like she's holding something back. Castle frowns uncertainly.

"Castle," I mutter. "Please."

His scowl deepens, but finally he nods as he squeezes my hand.

"Okay, *okay*," he sighs. "I'll call Cillian back and tell him he can sit tight."

Neve watches him leave the room. When he's gone, she turns back to me, that same white, scared look on her face.

"Neve?" I ask quietly. "What's—"

"I...I need ask you about something," she croaks.

I frown. "Okay?"

Her hands twist as she looks at me with a pained expression on her face.

"I wanted to wait until you were awake..."

"Neve, what's going—"

"I love you, Eilish, you know that, right?"

My brow arches. "I...love you, too?" I smile as her breath hitches and tears spring to her eyes. "Hey, hey! Neve! I'm *okay*! Look, it was just a mugging. I'm going to be fine—"

"The hospital wants to run a rape kit on you," she blurts in an anguished voice.

I go still.

"You..." She starts to cry. "I am *so* fucking sorry, Eilish. You had signs of sexual assault when you were admitted."

Shit.

This is going to be awkward.

I chew on my lip as I reach for her hand. "No one assaulted me, Neve."

"Eilish, you were unconscious. And I am *so fucking sorry*, but I think you need to—"

"I wasn't raped, Neve," I murmur. "I… I had consensual sex ten minutes before I got knocked out."

The room goes still and quiet. Neve blinks rapidly, her brow furrowing.

"I'm sorry, *what?*"

I smile weakly. "I…I've sort of been seeing someone."

Her lips purse. "Someone whom you decided to lose your virginity to?" she snaps.

"Yes. And?"

"And…that's a big fucking deal."

I frown, shrugging painfully again. "Maybe it's not to me."

"Eilish, are you joking? It's *always* been a big deal to y—"

"Maybe it's not anymore!" I spit back.

She frowns. "Wait, ten minutes before you were knocked out? Does this guy live above the bar or something?"

When I say nothing, her brows arch sharply.

"I'm sorry, did you have sex *in* the fucking bar!?"

I blush. I can't help it. Just like I *really* can't help the devilish way my lips curl up at the corners. Neve exhales with a whoosh, the tension visibly melting away from her face, replaced pretty quickly with a giant serving of "concerned older sister".

"*Seriously?*" She says sharply.

"Seriously."

She exhales with another puff as she shoves her fingers through her red hair.

"Look, I mean, get it, girl. Have fun. But..." Her brows furrow again. "This isn't you, Eils."

"Maybe it is now," I toss back.

She groans. "Jesus. Well, okay. But at least tell me who the hell this guy—"

She goes stock still. Her eyes widen and she slowly turns to look at the door, then back at me, her face white.

"*Hold the fuck on...*"

I wince. "Neve—"

"*GAVAN*?!" she blurts incredulously. "Are you fucking *serious*, Eilish!?"

"Can you stop yelling at me like I'm fucking child!?"

"I'm yelling at you like I'm *concerned* for you!" she hurls back. "Eilish, ever since the explosion, you've been—"

"What?" I snap. "Living my life?! Not being afraid anymore?"

"Reckless!" she blurts. "The word is *reckless*."

"Thank you so much for your concern," I mutter, looking away.

Neve sighs, taking my hand.

"I'm sorry. I love you, that's all. And this…scares me a little. A lot, actually."

I squeeze her hand back, smiling wryly. "I'm fine, Neve. I mean that. It's nothing sinister."

"Of all the men in New York, you had to pick *Gavan fucking Tsarenko?*"

I lift a brow. "Says the woman who married Ares Drakos? The crown prince of our arch-rivals?"

She smirks, but still glares at me. "That was…different."

"You're right, it was. We were *actively* about to go to war with the Drakos family when that happened."

She sighs, looking away.

"Just tell me this. Are you safe?"

"I am."

"Happy?"

I bite back a smile.

Way more than I should be.

"Yes."

She frowns, shaking her head before she looks back at me. "And do you promise that if that asshole tries anything, or hurts you in *any* fucking way, you'll tell me, so that I can murder him with a blunt instrument after castrating him?"

I snort. "Definitely."

My sister's lips twist. "I love you, Eils."

"I love you, too." I frown. "Look, can you…"

"*Not* tell Castle?" She makes a face. "Yeah, not a fucking *chance*. Do I look like I have a death wish? That's on you if you want to open that particular nuclear suitcase."

I grin. "Can you maybe not tell *anyone*? I mean, not yet. It's all pretty new, and I just—"

"Like you said," she says with a sigh. "You're not a kid, Eils. Tell or don't tell whomever you want, whenever you want. Okay?"

I nod. "Thank you."

Maybe this is a bad idea.

But also, more than anything, he's the one that I want here with me right now.

And maybe that makes this not such a bad idea after all.

18

GAVAN

WHAT THE FUCK *am* I doing with her?

My brow knits as I watch her from the doorway as she sleeps. Neve and Castle have left. Visiting hours are long over.

I don't care if they are or not. It's what separates the Bratva from organizations like the Kildare and Drakos families. Despite all of us existing and operating in the same industry —namely, crime—they still feel the need to walk on a certain side of a line.

As in, when visiting hours where over an hour ago, Castle and Neve *asked* the nurses for ten more minutes, which they were given.

I don't ask. I take. Or, in this case, bribe. Because right now, all I want is to be right here, with her.

I step into the room, crossing to sit on the little stool next to her hospital bed. She's going to be okay—just some scrapes and bruises, and a minor concussion.

Not, mind you, that any of that is "okay".

I've already spoken to Korol about putting the word out to find whoever did this to her. For one, obviously, because I want to bathe in their blood and screams. But also, I want some fucking answers.

Contrary to what Eilish has told me, the nurses, the doctors, and her own family, this wasn't an attempted mugging.

At all.

Maybe her story about "fighting them off" would hold more water if they *hadn't* knocked her unconscious. But they did. And yet, for mysterious reasons, once she was knocked out these would-be muggers neglected to steal her Chanel bag, the four hundred dollars in cash inside that bag, her credit cards, phone, iPad, matching Tiffany's earrings and necklace, or her Cartier wrist-watch, itself alone worth four thousand dollars.

Either Eilish managed to run into the world's worst fucking thieves, or my personal theory is right: someone wanted to hurt her—either just to *hurt her*, or, more likely, to send a message. To her family, or maybe to me.

Any of those scenarios turns my blood to fire. And when I find whoever did this to her, I'll turn killing them into a spectator sport.

"Hi."

My gaze snaps from her hand, which I've been holding tightly, to her eyes, which are now open.

"How do you feel?"

"Groggy," she mumbles, considering. Her face scrunches up. "Achey. And my head still hurts a bit."

I frown as my other hand raises, gently pushing back her hair. Eilish smiles quietly before she makes a face.

"Guess I should have taken that ride with you, huh?"

My jaw sets. "Yeah. You fucking should have."

She smiles wryly. "I did have a very nice night before...you know, this." She points at the swelling on the side of her head. She giggles. *"Beside that, Mrs. Lincoln, how was the play?"*

I frown deeply. "I'm not sure I'm ready to joke about this."

She shrugs. "Oh. I guess I am."

My eyes search hers. "Who did this to you? This is *me* asking, not Neve or Castle."

She frowns. "You think that means I have a different answer?"

"I was hoping it might."

She smiles and shakes her head. "Sorry, same answer. Just two guys who wanted to take my bag." She shrugs. "It's New York. Muggings happen."

I nod, smiling as I stroked her hair.

She told the intake nurses it was one mugger.

She told her sister it was three.

Now it's two.

I know she hit her head, but still. Something isn't adding up. But I'm not pushing the issue. Not yet.

When she yawns, I smile and squeeze her hand.

"Get some rest, Eilish."

She nods, her eyes closing.

"Isn't it past visiting hours?"

"It is."

She smiles, her eyes still closed. Her hand squeezes mine back.

I stay like that until she's sleeping peacefully. When I slip my hand from hers and step out of the room, Korol and my other highly trusted guard, Isaac, are right there.

"I've got two guys by the front doors, one on each floor, and two more on the roof," Korol says quietly. "*Nobody's* getting in here."

I turn to let my gaze stab through the window of her private room and land on Eilish's sleeping form.

This whole thing with the two of us started as revenge. It was about payback, no more.

Now, it's just about her.

What the hell is happening to me?

19

EILISH

"WHAT THE FUCK are you doing here?"

Gavan frowns as I sashay into his office and close the door behind me.

"It's eight o'clock on Monday morning," I shrug, biting back a grin.

It's been four days since I got jumped outside of the bar. Three since being sent home from the hospital. At home, a rotating cast featuring Neve, Ares, Castle, Callie, Hades, Elsa, Kratos, and even Dimitra Drakos as the occasional guest star has been taking care of me and dropping in to check on me.

It's been wonderful. And nice. And kind.

And *so boring*.

Also…and this might be a problem…after four days of *not* being made to moan and writhe my way to orgasm by Gavan, after it being an almost daily occurrence now, I'm…antsy.

Needy.

We've texted, and chatted on the phone a few times. But it's not the same. It's not what I *need*.

Like I said: it's a problem.

"You should be resting," Gavan grunts, scowling as he drums his fingertips on the desk.

I frown. "I'm fine."

"You should go home and rest anyw—"

"Are you sure?"

Biting my lip, I drop the short trench coat I've worn into his office. Underneath it, all I've got on is heels and a black lace lingerie set, complete with stockings and a matching garter belt.

Gavan's eyes go the color of liquid steel. His jaw grinds in a way that makes the veins on his neck pop as I casually saunter toward him, a saucy grin on my face.

"I don't know… *Should I* go home? *Sir?*"

His eyes drag over me as I get closer and closer, his nostrils flaring.

"I'm not hurt anymore," I purr, feeling empowered and sexy in a way I've never felt before as I slide between the chair he's sitting in and the edge of his desk. "And I'm sure I'm *so* far behind on my work—"

In one motion, he's lunged out of his chair, pushed my ass back onto the edge of his desk, and grabbed a fistful of my hair as he slams his mouth to mine. And, okay, I *am* still bruised, and I wince a little at the ferocity of his kiss.

But I also don't care. Honestly, I kind of love it.

I moan as his mouth devours mine, my fingers shaking as I start to pull at his shirt buttons and shove his jacket from his shoulders as he shrugs it the rest of the way off. My fingertips slide over his rock-hard body, moaning into his mouth as his hand slides up my thigh to cup my wet, throbbing pussy.

"Did someone miss me?" he growls, his mouth dropping to my neck.

"*Yes*," I choke, moaning as he pulls away to hook his fingers into my panties.

He yanks them down my legs and over my heels, and I gasp as he shoves my thighs apart before diving between them.

Oh, fuck yes...

It's like balm on an aching burn. Like a medicine I've been needing. His tongue drags up through my slickness, making me cry out as he takes my clit between his lips. My hips rock up to meet him, my hands sliding through his hair as he sinks two fingers deep into me and curls them against my g-spot.

Gavan's tongue lashes my clit, the low rumbling growl in his chest sending vibrations through my body that leave my toes curling. He grabs my legs and pulls them over his shoulders, devouring my pussy like a starving man.

My head drops back, my back arches...

...And then I groan in protest when he pulls away *just* before he makes me come. Before I can say a word, I'm suddenly gasping as he drapes me back across his desk, stands, and sinks every inch of his cock—already out of his pants—balls-deep in my throbbing, soaked pussy.

The explosion is *instantaneous*. The second he rams into me, it's like pulling a trigger. I cry out, writhing on his desk as my legs wrap tightly around his waist. I claw at the desk beneath me, choking on my own release as the rush I've been craving for days ignites through every nerve in my body.

"There's my good girl..." Gavan growls, his shirt open, his muscles rippling as he fucks me. The fact that he's still got his pants on somehow makes it even hotter. And as he starts to pound into me, my eyes roll back as another orgasm already begins to build deep inside.

I moan when he brings my legs up, hooking my ankles over his shoulders as he buries his fat cock in me to the hilt. I cry out, whimpering. The position allows him to drive even deeper, making my toes curl and my eyes roll back in my head.

The phone on his desk rings. Gavan glares daggers at it, picking it up and then slamming it back down, hanging up. I whimper, breathing heavily as he starts to fuck me again, when there's another interruption.

This time, it's the intercom.

"Mr. Tsarenko?" Rachel's voice buzzes through the speaker.

Gavan clamps a hand over my mouth and rams into me even harder.

"What is it, Rachel?"

Jesus. He doesn't stop fucking me. He doesn't even *slow*.

"There's a call for you. Mr. Volkov. He says it's urgent?"

Gavan frowns, his cock still sliding in and out of me with hard, wet strokes.

"Which Volkov?"

"The older one. Yuri."

"Put him through."

I can only stare as he picks up the telephone receiver and cradles it against his shoulder—and my ankle. His eyes lock with mine, a dark smirk on his face. He keeps one hand over my mouth and I moan wildly into it as he starts to rub my clit with the other, his cock pistoning in and out of me the whole time.

"Yuri," he growls. "What…"

Rage clouds his face as he listens. His jaw clenches, and I whimper as suddenly his thrusts become even more brutally hard.

"*What?!*"

Part of me thinks I should be furious that he's so casually fucking me while he's on a business call. Except, it's also hot as *fuck*.

I have no idea what he's talking about, or what's even wrong. But as his face grows more and more livid, the way he's fucking me becomes more and more vicious, to the point that I'm clinging to the edge of the desk for dear life, biting down hard on his hand as the orgasm builds like a wave inside of me.

"*No!*" He snaps into the phone. "No, *fuck that!*"

Fuck me.

Fuck me. Fuck me. FUCK. ME…

The world blurs. It feels like I'm floating as he grits his teeth, still cradling the phone. I have to cover my own mouth as he grabs my hips with both hands in a bruising grip and starts to absolutely fuck the living *hell* out of me, his hips slapping against my ass hard and fast as his veins thicken and his muscles bulge.

"That. Is. Completely. Un. Fucking. Acceptable. Yes, obviously we cancel."

I'm about to come. He rams into me hard with every punch of his words, and suddenly, there's no stopping it.

"I have to call you back, Yuri."

He all but breaks the phone when he hangs up. And if I thought I was getting fucked before, now that his full attention is on me, I realize just how wrong I was.

Suddenly, it's like fucking a machine.

Reality shatters around me. I scream into my hand as I dig the nails of the other into his forearm. And suddenly, I'm coming so hard my vision cuts out for a second.

The orgasm tears through me like liquid fire, engulfing me, charring me, leaving me a burned-out shell as I collapse onto the desk gasping for air and twitching from the aftershocks.

Gavan slows and finally stops, giving me time to breathe as he leans over to kiss my breasts, my nipples, and my ribs.

Suddenly, there's a commotion outside the door.

"Sir! *Sir*! I'm afraid he's busy at the moment! SIR!!!"

Footsteps pound toward the door.

Oh fuck.

I scramble off the desk as Gavan glares at the door and quickly buttons his shirt. I'm about to make a mad rush to his bathroom, but there's no time. In a second, I've made my decision, ignoring Gavan when he hisses "What the fuck are you doing" before I dive *under his desk.*

Gavan sits heavily and yanks his chair against said desk just as the door slams open.

"Mr. Tsarenko!" Rachel pleads. "I am *so* sorry! He wouldn't—"

"It's fine. That'll be all, Rachel, thank you."

I have no idea who just walked in, but I hear a low, masculine chuckle as the door shuts.

"The concept of knocking first is something most six-year-olds have mastered, Abram," Gavan growls.

The man snorts. "I didn't come here to be insulted.."

Under the desk, as my eyes adjust to the darkness, I suddenly flush.

Right in front of me is Gavan's very erect, swollen cock, still out of his pants.

I grin salaciously.

Don't even. What the fuck are you thinking?

What I'm thinking is that new Eilish has fully embraced herself.

Gavan jolts, coughing as my fingers wrap around his cock.

"Then what the fuck *did* you come here for, Abram?"

"I was coming to talk sense into you," the other man hisses with a Russian accented voice. "Until I just learned as I got off the goddamn elevator that you and that Volkov coward canceled tonight's Council meeting."

"No shit," Gavan grunts, clearing his throat again as I start to stroke his dick. "Someone just tried to firebomb Viktor's *hotel room*, Abram. I literally just got off the phone with Yuri."

"Viktor is fine."

"His wife and *son* could have been in there!" Gavan barks.

"And that's precisely why we need to have this fucking vote!" the other man roars. "To put a stop to this Drazen madness! Wake the fuck up, Gavan! It could be my house next. Or yours! I've heard rumors of there being a girl in your life these days. You want anything to happen to her?"

Gaven stiffens, his thighs clenching as I lean forward and lick the tip of his cock like it's the most delicious ice cream cone.

"Be very careful what you say next, Abram."

"I am merely saying, this is getting out of control."

"We don't *know* it's—"

"Here!"

Something light hits the desk.

"Another fucking calling card," the man growls.

I grin to myself, licking the crown again, just to tease him.

"Drazen is *here*, Gavan. And if you, Yuri, and Viktor don't stop acting like frightened old women…"

I gasp as Gavan suddenly reaches under the desk, grabs my head in his hands, and pulls my lips right up to his cock. My mouth falls open in shock, and suddenly, he's thrusting inside, hard.

And *fuck*, is it outrageously hot.

I was only trying to tease him a little, assuming he'd push me away. This... This is unexpected. And very, very erotic.

"Then we'll all go up in flames!"

"Listen to me carefully, Abram," Gavan growls as he starts to fuck my mouth with discreet, shallow thrusts, his gorgeous cock leaking precum all over my tongue.

"Yuri, Viktor, and I will assess the situation and *deal with it accordingly*. But if you think we're going to let you use chaos and uncertainty to hand you our armies, you're completely delusional."

My hand drops between my legs, rolling my clit between my fingers as Gavan's cock swells harder and thicker in my mouth.

"I am merely trying to—"

"You are merely trying to *seize control of the entire High Council*," Gavan snarls. "And while Viktor and Yuri might be content to be polite to your face about it, I am *done* trying to tiptoe diplomatically—"

Thrust.

"Around."

Thrust. Thrust.

"You wanting to play games."

Thrust. Thrust. Thrust.

My eyes squeeze shut as I start to come.

"*Dictator*," the other man hisses. "Don't make the mistake of making an enemy out of—"

"Abram, get the fuck out of my office."

Thrust.

Thrust.

"*Now.*"

"Fuck you."

There's the sound of footsteps stomping across the room, followed by the door opening and then slamming shut.

Gavan groans, sliding back from the desk. He grips my hair with both hands, his eyes wild and his jaw clenched tight as he fucks into my mouth over and over, until suddenly he explodes with a long, loud, toe-curling groan of pleasure that sends ripples through my core.

Cum *blasts* out of his cock, rope after thick, hot rope, exploding down my throat.

Grinning, my face flushed and my body tingling, I shiver with pleasure as he pulls me up and into his lap a moment later.

"What was that all about?"

He shrugs, making me gasp as he suddenly pulls my thighs to either side of his. The steel in his eyes goes molten as he centers his thick head against my eager pussy.

"Who cares."

He sinks into me, making my eyes roll back.

Who cares, indeed.

20

EILISH

It's been two weeks since the mugging. After assuring Gavan I was fully healed, we've gone right back to it: hard, brutal, explosive sex that I crave like a drug. Tied up. Bent over his desk. On his kitchen counter. Against the glass wall in his living room, looking out over the city.

There are times that it scares me just how comfortable I've become with it. I don't see Gavan as a tyrant anymore, I see him as—

Well, okay, he's still a tyrant. But he's a tyrant that I am, for all intents and purposes, *dating*.

Kind of. Sort of. Maybe?

I don't know. It's confusing. But for the time being, it's a ride I don't want to get off just yet. And that's fine.

Callie gives me a sharp look over the book in her hands when I step into the library of the Drakos family estate.

Okay, even "estate" doesn't quite give their place the right amount of gravitas.

Though they later moved to London for a while, Callie and her four brothers—Ares, Hades, Kratos, and Deimos—were all born here in New York. And they were all raised in this *massive*, breathtaking home on Central Park South that I've just walked into—a neoclassical mansion from the British countryside, as in it was *literally* a mansion in England that Callie's great-grandfather had moved brick-by-brick and rebuilt on the roof of a forty-story building overlooking Central Park. It has grounds, gardens, and *two* pools.

It's ridiculous.

Currently, though, with Ares and Hades happy in their own places, and Deimos back in London overseeing the Drakos operations over there, the only full-time residents of the sprawling mansion are Callie, Kratos, and their grandmother, Dimitra.

"Well, well, well…" Callie drawls, glaring at me.

My mouth goes small as I look at my feet. "I'm sorry."

"For which part, exactly? Disappearing from the face of the earth for the last two weeks—after, I might add, that I took such good care of you after the hospital? Or for not freaking telling me that you were dating *Gavan fucking Tsarenko?*" She eyes me up and down. "Or, wait, is it some *other* cataclysmically huge thing you've decided not to tell your best friend about?"

I sigh as I cross the room and sink onto the couch next to her. "Okay, I deserved that."

She pouts. "Yeah. You do."

"Thank you for taking care of me after I got discharged. Really. I've just been so busy with…you know, life?"

"By which you mean screwing Gavan."

My face heats. Callie smirks.

"*Fine,*" she mutters. "I suppose I can forgive you, on one condition."

I grin. "Which is?"

Her grin is even bigger. "That you fucking tell me everything right this *instant.*"

I make a pained expression.

"Oh, come on, Eilish!" she sighs. "I'm not Castle with his overprotective big brother energy. And I'm not Neve with her concerned sister routine—" She stops suddenly and glances at me. "Did she and Ares land okay, by the way? Ares is a dick and never texts me back."

I smile. "They're all settled."

Neve and Ares have just arrived in London for a few weeks so Ares can catch up with Deimos on some business stuff. There's talk of an alliance with a powerful Spanish mafia family, too, I think.

"Good." Callie eyes me again. "So. Let's hear it."

It's impossible to tell her *everything*, because I'm not going to mention the egg, and I'm sure as shit not mentioning what happened in the past that Gavan knows.

So I give a condensed, Cliff Notes version. One where I first connected with Gavan through a "corporate internship program" at school.

"It's just…fun," I shrug, blushing. "That's it. We're just casual. No high stakes or anything."

At least, that's what I keep telling myself.

Callie grins salaciously. "Fun? Uh, *yeah*, I bet. I mean sweet Jesus, look at him," she snickers. "That *looks* fun."

I blush fiercely. "And, I mean, yes, there's been some bad blood in the past. But it's not like we're at war with the Reznikov family or anything."

She nods, thinking. "No, for sure. And that's great that he can move past the bad blood in the past. That's big of him."

I frown. "Well, a lot of that stuff a few months ago, including the Banshee, was Leo Stavrin, his old second in command. And he was acting without orders from—"

"Oh. No, I didn't..." Callie frowns. "I didn't mean that. I meant from like two years ago."

My brows knit. "What happened two years ago?"

Callie's face suddenly pales. "Are you joking right now? Because that's not very funny."

"Callie, I honestly have no idea what you're talking about."

She sucks her bottom lip between her teeth, gnawing on it as she looks away.

"Callie," I press. "What bad blood—"

"She means when your family and the Reznikov Bratva almost went to war, Eilish."

I glance up sharply to see Dimitra standing in the doorway. A small, frail, elderly woman, it would be easy to discount her as just a little old lady.

Which would be *incredibly* foolish.

237

Dimitra may be tiny and old, but she's a hurricane. A force of nature to be reckoned with—and you don't want to get on her bad side. Thankfully, she considers me as much family as she does her grandchildren.

She smiles sadly, stepping into the library as I frown in confusion.

"I...don't remember that happening?"

She shakes her head. "No, because it never actually came to that." Her face darkens. "There were rumblings and rumors. But Konstantin and Gavan backed down from aggression after your father passed just a few months later."

I frown. "I don't understand—"

"Eilish, *poulaki mou*," she sighs quietly, her face strained. "I wish you had already known this."

"Known what?"

Her lips purse. "It's believed that two years ago, your father killed Vadim Tsarenko, Gavan's adoptive father."

Oh my God.

****

I'm not expected at Gavan's office today. I had a lecture class and an advisor meeting and he told me I was off the hook. But the lecture got out early, and my advisor had to cancel last minute.

Rachel smiles when I walk in. She's still not exactly my best friend, but she's warmed to me, given that I'm coming in so often.

I also think she one thousand percent knows *exactly* what's going on with Gavan and me. And the fact that she hasn't ever cracked a joke, smirked, or made a single comment about it whenever she sees me makes me like her even more.

"I think he's in a meeting, but…" she shrugs. "I'm sure you can go in."

"Thanks," I grin, sliding a box with a cupcake from Magnolia Bakery across the receptionist desk to her.

She groans, beaming at me as she shakes her head.

"You're evil."

"And you're welcome."

Upstairs, I head to Gavan's office. I'm not going full scandalous today with the trench coat and lingerie deal again. But I *am* remembering the time a few weeks ago when he fucked me across his desk while on a business call. Because that was outrageously hot.

My face is still throbbing with heat at the memory when I twist the knob and swing the door in.

Instantly I freeze.

Gavan isn't alone.

His eyes snap to mine from where he's standing by the windows, a cold, drawn, grim look on his face. I'm not focused on him, though. I'm focused on the gorgeous, dark-haired older woman standing *intimately* close to him.

With her hand on his chest.

With her lips close to his neck.

A dark, malevolent green mist clouds my vision. My teeth grind tightly, and a horrible feeling knots in my stomach.

The woman turns to arch a perfectly manicured brow at me, smirking coldly.

"What are you doing here?" Gavan growls stiffly.

"I—"

"*You* must be little Eilish," the woman purrs, grinning at me like a tiger. She smirks another haughty, sneering smile at me before turning back to Gavan and patting him on the chest again, letting her hand linger there far too long for my liking.

"Lovely to see you, Gavan," she murmurs seductively, turning to wink at me. "Let's not go so long next time, shall we?"

She smirks again as she brushes past me and sweeps out the door. I'm left staring at Gavan, his face darkening as he turns to stride over to the couches.

"You weren't expected today."

My lips purse. "Who was that?"

"No one."

My eyes flash. "No one? She seems to think she's someone."

"Let me rephrase: she's no one you need to be concerned about," he snaps as he sits heavily on the couch. His gaze raises to mine, full of fire and hot steel as he brings up a hand and crooks two fingers. "Come here."

I'm still glaring at him as I walk over.

"On your knees," he hisses.

I freeze, my scowl deepening as I glance down to see the bulge tenting his pants.

Oh, fuck you.

He's hard. What? From *her*?! And he wants *me* to take care of it for him?

Yeah, fuck everything about that.

"No," I hiss quietly.

Gavan scowls icily. "Excuse me?"

"I said no."

I gasp as he suddenly stands, shivering when his hand cups my jaw firmly to jerk my face up to his.

"*That word*," he snarls. "Is not in your vocabulary when it concerns me."

"It is today," I snap.

His eyes turn cold and malevolent in a way I've never quite seen before.

"And if I take you anyway?"

There's a sensual sharpness to his words, terrifying as they are.

"If I take what is mine, regardless of your opinion?" he continues quietly.

I shiver but hold firm.

"That's not part of our deal."

"Our deal is that I can—"

"If you want to force me, go ahead," I blurt coldly. "But it will *not* be willingly!" I'm shaking as I jab a finger into his chest. "There's free use, and then there's this. I didn't sign up for THIS."

Without another word, I spin and march for the door.

241

"What the fuck are you—"

"Discovering I have a spine!" I whirl back and blurt at him. "That's what the fuck I'm doing! This is me having a back-bone and showing some self-respect."

I slam the door shut behind me. I manage to make it past Rachel and her still-untouched cupcake before the tears start to fall.

Outside on the street, I grit my teeth as I choke back the sobs. I angrily wipe my damp eyes on my sleeve before I look around for a taxi.

"Oh, you poor, poor baby."

I stiffen, my pulse thudding as I turn. The woman from Gavan's office is sitting on a bench near the front entryway to the building. Poised, regal, and—much as I hate to say it—gorgeous. She's one of those women who's probably pushing fifty but looks more like a surgically enhanced thirty-five. She effortlessly flips a lock of dark hair back from her face, and her full, dark red lips curl as she grins maliciously at me.

"Did you think you were something special?" she laughs coldly. "Get in line, darling. You're merely one of several. Although I wasn't aware he was going through a blonde phase these days.

I feel sick. I want to scream at her, or physically attack her.

But that won't change the fact that what she's saying is something I've been trying to ignore for weeks and weeks now.

Gavan and I *are not* "a thing". This isn't a relationship. We're not even fuck buddies or friends with benefits or whatever else you'd want to call it.

We're completing a transaction: his silence for my submission.

And I mean, *look at him*. The man is beautiful...captivating... just the right amount of dark and broken, insanely powerful, dangerous, *and* rich beyond belief. And there's the thing I've so desperately avoided thinking about for more than a month.

...There's no way I'm the only one.

How *could* I be?

The woman's brow furrows. "I'm not sure I see what he sees in you, to be honest."

My heart twists painfully in my chest.

"Though, obviously," she grins wickedly. "I see what *you* see in him. The man certainly knows what he's doing in bed. I mean, he fucks like a god, doesn't he?"

Her face darkens, her eyes slicing into me as I break inside.

"Oh, and by the way, you're welcome."

"For *what*?" I sneer.

Her lips curl. "For teaching him everything he knows."

She starts to laugh. She's still laughing as I turn and bolt down the street, the tears now flooding my face.

21

GAVAN

FUCK SVETLANA.

I hate that she was in here, poisoning the very air I breathe. I hate that she even crossed the Hudson from New Jersey into Manhattan.

I hate how I always freeze up when she's around. It's as if the very air leaves my chest, like it did when I was a kid.

I was a fucking kid.

Everyone has demons. But some are darker than others. Some have sharper claws, or a more vicious bite. And those are the demons and the darkness from my past I've never told anyone.

Not even Konstantin, my own brother. And definitely not Vadim. I couldn't.

When Vadim, an unmarried, unattached man was suddenly raising a baby boy—aka *me*—people had questions. The rumor began swirling that I was Svetlana's unwanted child, and that Vadim, being the good brother he was, had taken me in as his own.

Vadim never confirmed the rumor, obviously, because it wasn't true. But he never denied it, either. It was just easier than whatever complicated explanation he'd have to give otherwise about who I was and where I came from.

But those rumors made things not so easy for Svetlana. And she resented both Vadim and *me* for the sideways looks she got after I appeared on the scene.

That's where her cruelty came from, I'm sure of it. It's how she must have justified the abuse she heaped on me later.

But Vadim could and never would know of that abuse.

Back then, of course, I didn't know I was Kristina Reznikov's secret son. All I knew was that Vadim had found me one night when I was a baby, orphaned on the streets of St. Petersburg. I'd have died or turned into one of the walking dead you see on the streets of Russia—the unwanted children with darkness flowing through their veins and dimming their eyes.

He saved me from that nightmare. And in return I never said a word about what his sister Svetlana did to me. I decided it was the toll I would pay for the new life I'd been given.

A violent black knot twists in my chest. I stare at the door where Eilish just left. I know I should follow her. I *want* to follow her, want to tell her everything, for some insane reason.

But I can't.

I grit my teeth. Eilish probably has the idea in her head that Svetlana made me hard, and that I wanted *her* to give me release.

That couldn't be further from the truth.

Svetlana sucks the life out of the world around me. She brings nothing but coldness and darkness. After she left, and I locked eyes with Eilish, it was Eilish I wanted. I instantly craved her, like a drug—craved the goodness she brings to my life. The way she breaks down my barriers, even when she's defying me. Or maybe *especially when* she's defying me.

I wanted her just now because I wanted to forget. I wanted to lose myself in Eilish to purge the nightmares of Svetlana from my head.

I exhale, shoving my fingers distractedly through my hair as I march over to the safe and open it. Svet was in here bitching about the egg, obviously. And that led to questions about the empty display case.

I told her I was keeping it in my safe until our deal could be done.

It's not *technically* a lie. The Imperial Shield *is* in my safe. It's just that it's in there in about forty pieces, in a box.

I glare at the shattered bits.

I'm running out of time and runway to try to hold Svetlana off. Soon, she's either going to realize I'm bullshitting her, or not even care if I am. Then she'll simply move on with her legal attack on my company.

The fucked-up part is, she's got a great chance of winning that attack, too.

There are other ways, of course, that I could, I suppose you could say...*take care* of this problem. I've dreamed of about a thousand different ways I could kill Svet. Except she's not stupid, and employs a small army of security. In fact, just now in my office is the first time I've even seen her without at least three of her guards around her. I mean there were ten of the fuckers downstairs on the main floor, but still.

I should have killed right now and figured out the consequences later. Fuck.

Sinking into my desk chair, I grit my teeth as I tap Taylor Crown's contact number. This is a conversation I've been putting off for way too long.

"Gavan," Taylor chirps into the phone, all-business as always. "What can I do for you?"

"If there was no egg."

She pauses. "No egg?"

"If there *was* no Imperial Shield. What would that mean, concerning Svetlana and her deal."

She exhales slowly. "You *know* what it would mean, Gavan. Look, I know it's worth both a lot of money and has incalculable sentimental value to you. But, Gavan, given what's at stake here, just *give it* to her—"

"No, what I mean," I growl, "is if there literally *was* no egg. Not off the table. Not as if I'm refusing to part with it. If it didn't exist anymore. What would happen."

"*Jesus,* Gavan," she murmurs. "What happened—"

"Just tell me, Taylor. Please."

She takes a long, deep breath. "If there *was* no egg, then again, I'm afraid it would fall back to the unfortunate language of your father's will."

My eyes close.

"Unfortunate" doesn't quite cover it.

Years before he died, when I was a newly crowned prince, for tax and security reasons, Ironclad Holdings was created with Vadim listed as the owner. When he passed, that ownership formed part of his estate, which he left to me.

Except some fucking *idiot* of a lawyer worded the will to have Vadim leaving his estate specifically to "Gavan Tsarenko *and his family.*"

And therein lies the problem.

I might be biologically Kristina Reznikov's son. I might co-helm the empire with Konstantin. But legally speaking, Vadim adopted me, making me his family. Given that he has no other relatives aside from his sister Svetlana, it now means that miserable bitch is—technically speaking—my only living family.

Which means the company, according to that shit wording, technically belongs to me *and* the devil-cunt herself. And given that she can prove I purposefully denied her money Vadim left her, it puts me at fault, and allows her to take full control.

Unless I had other family.

Unfortunately, Konstantin doesn't count, as there's no legal record of Kristina being my mother. A blood test would prove it, but the horrible irony is that by being a good, decent man and legally adopting me, Vadim's sort of fucked me over here. Because now that adoptive son status outranks my half-sibling relationship to Konstantin.

Long story short, if I want to stop Svetlana, I need a family.

"If there's no egg, Gavan," Taylor says quietly, "then we're in big trouble. But we've been over this before. Just *find* someone. Literally anyone."

There's the final twist: legally speaking, "family" can just mean "wife".

"Walk out of your office right now and find someone on the street. Or your secretary, for fuck's sake!" Taylor pleads. "I'll draw up a contract and a *bulletproof* prenup. It would just have to last a few months to hold up to a court examination, and then this would all be over. You'd probably have to pay Svet some money, I won't lie. But the company and Koikov would stay firmly in your hands."

I close my eyes. Taylor exhales.

"This doesn't have to be hard, Gavan. Just find someone. Anyone. Literally a stranger will do."

Slowly, my lips curl at the edges into a dark grin.

"Thanks, Taylor."

"Wait. Gavan—"

I hang up, my pulse thudding loudly in my ears.

I don't need a stranger.

I have Eilish.

22

EILISH

I'm furious. But I'm almost more furious at *myself* for even being furious in the first place. And I *hate* that I broke down like that on the street in front of that...that...*cunt*. Whoever the hell she is.

A dark green monster churns inside me as I remember her words.

"I taught him everything he knows. You're welcome."

Jesus Christ, I want to go back to that moment and stab her in the fucking eyes. Then I take a breath and try and clear the rage from my system.

I mean, what the fuck. What am I, *jealous*? Gavan and I are *not* a couple. He's not my fucking boyfriend. We're not "going steady".

We've never once had a conversation about whether or not we were exclusive, even within the context of our arrangement. And I mean, the reality is, Gavan's a ridiculously handsome, dark and brooding, insanely powerful and wealthy guy in New York.

What stings the most is how naive I was to be blind to the fact that he'd have a whole harem of women out there who blush like I do when he beckons with those two fingers. Who drop to their knees and moan when he asks. Who—

"Whoo hoo! Elsa's here!"

I blink, mercifully ripped from the swirling black downward spiral of my thoughts at the sound of Callie's voice.

Seriously, *fuck* Gavan. And fuck that raging cunt who tried to be as shitty as possible to me yesterday.

Shaken from my sour thoughts, I look up and force a smile when Elsa Guin walks into Fort Defiance, one of my favorite brunch spots in New York even if it is way the fuck out in Red Hook. I haven't told Callie in so many words what happened yesterday. But she knows something's up. And she's an amazing enough friend that she dragged me out here for their famous French toast drowning in mascarpone, maple syrup, and candied walnuts, washed down with their signature marmalade gin breakfast cocktail.

She even somehow got Elsa—perpetually up to her eyeballs in work—to meet us. I grin as I stand and hug our tiny blonde lawyer friend, who's also Callie's soon-to-be sister-in-law, now that she and Hades are engaged.

"You made it!" Callie beams, embracing her before we all sit back down again.

Elsa grins at the breakfast cocktail we already ordered for her, taking a sip before she exhales luxuriously like she's on a tropical island vacation.

"*Oooh*, that's good," she sighs. "And hell yeah I made it. When you're about to make equity partner, it seems they dial your workload back a little so they don't burn you out," she snickers. "Plus, Hades took Nora to a classic car show out on Long Island. What else was I going to do?"

Callie shakes her head. "I don't want to know how you did it, but thank you for turning my brother from the perpetual child he was for the twenty-nine-odd years before he met you into a respectable adult."

Elsa snorts, shaking her head. "Please. I didn't do a thing."

"Does he still give oversized dildos as gag presents on extremely inappropriate occasions?"

Elsa's brows raise. "Um—what?"

Callie shrugs. "I rest my case, your honor."

I laugh along with the two of them, glad for the distraction from the dark mood swirling inside me.

"I love that he's so amazing with Nora."

Nora is Elsa's fifteen-year-old sister, whom Elsa basically raised herself from when Nora was a toddler, when Elsa herself was only eighteen. I had my doubts about Elsa *and* Nora moving in with Hades, even though Nora got her own floor at his place so the two of them could have their privacy. But I have to say, Elsa's right: my historically wild brother-in-law is *incredible* with Nora. He's been teaching her how to drive in his prized '67 Camaro Z28—a car he barely lets *Callie* even touch. And now it seems they're bonding over classic muscle cars.

"Well, what do you say?" Callie grins impishly at Elsa. "Am I going to be an aunt someday soon?"

Elsa blushes, biting back a smile. "We'll see."

"It's what I want for Christmas. You have to."

We laugh, devouring our brunch and possibly one too many breakfast cocktails. Callie and I drop teasing hints to Elsa about her upcoming birthday celebration, which is going to involve a private showing at the Metropolitan Museum of Art followed by a private dinner in the Renaissance gallery— none of which Elsa is aware of yet.

Eventually, though, Elsa has to take off, and Callie ends up leaving with her. I stay for one last drink before finally throwing in the towel. I'm walking out when I literally bump into someone. Blinking, I step back before I stiffen.

Shit.

I've somehow managed to avoid Britney Torres ever since the night I broke into Gavan's office. I never heard back from anyone in the Crown Society, which was obviously a disappointment, given the sort of doors it could have opened. But whatever. I sort of assumed my application was toast when I never reported back to them with the egg I was supposed to steal.

"Oh. Eilish." Britney gives me a withering look, her nose wrinkling like I'm a stinking pile of garbage. "*Hi.*"

She's with two other girls who give me the exact same look before pushing past me into the restaurant. Britney stays where she is, still sneering at me.

"Just to let you know, I'm *so* sorry, but your application to the Crown Society has been denied."

I smile, not meaning it. "Yeah, I sort of figured. Thanks. Bye."

I start to push past her, when she stops me.

"Yeah, well, just so you know?" she continues coldly. "The only reason we even entertained your attempt to join was that Brooks McKinnley is an alum, and he..." She shrugs. "Put in a word for you."

I swallow back the bile in my throat.

Britney keeps prattling on. "We were never going to *actually* let a criminal like you in." She shrugs as I glare at her. "Anyway, have a nice life, I guess. Maybe I'll see you on the news when you're going to prison someday."

She laughs as she shoves past me and into the restaurant after her friends.

"*Fuck off,*" I mutter, turning and pulling my phone out to get an Uber.

"Who the fuck was that?"

I almost scream. My phone flies out of my hand when I start...

...But *he* catches it.

My heart swells and twists. My pulse quickens and my face heats as a million different conflicting emotions surge through me. Gavan's leaning against the side of a black Range Rover, his gunmetal gray eyes locked on me.

I glare at him. "Here for the breakfast cocktails?"

He shakes his head. "Here for you, actually."

My brows knit. "And how exactly did you know I was here?"

"Because I've been having you followed."

He says it in such an easy, matter-of-fact tone. But I know it's not a joke.

His brows furrow as he nods past me with his chin. "And again I ask, who the fuck was that girl?"

"No one," I shrug, my lips twisting. "Just some bitch from school who loves to make my life miserable."

His eyes stab past me in the direction Britney went with a lethality that honestly scares me a little.

"Gavan," I swallow. "She's just being a cow. It's fine."

His lips curl. "What, did you think I was about to assassinate her on the street or something?"

I shiver. "I…don't know, truthfully."

He frowns. "Why?"

"Because sometimes you scare me."

Gavan says nothing for a moment. He just looks at me with this burning intensity as he sucks on his teeth.

"Get in the car."

I snort. "Uh, no thanks."

"It wasn't a request."

"Then I guess this is mutiny. *Bye.*"

I roll my eyes and start to walk away.

"Get in the car or so fucking help me God I will pick you up and throw you in myself in front of the whole street and everyone in that restaurant."

I glare at him. He just cocks his eyebrow and shrugs.

Goddammit.

Muttering to myself, I get into the back seat. Gavan shuts the door before going around, getting in on the other side, and raising the partition separating us from the driver. The SUV drives through Red Hook in silence, pulling onto the Brooklyn-Queens Expressway, then heading over the Brooklyn Bridge back into Manhattan.

It's only then that he clears his throat and turns to me.

"You're jealous about that woman you saw yesterday."

"*Nope.*"

Yes.

"Her name is Svetlana."

"Great," I snap, staring out the window. "I don't care—"

"She's my father's sister."

I frown, turning to him. "That was your *aunt?*"

Something menacing flickers behind his eyes. "She's my father's sister."

"Yeah, that means—"

"She is *not* my aunt," he snaps coldly. "Vadim raised me. For that, I call him father, even if he didn't sire me. Svetlana does *not* get the extension of being family to me."

I nod. "Okay," I say quietly. Obviously, Gavan isn't a fan. That makes two of us. But it's also *beyond* weird and unhinged that she clearly tried to get under my skin by implying she was his lover or something. All that bullshit about him "fucking like a god?" That she "taught him everything he knows"?

I mean, eww.

I frown as I turn to him. "I'm…sorry. For the way I sort of freaked out."

"You don't need to apologize."

"No, I do," I shrug. "I thought she was—"

"Another woman."

I nod.

"She's not," he growls quietly.

I smile wryly. "Well, yeah. But still. Even if she *was*, I'd have no right to act like—"

"Yes, you would." He turns to level a fierce look at me. "If it'd been me walking in on another man talking that closely to you, with his hands on you, I'd have thrown him through the window."

My core pulses.

Fuck, why is that so hot?

We cruise the rest of the way uptown in silence before the car pulls up outside the Kildare family brownstone. Gavan turns to me.

"There's something I'd like to talk to you about."

"Okay…"

"Not now. Tonight. I'm picking you up at eight."

A blush tingles through my cheeks. "Oh? For what?"

"For dinner."

My bottom lip sucks between my teeth.

"If that's okay with you," he grumbles. "It's not a date, in case you're wondering."

"Oh no, two people who fuck each other a lot having dinner alone together is…definitely not a date."

Gavan smirks. "Be ready at eight."

23

GAVAN

Fᴜᴄᴋ ᴍᴇ, she looks *stunning.*

I mean, Eilish always looks good—too good, actually. She's got a thing for fashion, and she obviously puts a lot of thought and effort into what she wears and how she presents herself when she steps out of the house every day. And I, being on the slightly OCD side of cleanliness and taking pride in how *I* present myself to the world—like that about her.

What can I say: I find meticulous attention to detail sexy.

But tonight, she's...*more.* The woman sitting across the table from me in our private dining room at Il Piatto Buono isn't the Eilish I've seen day in and day out in Dior office wear, or Chanel dresses on the street. Tonight, it's up another notch.

She's in an elegant black cocktail dress that wouldn't look remotely out of place on a red carpet or at a royal function. It's not overtly "sexy", and yet, she looks like sin in it—a knee-length, scooped back, sleeveless number that shows just enough cleavage to get me hungry, but not so much that I have to fire warning glares at the men around her.

I mean, I still *do*, though.

There's a knock on the door.

"Enter," I growl.

A waitress smiles as she steps in, showing me the label on the Domaine de la Romanee-Conti Burgundy before she opens it and pours a splash. I swirl, sip, nod, and wait for her to fill both our glasses before leaving again.

Eilish's brows shoot up as she glances at the bottle on the table.

"You have expensive tastes."

"Guilty."

She grins. I bite back mine.

There are a few reasons I've brought her here tonight. There's the one big one, obviously. But there are some other things I need to clear up first that I've dug up in the last day.

And by "things" I really just mean one specific one.

"I have to ask you something."

She takes a sip of her wine and nods. "Okay."

"What the fuck is going on with you and Brooks McKinnley?"

Instantly, she stiffens and looks away. My jaw grinds. I've found out who the smug little shit was whose nose I most likely broke at the bar that night. Brooks McKinnley, son of Senator Harrison McKinnley.

I've also found out that the senator recently made overtures to the Kildare family about marrying Eilish off to Brooks.

Obviously, that isn't fucking happening. But I want to know how that even gets considered in the first place.

"Well?"

"Well, what?" she spits. "Google him. What do you want from me?"

Well, this is going nicely.

"His father wants you two to marry."

It's not a question. She looks surprised for a second, then shrugs.

"And?"

"Why."

She rolls her eyes. "*I* don't know. Money? Power? Senator McKinnley wouldn't be the first politician my family had a business relationship with."

"Yes, but why *you*."

She frowns and looks at me curiously before smiling sarcastically. "I guess you didn't dig quite deep enough when you were prying into my past."

"Meaning what, exactly?"

Eilish rolls her eyes. "I'm sorry, is this really what you wanted to ask me about? Why you brought me out tonight? Because if I'd known the agenda for the evening, I'd have done something more fun, like slamming my head repeatedly against a brick wall."

"We're getting to the reason for tonight," I growl. "But I need some things cleared up first."

Like why Harrison is reaching out specifically to the Kildares. And, more importantly, why that little fuck Brooks had his goddamn hand on Eilish when I walked into the bar that night.

Why he looked way, *way* too cozy and familiar with her.

"Do you two have a history."

I almost don't want to hear the answer. Because it may force me to go out and level half the city on my way to finding Brooks so I can break him in two.

Eilish pales, her eyes getting a scared, haunted look in them that makes my hackles raise.

"I…" she looks down at her hands. "We used to go out. In high school."

I see *red*.

"*Did you now*," I snarl quietly. Eilish isn't even looking at me. She's still staring at her hands as they twist the white linen tablecloth in front of her, this faraway, cold look still in her eyes.

"It…" her throat bobs. "It wasn't good." Her eyes raise to mine. "If you're asking what I think you're asking, just know that I fucking *hate* Brooks McKinnley, end of story."

"Did you two ever—"

"*No.*"

Her voice is pure venom and her eyes lethal slits. "No. You already know, I was a virgin. You were there when that changed. Or don't you remember?" she hisses sarcastically.

"Look," I growl. "I'm only asking because—"

"Can we *not* talk about this?!" she blurts, standing abruptly. "Like, can we please talk about literally *anything* else?"

I go still. Then I nod.

"Of course."

For now. But now there are SEVERAL pieces of information I will either drag out of you or beat out of him.

She turns, about to head for the door.

"Eilish."

She whirls back, glaring at me. I raise a hand, crooking two fingers. Instantly, I can see the defiance making her eyes blaze like two flames. I can also see the heat in her cheeks, and the way her lip catches in her teeth.

"Come here."

She stares at me coolly, her arms folded as she stands halfway between the table and the door, her hip cocked.

"Please. Come."

I crook my fingers again. This time, she drifts over, still glaring at me. When she's standing right next to me, I push my chair back and pat the tablecloth in front of me.

"Sit."

She stares at me blankly. "What?"

"Sit."

"Gavan, I'm not going to—"

"I'm not asking. Sit."

263

Her lips purse. "We're in a restaurant."

"Yes. That I own. Sit."

She stares at me. "I'm sorry, exactly how many restaurants *do* you own?"

"Several. Now *sit*."

She swallows.

"*Please*," I add. "I didn't bring you here to talk about goddamn Brooks McKinnley."

"Well, that's nice to know," she mutters.

Goddammit. I'm fucking this up so bad.

"Well?" Eilish mutters as she slides her ass onto the table in front of me, demurely keeping her knees firmly together and her hands folded in her lap. "Why *did* you ask me here?"

"Because I have a counter-offer."

"Of?"

"Marriage."

You could hear a pin drop. Eilish stares at me, her eyes bulging out of her pretty face.

"I'm not asking for the reasons people usually ask," I continue quietly. My hands grip the table on either side of her knees as I sigh. "There's a complicated situation unfolding right now involving Svetlana—whom I fucking hate, if that wasn't made clear before—and my inheritance from my adoptive father."

She swallows, nodding.

"The short version is, Vadim left her a decent chunk of change when he died. But she's a bloodsucking cunt and fuck her, so I stole it from her. I denied her the money, and assumed she'd go broke in no time. Except now she's hired one of the best law firms in the country that specializes in estate conflicts. She also has proof that I basically broke the law to make sure she didn't get a dime of that money."

"*Basically* broke the law? Or—"

"That I absolutely broke the law," I admit, shrugging. "And she knows it. She was going to use that to come after my entire company until we settled on something else she wanted even more—something of Vadim's she'd always coveted, that he'd left to me. If I gave her that, she'd shut the fuck up and disappear forever."

Eilish arches a brow. "So have you given it to her?"

I shake my head. "I can't."

She frowns. "Why not?"

"Because you shattered it into pieces, Butterfingers."

Her eyes go wide, her mouth falling open in horror, her face paling.

"*Oh my God—*" Her hand flies to her mouth. "Gavan, I am...I am *so fucking—*"

"It's fine."

She shakes her head. "No, it's not."

It's going to be.

"So... What happens now?"

I clear my throat. "Now, she's coming after everything, including some assets that involve associates of mine, and their money." I take a deep breath as my eyes lock with hers. "So *now*, I need you to marry me, because it would erase any claim she has to what's mine."

She's silent as she chews on her lip, looking into my eyes.

"When?" she says softly.

"Soon. The sooner the better, actually." I shake my head, my hands sliding over her knees. "But you don't have to answer right now."

Eilish swallows, nodding.

"So that's why you brought me here."

"That's part of why I brought you here."

She smiles. God, she's beautiful.

"Why else did you bring me here? To show off another glamorous, Michelin-starred restaurant of yours?"

"Am I that obvious?"

"Maybe." She giggles. "Well, let me get back to my actual seat before they bring in this fancy dinner you want to wow me with."

"Actually…" I reach under the table and push a button, locking the door to the private dining room and alerting the staff that we are to be left alone. "I was planning on starting with dessert."

She frowns. "What do you—*Gavan!*"

Eilish gasps as I grab her knees and spread them wide apart. She tries to shut them, but I'm stronger, and when my hands slide up her smooth thighs, she whimpers.

"What are you...oh my God..."

She whines when my finger teases up her lips through her lace panties, her eyes rolling back in bliss. I slip my fingers under the lace, teasing up and down her bare, slick pussy before I peel her panties down her legs, slowly.

I let them dangle from her heels before I push between her legs and kiss and nibble my way up her thigh. Eilish squirms, and when I shove her back across the table in front of me, she gasps as glassware and cutlery crash and tumble to the floor.

"Gavan—oh fuck..."

She's propped up on her elbows, her face bright red and her breath coming fast as she watches me hover my mouth mere inches above her eager cunt. I lock eyes with her, making her wait for it as I drool on her pussy for a moment before slowly dipping my mouth to her.

"Oh. My. Fuuccck..."

She coos in pleasure helplessly as I lick her slowly and languidly, not hurrying. I take my time savoring the taste of her pretty pussy. I lap at every drop of her honey-sweetness. My tongue dances lightly around her clit, teasing her into a frenzy before I plunge it deep inside of her.

Eilish's legs shake. Her chest rises and falls, never breaking eye contact as I slowly work my tongue and lips over her sweet little pussy, taking her higher and higher.

I don't rush it. I don't demand, which is a change for me. But I do utterly subjugate her pussy and claim it as mine. I have her dancing on a fucking tightrope, and I keep her there for damn near close to twenty minutes, until I'm legitimately worried I'm going to break something in her head.

But still, I keep the pace slow. I keep the tip of my tongue teasing around her clit. Until suddenly, with one precise, tiny flick, Eilish's whole world comes crashing down.

She slams a hand over her mouth, biting down hard on heel of it as she wrenches and writhes. Her swollen, throbbing pussy explodes in spasms against my tongue, flooding my mouth with her orgasm as her thighs lock around my head.

Slowly and gently, I tease my lips up and down her thighs as she catches her breath. Then, with a smug grin, I stand between her legs.

"Well then," I growl. "Should we tell them we're ready for dinner—"

"Don't even think about it."

The look in her eyes is downright *feral* as she grabs me by the belt with one hand and the tie with the other. My pants hit the floor as she yanks my mouth down to hers. And when my swollen cock sinks into her, the rest of the world disappears.

Yeah, dinner can fucking wait.

24

GAVAN

"Sir?"

I frown. I've just gotten off a long, tortuous call with Yuri, Viktor, Konstantin—and Anatoli Sevgeny, who is currently helming the Kalishnik Bratva given that Marko remains in a coma. We were discussing the ongoing Council issues with Abram and his continued push for power wrapped in the guise of fear of Drazen Krylov.

And honestly, even though we're all on the same "side" regarding giving in to Abram's hysteria, we're becoming divided on where we stand on the idea that it's actually Drazen behind all the attacks.

Viktor, who's fine after the explosion in his hotel suite here in New York, doesn't seem to believe it.

"I have *many* enemies," he made it clear on our call. "Not just from being at the helm of the Kashenko Bratva, but also through our non-profit organization," he added, referencing the Free Them Foundation that he and his wife Fiona run, which liberates children around the world from human trafficking.

Fiona's contribution to the operations is liaising with local governments and lobbying Congress. Viktor's is actively hunting down the inhuman trash who trafficked the kids in the first place, and eliminating them with extreme prejudice.

Word is, he and his men have a fondness for wood-chippers when it comes to erasing child-abusing pieces of shit from the face of the earth. I see absolutely nothing wrong with this.

But, long story short, he's made some serious enemies.

Anatoli, in contrast to Viktor, seems the most worried about Drazen being a real person. Which makes sense considering his boss and good friend Marko nearly got blown to pieces. But as Yuri pointed out, we don't even know what Drazen *looks* like, never mind his handwriting. Which sort of negates the "signed calling card" left at the scene of the car-bombing.

Not to mention a similar card found at the scene of Viktor's hotel explosion—the second playing card that Abram himself so dramatically slapped down on my desk, while Eilish was *under it*, which didn't have a message written on it at all.

It *did* have another burn circle through the head of the king of diamonds, though.

Konstantin, who I wanted to be included in the call even though he's technically hands-off for the next year, is—surprisingly—on Anatoli's side in believing Drazen really is a threat, and behind the attacks.

And me? I'm not sure what I think yet.

In the meantime, we're all tightening security and actively putting teams of people out there to see if they can track Drazen down. Whether or not he's behind these attacks will become little clearer if we can prove he actually exists.

"Mr. Tsarenko?"

I frown, focusing my attention back to the intercom. "Yes, Rachel?"

"Apologies, sir, but you have an unscheduled visitor."

"Not today, I don't," I growl. The conference call and its subject matter has me riled up enough. The fact that Eilish has been buried in advisor meetings and other schoolwork for two fucking days in a row isn't exactly improving my disposition.

"Sir, I'm afraid he's quite insistent…"

"Please tell him I *insist* that he get the fuck out of the building until I can schedule him in." I pause, my mouth twisting before I exhale and rub my temples. "Rachel?"

"Sir?"

"Who *is* he, anyway."

"A Mr. Petrov. Stanislav Petrov."

I scowl. "*Who?*"

"He says he's an antiques appraiser?"

Shit.

"And I'm afraid he actually might have what looks like a legal document concerning—"

"Bring him up, Rachel," I growl quietly.

Fuck. Me.

This was going to happen sooner or later: Svetlana's goddamn expert, here to go over and authenticate the fucking Imperial Shield. I've been stringing that miserable fucking cunt along for weeks, and she's clearly gotten tired of it.

Or, she's smarter than I'd like to give her credit for and is starting to doubt I even have it.

Which is a problem.

Because she'd be *right*.

But sending this fucking guy away outright just now will only give that hunch of hers more weight. If I can send him back to that witch with a pretty story, I can possibly drag this out a little longer.

Until Eilish says yes to my proposal.

I know I could find almost literally any woman with a pulse to do this for me. Taylor Crown already has the contracts, watertight NDAs, and crystal clear prenup all drawn up.

But I don't want any woman with a pulse. I want Eilish. Even if it's a fake marriage that is just a means to an end.

And I'm not quite sure how to deal with that.

There's a knock at my door.

"Enter."

The door swings open. Rachel comes in first, biting her lip and almost, dare I say it, blushing as she clears her throat.

"Uh, Mr. Petrov, sir."

The appraiser steps in next, and my brows shoot up.

Okay, not what I expected.

When I heard "expert antiques appraiser", I imagined one of the fucking goblins from that bank in Harry Potter, or a hunched old man in tweed smelling like mothballs.

The man who walks in is neither of those. Tall, with an obviously muscular build, and a strong, sharp jawline.

He *is* wearing tweed, though.

"Ahh, Mr. Tsarenko!"

The appraiser beams widely at me as he crosses the room to shake my hand eagerly. His voice is heavily accented—Belarusian, unless my ears are rustier than I think. I keep my face neutral and my mouth a straight line as I firmly shake his hand back.

"I will not insult you and ask if this is a good time," he chuckles. "I know you are, how do you say, busy-busy! No time is good time, yes?"

I frown. "Look, Mr. Petrov—"

"Please, call me Stanislav. All my friends do."

He turns to wink at a blushing Rachel. *Blushing.*

"That'll be all, Rachel," I growl. She nods quickly and slips out of the room, closing the door behind her. When Stanislav turns back to me, he grins.

"I am not what you are expecting."

I incline my head. "Not exactly."

The man laughs. "What can I say, I'm an academic trapped in a footballer's body. It's a curse." He shrugs before lifting his brow gracefully. "But you, Mr. Tsarenko, are every inch what I expected."

I clear my throat. "Meaning?"

He laughs again. "Oh, all good things, Mr. Tsarenko. *All* good things, I assure you." He grins as he drags his gaze around my office. "You have wonderful taste, I must say." He whistles appreciatively. "In interior design, clothing." He looks past me at the Monet on the wall. "Art..." his grin curls. "Women."

I tense.

"*Excuse me?*" I hiss, sudden images of Eilish swirling through my head.

Stanislav holds his hands up, looking concerned. "I think you mistake my words. I simply make a joke." He clears his throat. "Your secretary is...uh...very beautiful."

My shoulders unbunch a little. My jaw stays tight, though.

"She's very good at her job. I'm not fucking her, if that's what you're suggesting."

Stanislav laughs heartily. "That is probably wise. And I assure you, I was not suggesting anything. I apologize if it came out as such."

He takes a deep breath. "Mr. Tsarenko, I think we're off on the wrong foot. I am sorry. I'm very aware of the legal disagreements between yourself and your aunt—"

"She's not my aunt."

He dips his head. "Again with the wrong foot. My mistake. I assure you, my only interest in any of this dispute is to authenticate the extremely rare piece you have in your possession. I must confess, I am a bit of a...how do you say…" he chuckles. "A *stan* for late period Imperialist Russian art." He almost giggles. "Stanislav is a *stan*. Get it?"

Jesus Christ. This guy is making dad-jokes while being a dead ringer for Henry Cavill. All the same, it's pretty clear that he's here because he's a nerd for Russian art, not because he's Svetlana's stooge. And that's good.

He smiles. "Now, I know you're a very busy man. Shall we get to it, so that I can get out of your hair?"

I take a deep breath, gesturing past him to the shelf with the empty glass display case.

"I wish you'd called ahead, Mr. Petrov. I'm afraid the building had a security breach a month ago. Since then, I've kept the Imperial Shield off-site in a very secure, private location."

I almost feel bad at the crestfallen look on his face. Like a little kid who just came charging downstairs to find his stocking empty on Christmas morning.

"Ahh, I see." He exhales, walking over to the glass case over the old wooden base anyway and looking at it fondly. "A shame. I would have loved to see it with my own eyes. You know the history of this particular Fabergé piece is quite fascinating—"

"I'm sure it is," I grunt. "But, as you said, I'm afraid I'm fairly busy today, Mr. Petrov."

He nods, smiling. "Of course, of course." His eyes drop to the base of the case, where I've taped the note from Vadim. His lips part in a smile. *"To my son. All my love."* Stanislav turns back to me, beaming. "You had a very generous father."

"I owe him everything."

"I am envious of you, Mr. Tsarenko." He chuckles. "And not just for your wonderful office view." Stanislav sighs, clasping his hands together. "Well then. Perhaps another time?"

"Perhaps."

He grins. "For now, I will tell Ms. Tsarenko that the Imperial Shield is safe and sound in your possession. Perhaps that will settle the matter until you complete your transaction with her."

I allow a small smile to curl my mouth. "I appreciate it. Thank you, Stanislav."

"Of course."

When he's gone, I stare at the empty glass case, my eyes reading the note from Vadim over and over. My cell phone buzzes.

It's Korol.

"We got 'em," he growls thickly, his tone heavy. "We found the pieces of shit who jumped Eilish."

My blood flows hot, the egg forgotten.

I LOSE track of time as I exact my vengeance. It's hours later when I finally step back from the limp, near-dead, blood-soaked men hanging from meat hooks in the basement of one of my properties deep in Brooklyn.

I'm shirtless and covered in blood. It's not my own blood, though. My muscles are still quivering from what I've just done to the two men who are quite literally begging for death.

They'll have to beg harder if they want my mercy, though.

Behind me, Korol sits back in a metal chair, drinking a beer. He offers the bottle to me, and I take a sip to wet my throat before I turn back to the two pieces of shit who dared to lay hands on Eilish. Who *hurt* her.

It's clear they're both nothing more than a couple of knuckle-dragging street thugs. But again, it's clear they weren't there to mug Eilish. Or else they'd have *taken* the several thousand dollars' worth of jewelry and other valuables on her person. No, this was done to hurt her. It was done to send a message.

It means someone hired these two fucks, and I want to know *who*.

So far, they've both been silent on that front. Which would almost impress me under any other circumstances—like, if they hadn't put Eilish in the fucking hospital.

"P...please..."

One of them men burbles blood and spittle from his savaged mouth as he tries to speak.

"What?" I snap. "Korol, did you hear anything?"

"Nah. I think one of these assholes just farted, boss."

I snarl, advancing on the one who just tried to say something, relishing the way he flinches. Or, tries to flinch, at least. He's dangling from his arms: one shoulder has dislocated, at least one of his legs is definitely broken, along with most of his ribs and his nose, and his face looks like a fucking horror show. Still, he's doing better than his buddy, who's drifting in and out of consciousness.

And who is now missing an eye.

"*What*," I rasp in the first man's face.

He whimpers, blubbering again.

"*Ple—please*," he chokes.

"Please *what*," I snap. "Please stop? Please kill you, to end your suffering?"

His head lifts up and drops pathetically again, like he's nodding.

"If you want this to stop," I snarl, grabbing a handful of his hair. "If you long for the sweet embrace of death, you know what I need to know."

He lifts and drops his head again in a small nod.

"*Okay...*"

The word croaks from his bloody lips. Next to him, his friend groans, and it sure looks to me like he's shaking his head. I snort.

"You're worried about any consequences from whoever hired you. I can understand that. But let me be clear. *Neither* of you is leaving this room alive. Ever. But today is just day one of...well," I smile. "Of however long I choose to keep you alive and in misery." I frown. "You hurt someone I care for. And believe me, I can make your stay in this basement, and this pain, drag out for *an eternity* should I choose to. There's no need to be afraid of whoever hired you anymore."

They both groan as I leer close in their faces.

"Be afraid of *me*, my friends. Be afraid of the pain I am prepared to inflict upon you for so long you will beg for Hell. Trust me," I hiss as stab my gaze into both of their faces. "*I am your devil now.*"

One-eye looks like he's fading out again. But the one who tried to speak before lifts and drops his chin again.

"*Tell me*," I snarl, leaning close. I pull the gun out from where it's tucked in my belt and wave it in front of him. "Tell me, and you have my word, I will let you die right now."

He nods again, a shell of a man. His lips move.

I frown, moving close. "What?"

"*Russian*," he croaks.

I laugh coldly. "You'll need to be more specific than that if you want this bullet—"

"*Draz…*"

I go still and cold as the word tumbles from his mouth.

"*Say that again*," I rasp.

"*Drazen*," he chokes. "*Drazen…Krylov…*"

The world turns red around me. My vision tunnels.

The gun raises in my hand.

"I'm a man of my word, shit-stain."

Two shots blast through the room, ending both of their miseries. I turn to Korol, who's looking at me unblinkingly.

"What do you want to do, Gavan?" he growls.

"I want to keep this quiet, and I *don't* want Abram getting wind of it," I mutter, glancing back at the carnage behind me. "Now—find someone to get rid of these two."

25

EILISH

I'M GETTING some reading done for class in the kitchen of the Upper East Side brownstone when my phone rings. I grin when I glance down and see Cillian's name on the screen.

"So, are you two just going to full-on move into that castle over there?"

He chuckles. "If Una has her way, it's a distinct possibility."

My lips spread wide and I gasp. "Really?"

A rumbling laugh leaves his throat. "*No.* Don't get me wrong, I could get pretty used to playing the King and Queen of Ireland over here. But there are things we'd both miss about New York."

As if on cue, Bones pads into the kitchen and rubs his face against my shin.

"Things like the fuzzy little houseguest I'm getting quite used to?"

Cillian chuckles. "He grows on you, doesn't he?"

"He's definitely growing. Horizontally, that is. Castle's feeding him way too much."

"Well, we're not staying forever. But we are extending the trip by another few weeks."

My brows shoot up. "Oh?"

"Yeah. There are a few old friends of mine I'd love to introduce Una to."

I grin. "Old friends of *yours*? You sure you have those?"

He chuckles. "One or two. Adrian and Celeste Cross reached out when they heard I was here. And we're going to meet up with Rose and Oliver Prince too."

I grin. Rose is another of Cillian's nieces, by way of his late sister, Saoirse. We've only met a few times, but I really like her. Her husband, Oliver, is cool too.

"Tell her hi from me when you see her. She should come visit New York again."

Cillian clears his throat. "Got a second? I wanted to talk to you about something."

"Sure thing. About what?"

"Gavan."

I swallow, my hand tensing around the phone as my mouth goes dry.

"I…"

"I can assume this is one of the reasons you've been avoiding coming back to the conversation about Brooks?"

"Amongst others," I say quietly. "Look, Cil—"

"Eilish," he sighs. "You're an adult. You don't need to explain yourself to me."

My brow furrows. "Well, I know this thing with the McKinn-leys could mean a lot to the family, politically speaki—"

"I don't give a shit about that. I mean, yeah, I've thought about it and what it could do for us. But you obviously despise Brooks—for reasons I'd actually be very keen to hear about sometime, if you'd like to share," he adds. There's a lethal edge to his voice.

Part of me has almost told Cillian a half dozen times before about what happened with Brooks. Or what's happen*ing*, really. Because Cillian's...well, *Cillian*...and I know what he is, and what he's capable of. He'd go straight to Brooks' house and literally skin him alive if I told him about what happened.

So yes, part of me has thought about that. Often. But the thing is, Brooks isn't just some regular trust fund brat douchebag. His father is a freaking Senator, for God's sake. And I also don't know how extensive the evidence he has against me is. It's bad enough that he has it at all. It'd be horrifying if he was killed and *someone else* got their hands on it.

"Nothing you need to go full Patrick Bateman about," I joke. "He's just a douchebag."

Cillian sighs. "Well then, that's all the conversation we need to have about it. Consider the subject closed."

"Cillian—"

"It's done, Eilish," he growls quietly.

I smile. "Thank you."

"But *that* brings us back to Gavan…"

My mouth twists. "Who told you? Neve?"

He chuckles darkly. "She wouldn't turn on you in a million years. I have…people."

"What, like spies?"

"Yes."

I swallow thickly. Cillian sighs.

"Again, you don't have to explain yourself. You can make your own decisions, Eilish. And for what it's worth, I respect Gavan." He grunts. "I don't *like him* very much, but I respect him. And if *you* clearly like him, and you're happy, and he's treating you well, and you're with him because you are *choosing* to be…"

"I am," I say quietly, blushing.

"Then I promise I'll keep my skinning knives tucked away in the cupboard."

I grin. "Thank you."

"Just make sure Gavan is aware that if any of those points above change, there's no measure I won't take and no line I won't cross to make him reevaluate his definition of pain and suffering."

That's not a joke, and it's not Cillian being all gung-ho macho.

That's who he is.

"Say hi to Una for me."

"Will do. Take care, Eilish."

****

It's been a couple of weeks since Gavan proposed to me. Or at least, since Gavan put a certain proposition on the table and let it sit there. And it's not that I've necessarily been avoiding the subject since then. I've just been…reluctant to bring it up.

Oddly, *he* hasn't mentioned it again, either. Even though I fully understand what's at stake for him and why he needs to get married in order to stop his aunt from seizing his empire.

I guess I'm just still confused why it's me he's asking.

I mean, why not some random girl? A girl whose family Gavan *did not* almost go to war with on more than one occasion in the past?

Or a girl he's not "with" in the first place because of blackmail?

All this, of course, leads me down the rabbit-hole of whether I'm "with" Gavan at all or not. Yes, it does feel like we've moved way past the whole blackmail thing at this point. But even so, what are we to each other?

Does frequently sleeping with someone with whom you are exclusive, with whom you also spend a fair amount of time, make you "with" them?

I blink away the confusing thoughts, stretching out in the huge, ridiculously comfortable bed in Gavan's bedroom—his *actual* bedroom. Like, the one he sleeps in. Not the one where he plays, where he took my virginity that first time.

Not to say that we haven't spent time in that one since as well.

The blackout shades on the walls of one-way glass windows are already up, bathing the room in morning light. I didn't actually sleep here last night, though.

We've never once actually spent the night with each other. It's become sort of an unspoken thing.

But this morning—I blush as I remember it—I pinged awake at five to a text from Gavan with a picture of a *huge* bulge in his linen sheets and the message "Come take care of this. There's a car waiting downstairs for you."

That was two hours ago. I've been in his bed ever since.

I reach over to the bedside table for my phone and the double espresso he made me earlier. It's taken everything I have not to make a crack about the tables turning—how after weeks and weeks of *me* making *him* coffee, usually in my underwear, today it was *Gavan* who strode out of the room, stark naked, only to return with an espresso he'd made *me*.

Next to me, Gavan's sitting up in bed, scrolling his phone as his hand lazily traces up and down my bare thigh.

It's disturbing how used to all of this I could get.

Have gotten.

Blushing, I go to my email. Instantly, my dreamy, grinning morning comes to a screeching halt.

"*Shit!*" I blurt, my heart sinking.

"What is it?" Gavan growls next to me, his hand instantly tightening possessively on my thigh.

I groan as I re-read the email. It's Elsa's birthday in a couple of days. I know Hades has something extravagant planned for the two of them for next week, but tonight Neve, Callie,

Nora and I were going to take Elsa to the Metropolitan Museum of Art for a private showing of the Impressionists wing, followed by a private dinner at the museum itself..

Except, the email I just got from a very apologetic museum director informs me that one of the museum's alarm sensors triggered early this morning, which means the entire place is on lockdown for the next day and a half pending a full security review.

My face falls as I relay all of this to Gavan.

"Ugh, I'm so annoyed! She *loves* Impressionist art." My brows knit as I try to think about how I could possibly save the evening. I mean, Elsa's pretty low maintenance. We could do literally *anything*, and she'd love simply being out with us.

But still—shit. I really wanted to blow her away with this.

"She likes the Impressionists?"

I nod glumly, paging through my phone looking for the number for the main office of the Guggenheim. It's modern art, but maybe if I can get hold of the—

"Would the Bijou Gala at the Musée d'Orsay work as a suitable substitute?"

I stiffen, sharply snapping my eyes from my phone to Gavan.

"I'm sorry, *what?*"

His brow cocks, a smug grin curling the corners of his mouth.

"The Bijou Gala, at—"

"I heard what you *said*," I arch my brows. "It's also one of the most exclusive art fundraising galas in the world."

"Indeed."

"And it's *tonight*."

"Correct."

"In *Paris*."

"A-plus for geography."

I grin as I playfully slap his arm.

"It also sells out a year in advance, and the tickets are a hundred thousand dollars each."

He rakes his fingers down his jaw, looking at me impassively.

"You haven't answered me. Would it suffice in lieu of a private tour this evening at the Met?"

I snort. "I mean, *yeah*. But it's not a realistic—"

Gavan reaches for his phone and starts texting someone. "Numbers. You, your sister, Calliope I'm assuming, as well as Elsa and her sister."

I stare at him. "Gavan, what are you—"

He barrels on ahead. "I'm going to assume there's not a chance in hell Hades or Ares allows their wife to get on a plane with me without coming too, so they're in." He frowns at the ceiling. "Castle can come, *if* he fucking behaves himself." He looks over at me. "Will your uncle and Una be joining us?"

"Uh, I don't—"

"I'll include them as maybes just in case. Then you and I, of course."

He finishes sending his text and then rolls his neck. The phone dings in his hand, and he nods curtly at it.

"Excellent. We're all set."

My eyes go wide.

"I'm sorry, what just happened?"

"We're in for the Bijou Gala."

My jaw drops. "*All* of us?"

His brow furrows. "Does Nora still pal around with Galina Kaminksi?"

"I...think so?"

"Ah. Then it's *ten* of us with two maybes." He texts again, and nods curtly at the instant response before dropping the phone. "We're set."

I blink. "How the hell did you just do that?"

Gavan smirks, yanking the covers from both of us.

"That Monet in your office..." I chew on my lip, blushing as he rolls over between my legs and wraps them around his waist. "That's a reproduction, right?"

His mouth lowers to my ear, making me gasp as he starts to nibble at the lobe.

"*Right?*"

"What do you think," he murmurs, making me gasp as his swollen cock head slips between my lips.

"I think..." I gasp, moaning, as he slides into me. "I think you just invited my entire family to Paris."

"I'm trying not to think about how many ways this might bite me in the ass later."

I giggle, grinning as I shift my weight and roll us over, with me on top of him. I groan as I slowly sink all the way down onto his huge, gorgeous cock and lower my mouth to his.

"Thank you," I whisper.

26

"ARE YOU FUCKING *SHITTING* ME?!"

I'm not a Buddhist monk. I'm not devoid of pride. When Eilish's friends and family pile out of the fleet of armored Range Rovers I sent to bring them to the airport, I allow myself a smug smile when Calliope gawks at the private plane sitting on the runaway.

My plane.

Behind her, Ares, Neve, and Eilish herself step out of the same car, looking equally as shocked at the size of the jet. So do Hades, Elsa, Nora, and Galina when they get out of the next vehicle. Kratos and Dimitra Drakos, who are taking the slots I reserved for Cillian and Una, who it turns out aren't able to make it, step out of the third car along with an extremely reluctantly impressed looking Castle.

There are private planes, and then there are *private planes*. I know for a fact that both the Drakos and Kildare families have private jets. But I'm certain their planes could fit *inside* the massive slate-black Boeing Business Jet 747-8i with

"Ironclad Capital" written across the fuselage in elegant gold lettering.

It's also not lost on me that this is the first time any of them are meeting me as Eilish's...well, whatever-it-is she's calling me.

In other words, it's the first time they're meeting me as not *just* the head of the Reznikov Bratva. The enemy. Just like it's not lost on me that the last time I was face to face with Ares, Hades, Kratos, and Castle, my men were leveling guns at them.

Neve breaks the tension first, walking right over to where I'm standing with a polite but hard look on her face.

"Thanks for the invite."

I nod. "Of course." Then I frown in surprise when she steps right up to me, her eyes unflinchingly piercing straight into mine.

"Before Castle or Ares or anybody else comes over here and tries to scare you about not hurting Eilish, you should know one thing."

"And that is?"

She smiles icily as she leans close, beckoning with her finger for me to lower my ear to her.

"I'll be the scariest motherfucker in the room if you ever hurt my sister."

I nod, my lips curling as she pulls away. "I have *zero* doubts about that."

Neve smiles a little less frostily and pats my arm. "Good. Then we'll get along great."

I chuckle as she slips back to the crowd of people staring at my plane. Ares immediately takes his wife's place in front of me.

"I'd like to believe I can trust you, Gavan."

I lift a shoulder. "Believe whatever you like. If I was going to come after your family or your empire, I probably would have done so already, don't you think?"

His brow furrows. "Didn't they teach you at business school that cockiness and smugness aren't good negotiating tools?"

"I'm not negotiating, and I didn't *go* to business school."

A smirk plays around the corners of his mouth. "Okay then, how about this: you seem to make my sister-in-law happy, and I'm choosing to believe that means I can trust you. Also, I met your father once, in London."

I blink in surprise. "I didn't know that."

He nods. "Vadim was an honorable man. I liked him, and he seemed to have the respect of everyone else in the room when we were introduced. I'd like to think that he raised you to be the same."

Ares puts out his hand. I shake it firmly, and he grins.

"Does this mean I can get on that sick plane now?"

I chuckle. "Be my guest."

Kratos, the giant among the Drakos brothers, walks his grandmother over, who gives me a sharp arch of her brow.

"I, too, would like to believe that you are a man we can all trust."

She clears her throat, offering me a Tupperware container filled with what looks and smells like fresh baklava.

"Mrs. Drakos—"

She shakes her head, holding up a frail-looking finger. "Before you make any promises, we have a saying in Greek. *Kalokagathían órkou pistotéran éche*. It's from the philosopher Solon, and it means 'Put more trust in integrity of character than in an oath.'"

I smile as I nod at her offered baklava. *"Na fováste tous Éllines pou férnoun dóra."*

Beware of Greeks bearing gifts—a reference to the ancient Greeks and their Trojan horse, which gained them entry into the walled city of Troy.

Dimitra grins widely, chuckling as she puts the Tupperware into my hands. "So long as you are kind to Eilish, who I consider one of my own grandchildren, there'll be no soldiers jumping out of my baklava come nightfall."

"That's a promise I can make confidently."

She nods, smiling.

"Nice plane," Kratos grunts, giving me a firm shake. "And thanks for the invite."

"No hard feelings about the parking garage basement, I hope."

He smirks, leaning closer as his grandmother steps out of earshot.

"Not exactly the first time I've had a gun pointed at me."

Elsa gushes an exuberant thank you, giving me a hug that elicits a venomous glare from her fiancé. Nora and Galina

293

blurt equally gushing thank you's before dashing up the staircase and onto the plane hard on Elsa's heels.

"Nice fucking plane," Hades mutters, stopping in front of me. "But seriously. The Bijou Gala? How the fuck did you pull that off?"

I shrug deprecatingly. "Called in some favors, that's all."

He glares at me. "You realize this means I have to up my fucking game next week for Elsa's actual birthday. Thanks a lot."

"Competition breeds innovation."

"Asshole."

I grin. "You're welcome to borrow the plane again for her—"

"I just might," Hades smirks back. "And don't think for a second I'll be topping off the tank before I bring it back."

I laugh as he gives me a strong slap on the shoulder and heads up the stairs.

Which leaves Castle.

Eilish's blond, built-like-a-fucking-Viking former bodyguard comes to a glowering stop right in front of me. The only reason this man's obsessive, compulsive need to protect Eilish and be up my ass about her hasn't pushed me into fury is because it's quite clear the love he has for her is brotherly, and nothing romantic.

But still. He needs to stop getting in my fucking face.

"Are we going to have a problem?"

"No, but only because Eilish went out of her way to convince me that you had nothing to do with the Banshee bombing, or Theo Petrakis getting lit on fire."

"Because I *didn't*," I growl in a warning tone. "And I'm getting more than a little tired of your veiled insinuations that I did."

He glares at me. "Don't think for a minute that I don't see something fucky with the way you and Eilish connected."

I glare right back. "So long as *you* don't think for a second that *I* don't notice the way you and Calliope Drakos have been doing everything in your power not to even look at each other since you stepped out of the Range Rovers."

Castle's jaw clenches tightly. "You have a vivid imagination," he mutters quietly.

I smile. "I'm sure that's all it is. But how about we keep our respective suspicions to ourselves for this trip and just have a good time."

Castle jabs a finger against my chest. "I want you to understand the ways I will hurt you if you fuck with Eilish in any—"

"I found the men who jumped her."

He pulls back and arches a brow. "You did?"

I nod. "I took care of them. It was very slow, and *extremely* painful."

He eyes me. Very slowly, his mouth relaxes. When I put my hand out, he takes it firmly.

"Enjoy the flight, Castle."

Finally, after I've gone through greeting them all, it's Eilish's turn to stroll over from where she's been leaning against one of the cars, an amused look on her face.

"That looked rough."

I smirk, wrapping an arm around her waist and pulling her against me. "Beyond brutal. But I'll live."

She bites her lip, turning to look up at the massive plane. "The plane, the tickets to the gala…" she turns back to arch a brow at me. "And Neve tells me you took care of the hotel rooms for everyone?"

I nod. She slowly shakes her head.

"This is…*wow*. I mean we've got a private jet. But holy *shit—*"

"You know millions, *solnishka*," I growl, relishing her little gasp when I pull her even tighter to me and drop my lips to her ear. "Let me show you *billions*."

I WON'T LIE: I'm gunning to impress. And if the full bar and dance club on the plane itself somehow didn't quite do it for anyone on the flight over to France, the fleet of Mercedes G-Wagons waiting to take everyone shopping before going to their hotels finishes the job.

I smile at the way Eilish and her friends go nuts when we arrive at some of Paris' most exclusive boutiques to find the perfect gowns for the gala. Kratos, still flushed from getting a little too deep into the whiskey on the flight over, gives me a firm clap on the back and a nod when his grandmother steps out of her dressing room looking like a Greek Dame Judi Dench on a red carpet.

"Hey, Tsarenko?"

I glance over to where Ares and Hades are sitting in the lounge of the boutique in the tailored tuxes I just bought them—cigars and drinks in hand.

"I know I'm being bought," Ares smirks. "But I'm not mad about it."

I chuckle as Hades comes over with a glass for me, giving me an approving nod. "Not fucking bad, man. Not fucking bad at all."

"You know I'm not actually trying to upstage you, right?"

He grins. "I mean, you *are*, but I know it's not intentional. I'm still borrowing that sick-ass plane next week."

"Deal."

He nods past me, to where a grouchy looking Castle is having the finishing touches on his tux taken care of by one of the in-house tailors.

"What do we think, buddy," Hades smirks at Eilish's former bodyguard. "You ready to drop that chip on your shoulder?"

Castle scowls. Then a familiar laugh rings out across the boutique, and we all turn to where Eilish is modeling an absolutely stunning green gown. She turns in front of the mirror, and when her eyes catch mine, her cheeks flush and her smile splits her face almost in two.

"*Thank you*," she beams. "I love it!"

Castle sighs, pulling my attention back to him.

"All right, all right," he grunts. "I yield." His gaze lands on me. "You keep making her smile like that, and we're good."

"I think I can manage that."

I turn to watch her twirl some more for her friends. And I can't look away.

At all.

This is becoming...*real.*

No, not "becoming".

It already *is*. And I don't know how to pretend I'm not happier about that than I've ever been about anything in my life.

27

EILISH

IT's hard to call it a Cinderella moment, because it's not like I grew up in rags, living with hardship. But even with the life I've had, the gala is next level.

Gavan was right: I know millions. But the wealth and glamour on display at the Bijou Gala at the Musée d'Orsay is truly that of *billions*. I might have grown up wanting for nothing, with nice cars, nice clothes, and all of that. But this is the world of the top elite. And that's why I feel like an actual princess as Gavan leads me through the evening.

There's ballroom dancing with music provided by the orchestra of the Paris Opera. We get a private guided tour through a few of the Impressionist collections of the museum, where Elsa almost starts crying at seeing some of her favorite pieces in the flesh. We meet royalty—like legit, actual royal figures. First there's an English duke whom Gavan seems to know personally. Then, there's a collective sound of our jaws hitting the floor when he introduces us all to Misha Tsavakov and his wife, *Princess* Charlotte

Bergendem of the Kingdom of Luxlordia, who is next in line to be queen.

It's a glimpse into a world not even Dimitra Drakos with her English mansion sitting on top of a forty-story building over Central Park knows. And it's *spellbinding*.

"Come here."

I arch a curious brow, blushing as Gavan takes my elbow and pulls me away from the circle where Neve and Callie are geeking the hell out talking to the world-famous model River Finn—who also happens to be married to Gavan's friend, Yuri Volkov, head of the Volkov Bratva family.

"What's up?"

Gavan smirks darkly as he spins me around so that he's at my back.

"The dress is perfect. But I got you a little something to finish it off."

I gasp as the cool string of diamonds drapes over my collarbones. He fastens it at the nape of my neck before turning me slowly to face a gilded mirror hanging on the museum wall.

My eyes bulge at the gorgeous choker—diamond and silver, with a stunning green emerald at the center.

"Gavan..." I swallow, my eyes locked on the necklace. I shake my head side to side. "I can't accept—"

"You already have."

I spin slowly to face him, shivering at the intensity in his eyes as he reaches up to cup my cheek.

"*Beautiful,*" he murmurs with a soft reverence to his voice. Suddenly, he's leaning down and kissing me.

And my world short-circuits.

We haven't actually done that before in public. But I don't freak. I don't second-guess it, or over-analyze. I just melt into the kiss, sinking against his chest as time loses all meaning around us.

When he slowly pulls back, my heart is thundering in my chest. His eyes are still locked on mine.

"I'm going to get us some champagne."

I chew on my lip, my face throbbing as I nod. "I...I think that's a good idea."

Gavan grins, his hand brushing mine before he turns and strides away toward one of the bars set up around the main gallery hall. I catch Neve giving me a sharply raised brow with a pointed smirk on her face. I roll my eyes and turn away, blushing as I meander away through another gallery full of sculptures by Degas and Rodin.

At the far end of the room, I step out onto a quiet terrace overlooking an empty inner courtyard. I inhale and exhale deeply, feeling something wild and freeing coursing through my veins.

This is no longer an "arrangement".

I think I've fallen for Gavan.

Actually, there's no "I think" about it.

I *have* fallen for him.

"I thought you were smarter than to insult me like this, Eilish."

The mood shatters like glass, the shards raking down my skin as my blood runs cold. I turn, and my face goes white as

I come face-to-face with Brooks McKinnley.

His lips curl dangerously.

This is the first time I've ever found myself alone with Brooks since that party I should never have gone to during my senior year of high school. And the second I realize just how alone we really are, my body begins to turn numb.

Like it did that night.

"What do you want?" I choke.

He glares at me. "Respect, for one. Eilish, I made you and your family a solid offer. An alliance with my family? Given the Senate committee my father oversees? Are you fucking *joking*? I'm your reusable get out of jail free card." He shakes his head angrily. "And yet, you ignore my offer. Worse, now I see you parading around like some Bratva whore with Gavan fucking Tsarenko."

My mouth tightens.

"Fuck you, assho—"

"I'd *watch* what you say to me," he snarls viciously, making my heart leap into my throat as I back away from him. "I don't take kindly to insults, Eilish." He sneers, nodding his chin at my choker. "Did *he* get that for you?"

"Yes," I spit back. "And *he* will be back any second. And when he finds you threatening me, you're going to realize what I've known for years about you—that you're an arrogant, pampered, spoiled fucking *idiot.*"

I almost choke as Brooks lunges at me, shoving me back and pinning me against the stone terrace railing. He looms over me, his hand wrapped tight around one of my wrists.

"Does he know you used to be *my* whore?"

Bile rises in my stomach like acid. I blanch as a wave of nausea spreads through me.

Brooks smiles cruelly. "You remember that night, don't you...*babe?*"

My lips curl into a sneer. "*I remember*," I spit venomously. "I remember you spiking my drink," I choke. "I remember you shoving me into that bedroom and trying to take my clothes off while I couldn't say no. While I couldn't fucking *move!*"

I was barely eighteen when Brooks dragged me to a "cool kids" party at the end of senior year. I remember him passing me a drink with a smile. I barely drank back then. Even so, two or three sips of a vodka soda later, the room was spinning. There must have been something in it. Enough to incapacitate me. Not enough that I don't remember *everything* that happened next.

When he led me upstairs and away from the party. When he pulled me into a bedroom and locked the door.

I couldn't move at all while he had me on the bed, trying to yank off my jeans.

Then he shoved his hand down my underwear and roughly tried to finger me.

All of this while I *could. Not. Move.*

Brooks only stopped that night because he got angry at "how fucking dry I was". I spent another two hours in that room silently crying, still unable to move. When I finally could again, I ran home, a fucking wreck.

Only to find Brooks waiting for me on my front steps. That's when he told me the dirt he had on me.

My shameful mistake.

I'd only gone out with Brooks in the first place because I was suddenly aware how uncool I was. How unpopular I was in school despite being—or maybe *because* of it—head of the class, academically. Brooks was cool, and rich, and popular, and he was nice to me. So we went out.

Then, when it became clear to him that I wasn't going to "do anything" beyond kissing, things got...weird. Pushy. Aggressive. What happened at the party was the final straw that sent me running from him.

But a few weeks before that, I'd done something stupid.

I'd given in when Brooks called me late one night, drunk, begging for me to "help him out". He was *horny*, he said. He'd been *so patient* with my "blue-balling", he said. And he asked —more like bullied me—into "assisting" him over the phone.

It was hands down the grossest thing I've ever done. I talked dirty—or at least made a cringey, terrible attempt at taking dirty—to Brooks while he jerked off on the other end of the line.

And then, that night on my front steps after he assaulted me, I found to my horror that he'd *recorded* that phone call.

That was his leverage. If I ever told anyone about what had happened at the party, he'd make sure the recording of me saying gross, horrible, porn-star things over the phone went public.

For the last three and a half years, I haven't told a *soul* about that night. Not even my sister.

Brooks sneers at me as he looms over me, my back still against the stone railing.

"A man can only take so much cock-teasing, Eilish. What you were doing wasn't fucking cool."

I blink, bile rising in my throat.

"I'm sorry, what I was *doing?*"

"You know damn well what the fuck I'm taking about. Teasing me. Leading me the fuck on. Giving me blue balls over and fucking over. C'mon, we both know you wanted me to fuck you. You were just being coy about it. And that's what that night was supposed to be. Instead, you fucking ruined it."

I stare at him. "Are you fucking *deranged?!* Brooks, you disgusting pig, you fucking drugged me and tried to shove your fingers into me! And then you got angry because I wasn't *wet!*"

Tears bead in my eyes like hot lead, my chest hitching as I try and suck in air.

"Get away from me," I spit.

Brooks shakes his head. "I don't like being ignored, Eilish. And I *will not* take some Bratva thug's sloppy seconds." He glares at me. "Have you fucked him?"

My lips curl. "*A hundred times,*" I sneer. "Gladly. Willingly. He's good. And *huge.*"

Instantly, I regret my decision to taunt him. Because Brooks' face goes *livid.*

"Maybe he'd like to hear you begging for *my* dick," he hisses. "We'll see if he even wants you once I play him that recording—"

It happens in the blink of an eye. Something dark surges into Brooks, ripping him from me and sending him flying across the terrace. The black shape is on him instantly, the dull sound of a fist pounding flesh echoing loudly in my ears.

Gavan is sitting astride Brooks' face, savagely beating the absolute shit out of him.

Instantly, the terrace is flooded with men in dark suits and earpieces, whom I realize are Brooks' security detail. But before I can even take a breath to scream, Gavan's whirling, leaping off Brooks, and diving right into the thick of them.

My jaw drops.

It's like watching a ninja fight. Or a vampire. Something not human that moves at impossible speeds and dodges every attack. He's like one of those samurais in a movie, in the middle of five assailants who can't even touch him.

It all happens very fast. One second, I'm staring at Gavan as he fights off *five* armed men. The next, he's the only one standing around five unconscious forms on the ground.

He looks up at me, his gunmetal gray eyes blazing. Then he whirls, storms over to Brooks, and yanks him up by the collar.

"*Where is it,*" he snarls viciously into Brooks' bleeding, terrified face.

"I—where's *what—*"

"The recording. Where. Is. It."

My eyes bulge in terrified disbelief. *What?* How does he...

Gavan's face is grim as he turns to level his gaze at me again. He winds up and punches Brooks hard in the mouth, knocking him to the ground. Then he walks over to me, taking my shaking hands in his.

"Please forgive me," he growls quietly, his jaw tight.

I shake my head. "For what?"

"I needed insurance," Gavan continues. "I needed something to bury him with."

He pulls a little device out of his pocket and pushes a button. I stare as Brooks' voice and mine rattle tinnily out of a small speaker.

"Have you fucked him?"

"*A hundred times.* Gladly. Willingly. He's good. And *huge.*"

"Maybe he'd like to hear you begging for *my* dick. We'll see if he even wants you once I play him that recording."

The terrace goes silent when Gavan touches the button again. I stare up into his eyes, my face pale.

"I—"

"*Forgive me,*" he growls again, his face pained as he takes my hands gently in one of his. The other reaches up and takes the emerald on my necklace between two fingers. He flicks something with his thumbnail, and when his hand pulls away there's a little black dot on his thumb.

A surveillance bug.

"*Please forgive me,*" he growls quietly again. "I had to have proof on him. Please understand."

Tears start to fall down my cheeks and I look away in shame. "I...*I'm so sorry,*" I choke. "It... It was years ago, and—"

"You have fucking *nothing to apologize for*," Gavan rasps with a dark edge to his voice that honestly scares me. He gently cups my face, tilting my head up to his. "Nothing, *solnishka*. Do you understand that?"

When I can't answer because the tears are streaming down my face too hard, all he does is close the distance between us in a blink and sear his lips to mine. And it's the best response I could have ever asked for. I sob as I throw my arms round him, kissing him as the past and the hold Brooks has had over me shatters and falls to my feet.

Slowly, Gavan pulls back. When he turns to a sniveling, bleeding Brooks, the look in his eyes is pure malevolence. He strides over to him and grabs him by the throat, making the spoiled little trust fund douchebag sob and bleat.

"I'm only going to ask you one more time."

Gavan flicks open a blade and Brooks' eyes bulge.

"*Okay!*" He sobs. "Okay! Okay, I'm sorry, okay!?"

"*Where is it.*"

"My phone! It's on my phone!"

Gavan snarls as he jams a hand into Brooks' jacket pocket, yanking out his phone.

"Where else."

Brooks pales.

"*Where. Fucking. Else.*"

"A safe! There's a safe!" he squeals. "In my condo!"

"Thought as much." Gavan's face is cold with fury as he calmly takes his own phone out and touches a button, putting it on speaker. The ringtone echoes out and the call connects.

"I'm here, Boss-man," a man's voice answers.

"You in?"

"Yeah," the man grunts. "It was easy. Minimal security. I'm standing in the McKinnley kid's living room."

Brooks' face turns the color of ash.

"Good," Gavan growls. His eyes narrow at Brooks. "Where's the fucking safe. Do not make me ask twice."

"Th—there's a signed poster of Yankee Stadium," Brooks stammers. "In the st—study. It's behind—"

"Combination. *Now*."

Brooks starts to weep. "It's a keypad password. Seven-nine-nine-six-two-zero."

Gavan smiles thinly at the phone. "You got that?"

"Got it," the voice rumbles through the speaker. "One sec."

A second later, there's a soft beep and a clicking sound.

"Safe's open, Boss-man."

"It's…it's on a little blue flash drive," Brooks whimpers.

"Take everything, Korol," Gavan snarls, still glaring at Brooks. "And I want the small blue flash drive secured. Clear?"

"Crystal. I've got it all."

"Now find his home computer."

Brooks' eyes threaten to pop out of his head.

"*Wait—*"

Gavan laughs coldly. "Make that *definitely* find his computer."

"Got it," the man on the phone answers after a second.

"Password," Gavan glares at Brooks. When the asshole hesitates, Gavan presses the edge of his knife against Brooks' throat. "I will not ask again, fucker."

Brooks looks like he's going to throw up.

"It's *whitepower.* One word, all lower case."

Gavan stares at him incredulously. "Seriously?" He shakes his head. "Jesus, the ways I'm going to fuck with you, you little shit. Korol. You got that?"

"I'm in, Gavan."

"Copy everything. Delete any cloud backups."

"Doing that now. One sec."

Brooks looks like a shell of a man as he slumps on his knees on the ground, bleeding from the face. The man on the other end of the phone whistles.

"Christ, there's some...I dunno, man, I'm not looking at this shit. But the motherfucker's got some questionable-looking porn folders on here."

Gavan's face swirls with rage. "*Copy it all,*" he snarls.

"Done."

Gavan hangs up the phone and quietly slips it back into his pocket. Brooks is sobbing on the ground.

"*P-please!*" he chokes, looking up piteously at Gavan. "Please!" Don't kill—"

"Jesus. I'm not going to kill you," Gaven spits venomously. "I'm going to fucking *own you,* you little fuck. And I'm going to own your *father,* too. And he's going to know exactly why I own him."

Gavan's eyes swivel to mine, holding my gaze for a second as something dark and surging swirls behind them. Then he turns back to Brooks.

"No—I'm not going to kill you," he murmurs, a lethal heaviness in his tone. "But you did touch what's mine. You *hurt* what's mine." He lets his words sink in. "Lie down."

Shaking and whimpering, Brooks does what Gavan says.

"Hold out your arm."

Brooks starts to sob even harder. Gavan snarls and bends down to yank Brooks' arm out for him before gagging Brooks with his own tie.

"I'd bite down hard if I were you."

Gavan stands, looks at me, and then turns back to Brooks. His foot stamps down, hard. Brooks screams into the tie in his mouth, trying in vain to wrench his arm away. But Gavan stops him, kicking Brooks' wounded arm back out across the stone floor and stomping on it again.

And again.

And again.

When he's done, Brooks could very well be in shock as he hyperventilates on the ground. His arm is bent askew in four different unnatural angles, and his fingers are nothing more than red pulp and gore.

Gavan wipes his bloody shoe on Brooks' jacket before leaning down close to him.

"I haven't killed you or cut off your balls because this is about sending a message to your father, not starting a war with him. Now, here's what's going to happen: when they wake up, your guards will say whatever you tell them to say. I'd make very sure to get your story straight. If you ever try and come after Eilish again, or her family, or her friends, or if God forbid you're supremely fucking stupid enough to try and come after *me*, the ways in which you will regret it are *vast*. You will *beg* me to shatter your arm again instead of what I'll actually do if I so much as hear of you looking at, speaking to or about, or even *thinking of* her ever again. You will nod if you understand."

Brooks manages a weak nod of his head before Gavan winds up again and knocks him out cold.

My pulse is roaring. My entire body is tingling with this weird, vibrantly throbbing, almost *erotic* thrill as I watch Gavan stand up, turn, and stab his eyes into me.

Suddenly, I'm consumed with an almost heart-stopping need for this man. A desire that threatens to engulf me in flames. His eyes surge with power, possessiveness, and lust as he storms across the terrace, grabs me hard, and yanks me against his rock-hard body as his mouth slams to mine.

"*I would fucking kill for you. Never forget that,*" he snarls. I hungrily kiss him back, whimpering as he scoops me up into his arms and carries me away.

28

EILISH

THE HEAT ROARING through my veins is primal. The need for him is fierce and savage. And when we slam together, it's like two unstoppable forces of nature exploding together.

We stagger through the doorway of a dark room, my head flung back as Gavan's mouth devours my neck. He kicks the door shut behind us, plowing across the room and knocking over a chair before my back hits a wall.

My hands tear open his shirt, hissing with need as I rake my nails up and down his chest. The dress slips from my shoulders, and he untangles my legs from around his waist and sets me on the ground so it can fall from my body completely.

I moan as he spins me around, pressing my face and chest against the wall as he takes a handful of my hair in his fist and runs his teeth down my neck. I shiver, my nipples hardening against the cool, glossy wall before I realize it's not a wall at all.

It's a window.

My eyes open just as Gavan's hand slides over my waist to slip into the front of my soaked panties.

I scream, and it lodges in my throat as I try to scramble back. But Gavan growls, holding me firm and keeping my body pressed to the floor-to-ceiling glass overlooking the gala below.

"It's a mirror on their side, *solnishka*," he rasps darkly into my ear. "I'd never let a single pair of eyes besides mine see you like this."

He nips at my neck, then drags his mouth closer to my ear as he grinds his thick erection against my ass.

"If this wasn't one-way glass, I'd have to blind every person in attendance."

His fingers plunge between my legs, making me moan as they drag up through my slick lips. He rolls my clit between his fingers, tearing another whimper from my mouth as his other hand slides around to pinch and tweak my nipples.

"Hands against the glass, *solnishka*," he rasps into my ear.

Gavan kisses, bites, and sucks the back of my neck. He drops lower, taking his time as he maddingly slowly trails vicious kisses down my spine. His fingers curl deep into my pussy, stroking my g-spot as his palm grinds against my clit.

He moves lower and lower, biting and kissing my tender skin as he peels my thong down, leaving it tangled at my knees. His teeth sink into first one butt cheek and then the other, bringing a cry of pleasure to my lips as he strokes my pussy.

"*Reach back*," he growls thickly. "And spread yourself wide for me."

I groan, flushing with the heady mix of embarrassment and arousal that he always manages to bring out in me. My cheek rests against the cool glass and I do as he says, reaching back to spread myself open as his mouth teases against the back of my thighs.

His fingers slip from my pussy, rolling my clit in blisteringly slow circles as his face presses between my legs. I choke in pleasure, fogging the glass with my moans as he tongues my eager pussy. My knees threaten to buckle, and my nipples are hard and electrified against the window as Gavan devours me from behind.

"*Such a good girl,*" he growls into my pussy. "Such a good, eager, greedy little fuck-toy."

He nips at my inner thigh, making me whine in pleasure. His tongue drags up and down my wet lips before pushing in deep, making my eyes roll all the way back in my head as he fucks me with his tongue.

When it slips back, and higher, my eyes widen.

"*Gavan...I...ohmyfuckinggod...*"

It's not the first time he's dragged his tongue over my asshole. But it's never been when I'm so lewdly exposed like this. Even though I know no one can actually see me like this —back arched, hands spreading myself so brazenly, moans of pleasure falling from my lips as Gavan tongues my ass—the thrill of it is like a drug hitting my veins.

I groan, my face bright red as I look down from high above the main floor of the gala at all the people swirling and mingling below.

315

Not one of them realizing I'm about to come in an explosive release with Gavan's tongue in my ass and his fingers rolling my clit.

When I tumble over the edge the window fogs even more as I gasp against it. My fingers dig into my own flesh, my body rippling and shuddering as the orgasm tears through me. I'm still catching my breath as he suddenly stands, and before I can even turn around, I feel his thick, swollen head press hotly to my dripping opening.

"Are you going to be a good girl for me?"

I whimper, nodding feverishly as I pant against the window.

"*Yes, Sir*—oh *FUCK!!!*"

He sheathes himself in one thrust, burying every single thick inch of his cock deep in my pussy as my body tightens and clenches around him. He's *so* fucking big, and even if I'm used to it at this point, the rush I still get when he just rams in like that always takes my breath away and has my toes curling.

Gavan growls into my ear, grabbing my hands and shoving them up against the glass. My fingers splay, his own interlocking with them as he pins me to the glass and grinds deep. His hips roll, his gorgeous dick sliding out of me inch by inch, dragging over every roaring nerve ending only to drive right back in with a force that pins me to the glass.

And then, Gavan truly starts to *fuck* me.

It's a possessive, consuming, *conquering* fuck. For both of us. He pounds into me like he's making a point—like he's fully laying claim to what's his. And I thrust back, arching my spine and greedily pressing my ass against his hips to take every inch of him, like it's a drug I need to keep breathing.

He rams into me harder and faster, his abs smacking my ass and his balls slapping my clit. His powerful, inked hands pin mine up and on either side of me against the window, nailing me to the glass as he fucks into me, leaving me shaking and quivering and about to explode all over again.

"Now be a good little fuck toy and come all over this big cock, *solnishka*. I want this pretty pussy dripping all over my fucking balls. I want it never *ever* to forget to whom it belongs. I want your cunt lonely for my cock and missing it whenever I'm not deep inside it."

My mouth goes slack as my eyes roll back. One of his hands slides down my arm, briefly lingering at my breasts to pinch and roll my nipples before dragging it down my body to grip my hip. He slides it between us, and when I feel his thumb drag over my asshole, my eyes bulge.

"*Gavan…*"

"I'm going to fuck you right here, Eilish," he groans into my ear as his cock rams into me over and over, bringing me to the edge of my sanity. "I'm going to make your tight little virgin hole *mine*, just like the rest of you. So be a good girl and make my cock nice and wet with your greedy pussy. Because I'm going to take your ass next."

I've never been an act I've actively fantasized about. But in this moment, I can't think of anything I want *more*.

There's a primal hunger in me that wants—more like *needs*—him to take me everywhere. To mark me as his everywhere.

To fuck me in every possible way.

To have *all of me*.

His thumb presses down, dragging a whine of pleasure from my throat as he slowly starts to open me up. I can feel myself tensing a little. But as I breathe deeply, and as the consuming need for him explodes through my core, my muscles relax. Slowly, his thumb sinks into my asshole as his cock fucks in and out of my pussy.

It starts like the first shudders of an earthquake. Then the tremors get bigger, and harder, and more terrifying, until suddenly, my world is shattering around me.

It's a sensation I've never felt before—being *so* fucking full of him in both of my holes. The filthy, animalistic desire for *more more more*. The need for him to take me every single way he wants, until all I know is him, and his domination over me.

His cock fucks in and out as his thumb sinks deep. And when his teeth bite down on the tender skin of my neck, I lose all control. I scream in pleasure against the glass, my body trembling and rippling from my orgasm. My toes curl in my shoes, my legs shaking as the release explodes in a rush through my core.

Gavan slows his thrusts, taking a fist of my hair and pulling it aside to tease his lips down the nape of my neck.

"*Good girl,*" he murmurs.

Slowly he slips his cock from the dripping wet slickness of my pussy and his thumb from my ass. The pulsing, swollen head slips higher, and my mouth goes slack as I feel it nestle hotly between my cheeks, right against my most private place.

"*You're fucking mine,*" he rasps darkly into my ear. "No one else's. Not now. Not fucking *ever.*"

I shudder, my head swimming almost like I'm drunk on him as I twist my neck around to glance back at him.

"Take all of me," I choke breathlessly.

He reaches around, cupping my jaw with one hand and rubbing my clit with the other. His hips roll, his muscles tightening as he starts to add pressure. I whimper, biting my lip and choking for air as I feel his head, so big and thick, press against my impossibly tight hole. But I'm still wet from his tongue. And his cock is slick and glistening from my pussy. And I want him *so fucking much.*

And slowly, ever so slowly, I feel myself start to open.

"I'm going to *have* all of you…"

Oh my fucking GOD…

The breath catches in my throat as Gavan's huge cock opens my tight ring and begins to sink deeper into my ass. I bite down hard on my lip—hard enough to taste copper. When he pauses, I shake my head.

"Please don't stop…"

Out of the edge of my peripheral vision I see his eyes blazing with lust. His fingers roll my clit, flooding me with pleasure and allowing me to relax enough for him to slide another inch further in. He keeps going, easing inch after thick inch of his gorgeous cock deeper and deeper up my ass. My eyes roll back, my face caving in the sinful pleasure of Gavan taking my last virginity. He groans, biting down on my shoulder as he finally manages to push the rest of the way inside.

"Now you're all fucking mine."

He starts to rub my clit harder with one hand. The other one wraps around my throat as he starts to ease out of me. I whine in pleasure, feeling my body clench down hard around him. The friction of him dragging out of my ass sends explosions through my nerve endings that almost send my brain short circuiting.

He slides back in, then out, slowly building in power and speed. And I fucking *melt*.

This shouldn't feel this good.

This shouldn't make me ready to come again already.

This is dirty.

But holy *fuck* does it feel good. I cry out against the glass, reaching up and back to wrap my arms around his neck behind me. I cling to him, moaning over and over as Gavan fucks me hard against the glass, his cock plunging in and out of my ass.

Consuming me.

Conquering me.

Blurring my reality and melting the world away until all I know is him and me and our fucking.

When I come, it's unlike anything I've felt before. It's like I enter a blank, white space where only he and I exist. My body convulses, shuddering and detonating from the force of my orgasm. Gavan groans, biting my neck as he buries his cock in my ass to the hilt and explodes deep inside. The hot jets of his cum spilling into me send me over the edge once more.

Into pure oblivion, and the sweetest sin.

29

GAVAN

It's quiet in the hotel suite. In bed, under just a light sheet, Eilish curls against me, her cheek and hand against my chest and her breathing so regular I wonder if she's faded off to sleep.

We left the gala a few hours ago, after some hastily blurted goodbyes with a blush on her face and a fierce wildness in her eyes. Since then, after soaping up every inch of her body, I've spent the time *worshipping her*.

With my mouth and my tongue. With my fingertips. With my cock, which doesn't seem to be able to go down around her no matter how many times I pump her full of my cum.

And tonight, she finally asked me.

I know the look I've seen in her eyes when they catch *my eyes* lingering on her scars. Tonight, both of us sweating and panting on the sheets and my finger tracing the one on her thigh, she finally rolled over and just asked.

"Do you stare at them like that because you hate how they look?"

The words cut like a blade. Because it's the furthest thing I think of when I see her naked in front of me.

"They're a part of you, as my scars and my tattoos are a part of me." I shook my head. "No, *solnishka*, I don't hate how they look on you, because they're *you*. But I hate that the pain and the fear they gave you is because of me."

She shook her head, sliding close to drape over my chest, her face hovering over mine.

"Not you. Leo, acting outside of your orders."

"Leo who *worked for me*," I growl. "Who *I* put into a position where he was able to do that to you."

She just shook her head again. "I've never blamed you for them. Even when I didn't like you."

I raised up to kiss her then, but her face darkened as she looked away.

"I still think they look ugly," she said quietly.

"Then let me show you how beautiful every inch of you is to me."

After that, I spent an hour kissing and licking the smooth pink skin of the scars on her shoulder and then her thigh, before plunging my tongue into her pussy until she came.

Now, hours later, we're lying tangled together with just the faint moonlight streaming in through the white curtains at the window leading out to the balcony.

There's a calmness in my soul as I lie with her, my fingers stroking her blonde hair, that I'm not sure I've ever felt before. It's like the fight to shove away something heavy that I've had inside me since the day I slid screaming into this world is finally at an end. Or at least it's shut the fuck up for a moment.

A moment that I'll savor.

Eilish stirs next to me. Slowly, she disentangles herself and sits up in bed, hugging her knees.

Her shoulders shudder with a heavy breath, and I frown.

"Eilish—"

"He killed my mother."

I sit up.

"My dad, I mean," Eilish says quietly. "She died young. Neve and I were only eleven and nine. And we were always told it was just one of those random things. A brain aneurysm. But I found out later she knew he'd been cheating on her, for years and years. She was going to leave him, with Neve and I…"

She turns her face just enough for the moonlight to glint off the pained look etched into her face and clamped jaw.

"…So he killed her."

Her voice is leaden, her body stiff and clenched.

"He injected an air bubble into her bloodstream, which popped in her brain." She turns her head a little more, the green in her eyes glinting like venom as she looks at me. "That's why I did what I did that night. What you saw…" Her eyes shut as she shakes her head at the memory. "I just… I wanted him to die."

She shudders, drops her head, and looks away.

"Does that make me a terrible person?"

"*No*."

I know this kind of pain and regret. And I know it doesn't always get better from physical touch or closeness. But just the same, I'm incapable of seeing her like this without doing something. I reach for her, just lightly putting my hand on her back and rubbing. Her muscles unbunch a little, and she melts back against my hand.

"No, it doesn't," I repeat quietly.

"Neve doesn't know. I mean, neither of us were close with him at all. But she doesn't know about any of it. The cheating, or—"

She stiffens again before she turns to look at me with a haunted expression in her eyes.

"Gavan…" she swallows. I can see the question in her eyes before she even asks it.

"Did my father kill yours?"

Her voice is frail and so fucking tiny when it croaks out that I almost want to lie to her.

But I can't.

"*Yes*."

Her whole body crumbles in on itself, her face falling, a haunted look in her eyes.

"*Oh my God, Gavan…*"

"They met alone in a warehouse in Queens. I have no fucking idea why," I growl, feeling like my voice is coming from somewhere outside my body. "And I don't know what about, but they argued. Then Declan pulled a gun and shot him."

She starts to cry, taking my hand in hers as we both sit there cross-legged on the bed.

"He called me," I choke. "I drove faster than I've ever driven in my entire life, and I got to him, but it was too late." I swallow the lump in my throat. "He died in my arms."

Tears roll down her cheeks as she reaches for mine, touching my face with so much anguish in her eyes that it breaks my heart.

"Why…" she keeps her face turned away from me. "Why didn't you slaughter my family for what my father did?"

A wry smile twists my lips.

"Vadim asked me not to. He used his last breath to look me in the eye and tell me revenge was a fruitless battle that nobody wins."

Her face is haunted when she looks up at me. "So you didn't come for revenge…"

I laugh coldly. "I did, actually." My mouth thins as my eyes lock with hers. "In the end, I didn't listen to Vadim. I was planning to kill Declan the very night he died. *That's* the reason I was there, Eilish," I say quietly. "At the meeting where he and Vasilis Drakos died. I was there to ambush your father and put a bullet through his head. And then…"

"And then he was shot anyways," she finishes quietly.

I nod.

"Then I saw you, running out to pick up the casings, burning your finger on one that was still hot."

"I…I was outside when the shooting happened," she whispers. "And when I ran in…they were dead. My father… Vasilis…poor Jason Adamos, who was there alongside Vasilis."

My hands take hers. "I saw what you did, you know. I saw you walk over to Declan's body and spit on it."

She swallows, her lips pursing. *"He was such a bastard,"* she chokes out.

"I know, *solnishka*."

When her chokes turn to sobs, I pull her into me, cradling her in my arms as I lean back against the headboard.

I'd say it happens suddenly. But that would be a lie. The truth is, the dam began cracking and splintering the first time I ever laid eyes on her. Or the first time I touched her, and tasted her lips.

But it's in this moment, holding her as she cries, after baring her soul to me, that the walls around the blackness in my heart finally tumble the rest of the way down, and I can tell her everything.

"It started when I was thirteen."

It feels like a serrated knife is being twisted into my very soul. But I don't stop.

"When Vadim came home with this random baby boy, and no mother, people had questions. There were rumors that I was actually Svetlana's kid, that her big brother was doing her a solid and raising the bastard she never wanted as his own."

Eilish goes still in my arms.

"Vadim didn't confirm those rumors. But he honestly didn't do much to deny them, either, because it told a plausible story." My eyes close. "Svetlana *hated me* for it. Hated me for being the reason people looked at her like she was a whore and a derelict mother. When I was a bit older, Vadim was traveling a lot, working for Konstantin's dad. So I got dumped here in New York for most of middle and high school."

Black rage and red mist swirl together inside me as I look away.

"I was thirteen the first time she told me how it was all going to…work."

My eyes close.

"The first time she took me to her bed."

Then I tell her. I fucking tell her *everything*. About the abuse. About the nights I tried to block out. About the self-loathing, and the drinking and the drugs that started early because they numbed the pain and the shame of my day-to-day, hellish existence.

Eilish weeps, throwing her arms around me and holding me so tight that my own eyes finally bead with tears.

I've never told a single soul about any of this. Not Vadim. Not Konstantin.

Nobody.

But when I tell her, it's like the fucking mountain that's been sitting on my chest suddenly crumbles to dust. Eilish is crying when she cups my face in her hands and kisses my forehead, and my cheeks, and my nose, and my eyelids.

And I swallow back the lump in my throat, breathing deep with the mountain lying in ruins at my feet. Slowly, I reach up and take her hands in mine, looking into her red, swollen eyes.

"Why are you crying, *solnishka?*" I whisper.

"Because the idea of someone hurting you when you were so young breaks my heart."

Another sob rips from her lips as I take her face in my hands and kiss her with every ounce of my soul. Kiss her to forget the past, and embrace the now.

To let go of my hate and drown in an emotion I've never felt before.

I have no idea how long we stay like that, just holding each other, my lips seared to hers. Breathing each other's air. Being each other's life raft in an ocean of pain.

"Gavan?" she finally whispers, pulling away. "I... There's something else. I wanted to tell you, I just... I didn't want you to worry or..."

I frown, stroking her cheek. "You can tell me anything. Always."

She swallows. "The men who jumped me that night..." she chews on her lip. "They... It wasn't a random mugging. They told me to stay away from you. They said the next time I..." her voice breaks.

I lean down to kiss her hand.

"They said the next time I decided to be a 'Reznikov whore', there would be bigger consequences."

My teeth grind so hard I almost crack my molars. And instantly I want to dig those fuckers up and make some sort of deal with the devil to bring them back to life so that I can torment them for another *decade*.

"I'm sorry," she blurts. "I didn't want to start anything—"

"They won't ever hurt you again."

She goes still and gasps, her eyes widening.

"I found them," I growl quietly.

"Did you…"

I take her hands in mine, raising them to my lips. "I told you before: I would, and *will*, kill for you, Eilish."

I pull her into my arms again, letting her cry a little more into my chest before her breathing turns deep and regular. She sleeps against my chest with her face in the crook of my neck for a little while before I get her settled in the bed and slowly slide out of it.

Naked, I pour myself a glass of vodka from the bar cart and pad outside to the balcony. Leaning my elbows on the railing, I breathe in the scent of Paris, looking across the Champs de Mars at the Eiffel Tower glowing in the moonlight.

I will kill for her.

Because I'm in love with her, as I have been for longer than she knows. Longer than I've been willing to admit to myself.

The truth is, I fell in love with her the night Declan died—when I saw her burning her fingers picking up the evidence and taking a moment to spit on his corpse.

That's the moment I realized she was more like me than I would have ever guessed in a million years.

I wonder: did I fall in love with the woman I was supposed to hate because I caught a peek of the darkness she kept hidden inside? Or because of the goodness she so gracefully wrapped her pain in?

Either way, there's no going back now.

A few minutes later, I smile as I hear soft footsteps behind me. Her arms slide around my waist, and she kisses the middle of my back before her cheek presses to it.

Slowly, I turn and wrap my arms around her. Then, she frowns slightly.

"Why didn't you just pick anyone to marry you? I mean for the legal battle with that fucking cunt."

I grin at the venom in her tone when she mentions... well...*that fucking cunt.*

"Because I didn't want to marry just anyone," I say quietly.

Her face heats as she bites her lip.

"Then why haven't you pressed me for an answer? I mean, surely time is of the essence, and—"

"My mother married for duty," I murmur gently. "For family. Because she *had* to. I didn't want that for you. I..." I look away.

"What?"

"Nothing."

Eilish leans close and kisses my chest. "Tell me. Please."

I take a breath before turning back to her. "I wanted you to marry me because you *wanted* to." My eyes burn as they lock with hers. "Because you loved me," I growl quietly. "And I wanted to give you the time to maybe, just fucking maybe—"

"I don't need any more time."

She leans up on her toes in an instant and crushes her mouth to mine.

"*I'll marry you*," she whimpers fiercely into my lips. "*Because I love you.*"

30

GAVAN

WE STAY four more nights in Paris. Everyone else I send home. But Eilish and I?

We just fucking disappear.

I mean, yes, a lot of those four days are spent fucking—in bed, or the shower, or out on the balcony, making each other explode. But it's more than that. For the first time in my life, I actually do real *couples shit*.

We go out to have fantastic dinners with amazing wine. We take long walks along the Seine and through the Luxembourg Gardens. We do all the stupid tourist shit like selfies under, or at the top of, the Eiffel Tower. Or putting a lock with our names written on it in Sharpie on the Pont Des Arts footbridge over the river.

We do all the museums, eat all the cheese, and drink all the red wine. It just might be the best four days of my entire life.

Eventually, of course, we have to go back to the real world. Still, when the Range Rover pulls up beside my plane on the runway, we're both grinning like idiots.

We might be going back to the real world, but the real world just got a whole lot better.

The driver is just shutting off the engine when my phone rings.

"Mr. Tsarenko."

I frown. The voice is familiar, but I can't place it.

"Who is this?"

"You might want to be alone for this conversation."

I don't fucking like this. I *hate* bullshit like this. I'm also curious as to how this person even got my goddamn phone number.

I put the phone down and turn to smile at Eilish. "I have to take this. Get comfortable on the plane. I'll join you in a second."

"Okay." She grins, leaning over to cup my face and kiss me softly. "I'll be waiting for you."

She slips out of the car, and I allow myself the indulgence of watching her ass as she climbs the stairs to the plane before turning to my driver and raising the partition between us.

"Who the *fuck* is this," I growl quietly into the phone.

The man on the other end chuckles chidingly. "*Manners*, Mr. Tsarenko." I frown, again trying and failing to place the voice with the Eastern European accent.

"I'm not a fan of games. So if you're going to play them, whoever you are, this conversation is…is…"

I frown, blinking as my head starts to swim.

Something's wrong.

I try to swallow, but my throat has gone numb. The inside of the car starts to go cloudy and hazy. I try and reach for the door handle. When I pull, I realize it's locked.

"Open the door!" I yell.

But it's not a yell. My voice is barely above a whisper.

My blood runs cold. What the fuck is happening.

I turn toward the partition, almost slamming my face into it as I lurch for the button. When it raises, all I see is my driver collapsed over the wheel.

My vision blurs. My mouth feels cottony, and I slump sideways across the back seat.

Oh, fuck.

My gaze swivels out the window, and my stomach drops when I see the plane door closing. With a surge of adrenaline, I hurl myself at the door, kicking and then slamming my fists against the window with the last of my strength.

A man suddenly steps in front of me, on the other side of the window.

"Hello, Gavan," he rumbles through the phone in his hand into the one in mine.

My reality glitches. I can't understand why Svetlana's antiques appraiser is standing outside of my car.

"I'm sorry that we have never been properly introduced," the man growls with a thin smile on his chiseled face. "Allow me to remedy that. My name is Drazen Krylov."

Oh fuck.

Oh FUCK.

I blink rapidly, trying to force my vision to clear as I stab my gaze past him to the plane containing Eilish.

"I did say you had lovely taste, didn't I?" Drazen purrs. "In fashion. In office decor, and art." His lips curl. "In *women*."

My face goes livid, my lips snarling as I try to slam a hand against the window. But I'm too weak. The last of my strength feels like it's seeping out of me like blood from a fatal blow.

"You…" I mumble.

"You have something that belongs to me, Gavan," Drazen says quietly. "And now I am taking something that belongs to *you* until I get it back."

No…

"I'm texting you a location." He lowers the phone and hammers something with his thumbs before bringing it back up to his ear. "You have twenty-four hours to bring the egg to—"

"The egg…" I blurt, the world spinning around me. "Is…smashed…"

He nods. "Yes, I know. Some people just can't be trusted with nice things. Luckily, *I* can be trusted with *your* nice thing, so long as you do what I ask." He presses his forehead up against the window. "As I was saying. Twenty-four hours to bring the *pieces* of the Imperial Shield along with the stand it sat on to the location I texted you. Come alone. And please don't make me explain what will happen if you don't do exactly as I say."

The world starts fade.

Eilish.

Eilish...

"Sweet dreams, Mr. Tsarenko."

Me eyes drop closed, and when I sink under, I just keep on sinking...

31

GAVAN

FUCK TWENTY-FOUR HOURS. The second I come to, still slumped in the back seat of the Range Rover, I call Korol and have him grab the pieces of the egg and—curiously—the old wood and brass banded base it once sat on, and immediately fly over to meet me in Pisa, Italy.

The location Drazen texted me is a palazzo on the island of Elba, off the coast of Tuscany. He also included a reminder not to bring anyone else, not even my number two.

Normally, I'd tell anyone giving me orders like that to go fuck themselves. But he has Eilish. That's actually the very first thing I did when I woke up, even before calling Korol: bolt up the stairs to the plane to look for her, where I found both pilots and both stewards just waking up as well.

But no Eilish.

Roughly twelve hours after waking up, I'm glaring down at the lavish cliffside palazzo as the helicopter I just took from a private airfield on the mainland descends onto a stretch of manicured grass.

The Mediterranean air whips around me as the chopper rises back into the sky after depositing me on the lawn, leaving me grim-faced and brimming with fury as I stand there holding a metal carrying case containing what Drazen wants.

Okay, now what, you fucking psycho.

As if reading my black thoughts, the ornate front door of the palazzo overlooking the circular driveway and grassy yard where I was dropped off opens. Four heavily tattooed men in suits, carrying semi-automatic weapons, quickly surround me with barrels pointed right at me.

One of them takes the case from my hands. Another frisks me and then uses a wand to check me over for metal. When they confirm that I'm not carrying any weapons, the one holding the case steps forward.

"Follow me."

I trail behind him, flanked by the others as we file into the gorgeous, sprawling old Italian manor. They lead me through various sitting rooms and libraries, past enormous windows with staggering views of the Tyrrhenian Sea.

Finally, we step into a stunning inner courtyard filled with leafy plants, lounge chairs and couches, and a burbling marble fountain.

I look right past all of that at the man sitting sprawled in a huge wood and upholstery chair, like a smug king.

Drazen.

"Welcome to my home, Mr. Tsa—"

"You fucking—"

Four semi-automatics instantly level at me, stopping me cold. Drazen's brows knit and he stiffens, but then he sighs, waving his men off. They instantly lower their guns as he stands and ambles toward us.

"She is *fine*, Mr. Tsarenko. I assume you are wondering."

"Where the fuck is she," I spit viciously.

Drazen smiles, dipping his chin. "As I said, she is fine. And you will see her in a moment." He gestures for me to sit on one of the couches. When I don't move to do so, one of his men prods me in the back with a gun barrel.

"Sit, please."

"Is that a request or a directive?"

"*That* is just good manners, Mr. Tsarenko. Please, sit."

Drazen sprawls back in his chair. He's wearing cream dress pants and a crisp white dress shirt, open at the neck with the sleeves rolled up: his numerous tattoos are on display on his muscled forearms and his chest. He smiles a toothy grin, dazzlingly white against his bronze, sun-kissed face.

"Too hot for tweed?" I growl as I sit stiffly on the couch.

Drazen chuckles. "I do apologize for misrepresenting myself like that." He clears his throat. "Have you been to Elba before?"

"No."

He nods. "You know, this is where Napoleon was first exiled."

"I'm not here for a fucking history lesson."

He smiles, dipping his head again. "No, of course not."

"Are you working with Svetlana?"

Drazen's face sours. "Your au… Sorry, your *not*-aunt?" He shakes his head dismissively. "No, not in the slightest. Svetlana is…" he twists his fingers in the air next to his head. "Merely a blunt tool. A useful idiot, as they say." He nods as one of his men sets the metal case on the low wooden coffee table between us. "She wanted that egg almost as much as I did. So I used that to get close to you. I hope you don't take that personally."

"I take you abducting Eilish pretty fucking personally."

He nods. "That's more than fair. And again, I apologize for my means to an end. Taking her was not meant to hurt her or punish you, merely to *motivate* you." He turns and barks something in what might actually be Serbian, now that I think about it.

Seconds later, my face lights up when Eilish walks out of the house and into the courtyard.

My heart surges as I leap to my feet.

"A moment, Mr. Tsarenko."

Drazen is still smiling cordially at me. But he's also pointing a Beretta right at me.

"She will be freed in a moment. Please, sit."

I stare at him lethally. "You have what you asked for. Release her, *now*."

"Patience, please. All in good time. Sit down."

When I just keep glaring, his smile fades a little.

"*Sit down*, Mr. Tsarenko."

My eyes drag from him to Eilish. She's being led out by an older woman—without a weapon, thank God—who's dressed in a housekeeper's uniform. Eilish's hands are bound behind her, and there's a gag over her mouth. But I can see she's smiling at me through it as our eyes lock. Her head nods almost imperceptibly, as if to tell me she's okay.

When the woman leads her to a chair across the table from me and lowers her into it, I sit as well. Drazen sighs.

"*So* much better, yes?" He nods to the woman who brought Eilish in, and then to his men. "Leave us." Without question, they all file out of the courtyard. When we're alone together, Drazen cracks his neck and smiles. "Good. Now we can talk like civilized people."

I glare at him, but Drazen ignores me as he taps his fingers on the top of the metal case.

"You see, it's not just that I *desire* this egg. It's that it *belongs* to me. It's in my blood, Mr. Tsarenko. It's my birthright."

"You have an astonishing sense of entitlement," I hiss quietly.

Drazen chuckles. "I know you didn't come for one, but let me give you a brief history lesson anyway." He taps the top of the case again. "This was commissioned by Tsarina Alexandra herself, the last empress of Russia. *Imperskaya Gvardiya*, or in English the Imperial Shield Fabergé Egg. It was a gift for her favorite bodyguard, Ioaan Vasilyev. When the Bolsheviks were marching on the royal palace, Alexandra sent Ioann away with orders to flee the country with the egg and to meet up with her and her family in Paris. He did as he was told. Obviously, the Romanovs never got to France, since they were killed by the mob. And while he was waiting for news from Russia, Ioaan was murdered in his sleep, and the egg was lost."

Drazen's face darkens. "Ioaan Vasilyev was my great-great-grandfather."

My jaw tightens.

Fuck me.

If this is true, the fucking thing really *is* his birthright. Which doesn't change the fact that it's smashed into forty-odd pieces right now.

"The men of my family have bled and died trying to reclaim this," he growls. "My family should have been wealthy beyond measure, living as kings."

"You seem to be doing okay," I mutter.

Drazen smirks, lifting his gaze to the gorgeous palazzo around us. "Yes. I seem to have a penchant for the world of the Bratva."

I glare at him. "Running around committing crimes and trying to murder the heads of other Bratva families *does not* make you Bratva," I hiss.

"No, but I believe this does."

He undoes two buttons of his shirt, pulling it open to reveal a swath of tattoos clearly marking him as Bratva on his firm chest.

"Before you suggest I merely had these done for show, my grandfather started the Krylov Bratva family, modeled in the old ways, when he had nothing to his name. And that?" He stabs a finger at the box. "That birthright of mine is how I will build my modest kingdom into an *empire*, and how I will ascend to my rightful seat at the table of the Bratva High Council."

I smile coldly. "You certainly have a vivid imagination."

He chuckles. "We'll see."

Drazen stands and opens the metal case. He pulls out the Tupperware I've put the shattered pieces of the egg in and sets it aside before pulling out the weathered, grubby, wood and brass base it once sat upon.

I drag my gaze to Eilish, my eyes locking with hers. When Drazen deftly dumps the pieces of egg out onto the table, we both turn to look on in confusion.

Suddenly, Drazen raises his gun.

And starts to *smash*.

"What the *fuck*!" I hiss, staring at him like he's a crazy person as he uses the butt of his Beretta to start pounding the pieces of egg into nothing but dust.

…Except…not quite.

When he smashes one of the large chunks, a piece of black metal suddenly appears and clatters away across the table. Drazen smiles, his eyes glinting as he reaches over and holds it up to the light triumphantly.

I blink.

It's a *key*.

Drazen turns to the old wooden base, and rips the black metal stand out of the wood, revealing a hole in the box beneath it.

Holy shit. Not a hole.

A *keyhole*.

Eilish and I lock eyes before we both stare at Drazen, who is slowly inserting the key into the lock and twisting it with a small metallic clicking sound.

Suddenly, the top pops open.

"You see, Mr. Tsarenko," Drazen says quietly, picking the box up and staring into it with a dreamy, meditative look on his face. "It's not the egg that was my birthright. It was *these*."

My eyes bulge in disbelief as he turns the base of the stand over, and proceeds to dump a fucking *river* of gleaming, glittering *jewels* out onto the table.

What. The. *Fuck*.

Drazen smiles widely, gesturing with the gun in his hand. "A pity that the egg needs to be destroyed to open the box. But that is what a shield does, no? Much like my great-great-grandfather. A shield protects the…" he reaches into the box and grunts as he wrestles something heavy free before pulling out his hand and revealing a gleaming, glittering, diamond-encrusted royal crown.

He glances at me and smirks. "A shield protects the crown, does it not?" Drazen glances at Eilish, then back to me. He nods. "I have what is mine. Thank you. Now you may take what is yours."

He's barely finished his sentence before I bolt around the table and grab Eilish. I tear off the ropes binding her arms, then her gag. With a choked sob, she wraps her arms around me so fucking tight I almost can't breathe, clinging to me as she buries her face in my chest. I close my eyes, sucking in air shakily as I stroke her hair, before pulling back. Our eyes lock, and a half second later, my mouth is searing to hers.

But before any more of that, there's something I have to do.

"This is how I'll be ascending to the High Council, Mr. Tsarenko. Perhaps we'll see each other—"

I whirl and launch myself at Drazen, catching him off guard as my fist slams into his face. He groans, staggering backward with me on top of him as I pummel his face again and again before grabbing him by the collar.

Drazen groans, gritting his teeth. "Yes, I deserve that, for taking your woman. But ask her," he hisses. "I never once touched her."

My lips curl as I glance to the side, to Eilish. She nods.

"He didn't. Not a single one of this men did, either. There was that one woman who helped me around and fed me, that was it."

"Yaelle is strong," Drazen grunts. "She is the one who helped Ms. Kildare off of the plane, too."

I turn back to level an icy look at him. "If you're looking for mercy…"

I hit him once more before whirling and grabbing one of the last large shards of the egg from the table. I spin back and snarl as I press the sharp, jagged edge of it against Drazen's throat.

"You'll find none with me."

Drazen grunts, spitting out blood before smiling a bloody grin at me. "I'm not looking for mercy, Gavan," he growls. "I'm looking for *allies.*"

I bark a cold laugh. "You're insane."

"It's been suggested before." He shrugs. "You can kill me if you like. But I have a counter-offer."

"Which is?"

Drazen smiles thinly. "Definitive evidence of Abram Diduch falsely using my name to declare war on your precious Council. And I do mean *definitive*."

My eyes draw to slits. "I've seen your calling cards from the attacks in New York. And I know for a fact that you've used those before in other wars with your enemies."

He nods. "Yes, but so does Abram. My flare for the theatrics at times is not a secret. And unless I'm mistaken, I don't imagine it's hard to get your hands on a deck of cards in New York City," he says with a smirk.

I glare at him. He glares right back.

"You can kill me and accuse Abram, and go nowhere with those accusations. Or you can let me up, we can shake hands like men, and I will give you everything you need to stop him."

"That's it?"

"Not quite." He smirks. "I *will* be making a play to sit at that table. I am confident you will have a free seat soon enough. I don't imagine Abram will be staying much longer, not after you prove to the other Council chairs that he was behind the attacks on Marko Kalishnik and Viktor Komarov." His lips curl. "I want your *vote*, Gavan. And I want your support getting others to vote for me as well."

I eye him warily. "That won't be easy."

"You're a very persuasive man, or so I've heard." He smiles. "Oh, and I can also prove that Abram is bankrolling your father's sister's legal crusade against you, if that tips the scales at all."

My jaw grinds as a flash of rage explodes through my system.

Yeah, it just might.

"What do you say, Gavan?" He smirks. "The King of Diamonds would be a powerful friend. And I'm only half the monster I'm rumored to be."

"*Which half*," I mutter.

Drazen grins. "Why don't we find out? It's your call."

32

EILISH

GAVAN AND DRAZEN SHAKE hands before the older man passes Gavan a hard drive.

"Everything you need is on that. Oh, and since you may not have heard in your mad rush to get here, Marko Kalishnik is awake." Drazen smiles grimly. "I'm sure he'd welcome a chance to see what I have on Abram before he metes out his vengeance on the snake. My helicopter is waiting outside to take you back to your plane."

Gavan says nothing. He just nods, pockets the hard drive, and then walks directly over to me. He takes my hand tightly, not looking back as he leads me out of the courtyard, through the lavish home, and out the front door to the chopper.

"Where do you want to go?" he murmurs in my ear as we climb in. "Literally anywhere you want. My plane is waiting on the mainland."

I just smile as I slide in next to him and turn to look into his eyes.

"Home," I breathe as I close the distance between my lips and his. "I just want to go home. With you."

***

I'd love to say that we spend the whole flight screwing like wild animals. But the truth is, the second we sit down on that plane, we both crumble from sheer exhaustion and sleep through the entire nine-hour trip.

I'm still in a bit of a fog when we get back to Gavan's place, but I'm grinning from ear to ear, my hand tightly in his as we step through the front door.

Home. We're home.

"Now," he growls with a glint in his eyes that makes my core clench and throb. "What *ever* should we do now?"

I bite my lip. "Is going back to Paris for, like, another *year* on the table?"

I shiver as he pulls me close, taking my hands in one of his and cupping my jaw with the other.

"If that's what you want," he murmurs quietly. "Then yes."

I feel my cheeks heat. "You'd do that for me?"

"I'd do anything for you," he growls, looking right into my eyes. "Because I lo—"

His eyes start from his head as he grunts violently, suddenly toppling past my shocked face and dropping to the floor. I scream, whirling to help him, when suddenly, a claw-like hand is grabbing me, wrenching me away from him, and hurling me against the wall.

I hit *hard*, wincing as my back slams into a side table, knocking my head back against the wall and making me see stars. I topple to the side, pain lancing through my arm and wrist as I land just as the large glass vase on the side table explodes into shards around me.

But I'm not looking at my arm. My eyes have snapped across the entryway to Gavan. And suddenly, my throat closes with pure horror when I see the figure looming over him, holding a gun, leering at me.

"*You little bitch*," Svetlana snarls, her face twisted with demented rage as she waves the gun erratically in my direction. "Did nobody ever tell you not to touch what isn't *yours?!*"

When she turns back to a dazed, groaning Gavan, I *scream* in rage. I make an attempt to lurch to my feet, but my hands slide wetly across the floor as I slump back. When I glance down, the color drains from my face.

Oh God.

My arm is bleeding. Badly. Really, *really* badly, actually. Red ribbons drip from the ugly gash on my wrist courtesy of the shards of vase that I landed on. My gaze drags nauseatingly back to Gavan, who I'm just realizing Svetlana must have hit in the head with her gun. My face pales as she fixes her gaze on me.

"I'm going to enjoy this," she hisses quietly. And before I can even try to form a response, she's kneeling down next to Gavan and yanking a hypodermic needle from her pocket.

I see red.

"Don't you fucking touch him!"

When I go to move, pain explodes through my back from slamming into the wall and in my arm from the gash. Svetlana ignores me, biting the cap off the needle and grinning savagely as she plunges it into Gavan's arm. His eyes widen for one second, then he slumps to the ground.

I start to scream.

"*Get up*, you little cunt!"

I cry out in pain as Svetlana yanks me to my feet. She jams the gun against my side, shoving me further into the apartment and toward the staircase. I stumble, slip, and trip my way up the stairs with the gun pressed to my ribs, trying to bite back the pain throbbing in my back and head, not to mention the gash in my arm that feels like it's on fire.

Svetlana shoves me down the hallway, until suddenly, she's kicking open the door to Gavan's playroom.

I cry out as she kicks me against the edge of the bed, shoving me down onto it before she reaches up and yanks down a pair of cuffs on a chain looped over the crossbar. She snaps one around my good wrist, then snaps the other even harder around my bloody one, making me scream with pain.

Which she laughs at.

Then, leaving me hanging there by my wrists, she exits the room.

My vision swims, and the pain pulsing through every part of my body is almost overwhelming. But I twist around anyway, trying to look out the door as I scream his name.

"GAVAN!" I choke. "*GAVAN!*"

"Oh, don't worry."

I flinch, wincing in pain as Svetlana returns, half-carrying, half-dragging a nearly unconscious Gavan. She throws a wild smile at me as she staggers into the room under the dead weight of him slumped against her.

"He's here, honey," she spits. "And neither of you is going anywhere."

Svetlana dumps Gavan on the couch facing me. I pull against the cuffs on my wrists, ignoring the searing pain as I snarl at her.

"What the fuck did you do to him?!"

She turns to glower at him. "Nothing less than he deserves, the little snake. The *bastard* child nobody but my idiot brother wanted. The cancer that ate at my life!"

I ignore the pain again as I slam against the chains holding me tight. Svetlana just smiles again.

"I gave him a neurotoxin, that's all. Right now, it's going to work on his heart."

No…

Her lips curl demonically. "I'd say he has…I don't know, maybe fifteen minutes left until it stops beating altogether?"

"NO!"

Svetlana laughs and laughs as I strain and sob against the cuffs.

"Of course, that clock speeds up if he's…" Her eyes flash pure malevolence at me. "*Exerting* himself."

My lips curl into a sneer. "I know what you did to him, you fucking monster."

She smiles even wider. "Oh, do you now?" Her smile drops. "*Good*. Then this won't be a shock to you."

Suddenly, she's sliding onto Gavan's lap. I scream in rage and pain, yanking at the chains as she turns to half look at me. Her lips curl cruelly before she leans close to his face and licks his neck slowly.

It's like I'm being stabbed.

"Get the fuck away from him!!" I explode at her.

Svetlana just smiles even wider, her eyes gleaming with cold, sick cruelty.

"Oh, no-no-*no*, my dear," she sneers. "No, you see, he *knows* me. He remembers me and our time together fondly, I'm sure." Her eyes draw to slits. "I bet he even thinks of me when he fucks you."

Anguish rips from my throat as she chuckles, turning to look at a barely conscious, bleary-eyed Gavan.

"Don't you, my sweet baby boy."

She turns her gaze to me again. "Goodness, I bet he even fucked you in this very room. How…." She giggles. "Poetic."

She turns back to Gavan, setting her gun down on the couch next to him as she starts to unbutton her blouse while hot, thick tears flow down my face.

"What do you say, baby boy? One more roll in the hay for old times' sake before I leave you here to die together?" She sighs, undoing more of her blouse as she turns to grin at me. "That's what this will look like, of course. After I'm done here. A lovers' quarrel, ending in murder-suicide. How cliche and yet how fitting. And of course, there will be no more resistance to me taking the company. *And* the bank," she hisses.

I try and yank at my bonds again, but the pain sends a fresh wave of blackness over me. It's not just the pain. I'm weak. My shirt is soaked red. And when I look up, I see blood still pouring down my arm, and the blue of my veins through skin that's unnaturally pale right now.

It's not just the pain making my head swim.

I'm losing too much blood.

"I'm going to enjoy this, Eilish," Svetlana purrs maliciously as she shrugs off her shirt. "I've never been an exhibitionist. But I think I'm going to enjoy making you watch me fuck him right in front of you."

Something inside of me snaps, brutally. Maybe it's partly the realization I'm about to die and have nothing to lose. But even more, it's looking at this monster in front of me, *once again* about to hurt the man I love so deeply.

I think that's what makes me break.

I yank on my arm. I ignore the blinding pain and yank again, and again, and again, until I'm almost throwing up from the raw feeling exploding through my wrist. But slowly, with all the blood dripping down my arm, the cuff around my wrist begins to slip off.

And suddenly, one arm comes free.

I bite back the cry of anguish, cradling my bloody wrist before I grit my teeth and force my arm back up again. The cuffs are for playtime, not restraining criminals. And because of that, there's a release mechanism on the side.

With a clumsy flick of my numb fingers, my other wrist falls free. In one motion, I lunge off the bed, stagger across the floor, and fall onto the couch.

I'm in a foggy daze. But my fingers wrap around the gun. And when I twist around, I use the rest of my strength and my consciousness to level the barrel right at Svetlana.

Her eyes bug out as she scrambles off Gavan's lap. But then she swallows thickly, and her lips curl.

"You won't shoot me," she sneers.

My heart beats heavy and slow, my vision dwindling.

I don't have much time.

"Look at yourself, honey," Svetlana jeers. "You're a goddamn fucking *mess*. And beside that?" She laughs coldly. "You're no killer."

She walks back to Gavan again.

"*Get away from him*," I croak.

"Or what?" She barks, reaching out to run a finger up his arm, taunting me.

"*Get away from him!*" I groan again, feeling the last of my strength begin to ebb away.

Svetlana laughs again. "You're *not* going to pull that trigger, honey. Because you're not a—"

The gun explodes in my hand. Svetlana's head jerks back, taking the rest of her body with it as she topples over dead on the floor.

"*Yes I am.*"

The gun drops from my slick, sticky fingers. My head lolls to the side as I crawl and inch across the couch until I'm right next to Gavan. I reach up, cupping his face as a single tear falls down my cheek.

"I love you so much. I...I love..."

Then I'm falling into darkness. And falling.

And falling.

33

GAVAN

GET UP.

Get. Up.

Get UP.

My brain synapses begin to fire. Through the dull haze slowing everything down, my dry eyes swivel in their sockets until my gaze falls on the girl sprawled next to me—

Fuck. No.

GET. UP.

It's like screaming into a void, trying to get my muscles to listen to me. I feel like I'm trying to run underwater, with weights tied to my limbs. Like I'm trapped in a pool of something viscous and sluggish, like syrup.

But when my eyes lock and slowly manage to focus on Eilish —looking so pale and broken and so fucking *bloody* next to me, the very last of my reserves kick in.

GET. THE. FUCK.

UP!

I lurch, my limbs like four logs as I slide off the couch. I roll, my nostrils flaring as I dig deep for even a shred of energy. Whatever was in that needle Svet stuck me with, it's making everything go in slow motion. I can feel my heart beating, but it's sluggish and slow.

Not just slow.

Slow*ing*.

My pulse is literally slowing down as the seconds tick by.

Fuck. I'm running out of time. And when my eyes drop to the horror show of Eilish's gashed wrist, the full truth hits me.

So is she.

My phone's not in my pocket. I vaguely remember Svetlana tossing it across the floor downstairs before she dragged me up here. And I don't see Eilish's bag anywhere.

I have to move. I fucking *have to*. My teeth grit, my hand sliding across the floor and grabbing hold of some fabric— Svet's shirt, I'm pretty sure. I drag it over, making my arms work somehow as I slump against the couch to wrap the fabric around Eilish's wrist, tying it as tightly as my muscles will allow.

It's not much. It's not going to save her life. But it'll buy her some time.

It'll buy *me* some time.

I wince when my face hits the floor after I fall from the couch. One arm shoves forward, my fingers curling against the floor and my feet kick dully as my body inches across the room.

I groan, digging even deeper, trying to find any possible drop of *anything* I have left in me. I shove forward, my nails splintering, my feet scuffing on the floor as I drag myself out the door.

I inch down the hall. My vision goes black for a second when I reach up for the doorknob to the guest room. I fall flat on my face, and feel my lip split open. But I ignore the pain. I ignore every fucking thing and other thought in the world except the fact that I need this if I'm going to have a single shot of saving Eilish.

The contents of the drawer in the ensuite guest bathroom tumble over my chest when I yank it right out. My eyes lock on the one thing I came for. And with a strength I almost no longer possess, I reach across the bathroom floor and curl my numb fingers around it.

If Luna's heart were to ever stop while she was at my place, a shot of this adrenaline would restart it enough to get infant CPR going and save her.

My heart hasn't stopped yet.

But it's going to, in a matter of minutes.

I thumb the cap off the pen. My vision goes dark again at the edges as my blood starts to feel like maple syrup in my veins.

This isn't going to be pleasant.

My fist slams against my neck with the *very* last ounce of my strength. The needle jams into my artery as I shove down the plunger.

Holy fuck.

If your heart has stopped, adrenaline will get it pumping again.

If it *hasn't* stopped yet, a shot of adrenaline is like mainlining thirty-thousand volts. And when that shit hits my blood-stream and surges into my heart—

Holy. Fucking. FUCK.

I lurch upright like something out of a horror movie: my eyes are bulging and wild, and a demon roar is screaming from my throat. It feels like my skin is on fire—like my heart is pounding a million miles an hour.

But I'm fucking ALIVE.

Whirling, I grab the second and third epi-pens off the floor, silently thanking Lukas for his over-protective nature when it comes to Luna.

One of these things is a child's dose.

Two will take care of an adult.

Three is my insurance policy.

I scramble to my feet, my eyes bulging wide as I steel myself and slam the second pen into my neck.

Fucking HELL.

Pure energy explodes like napalm through my veins. I lurch, slamming into first one wall and then another before I crash out through the bathroom like an unsteady bull. Whatever Svetlana gave me is still fucking me up. But I can move. I can breathe.

I can save Eilish.

It takes everything I have not to rush to her first. But she needs more help than I can give. I half-run, half-fall down the stairs, groaning as I slam into the ground at the bottom and charge like a drunk across the floor. My phone is smashed. But I grab Eilish's bag off the ground amidst a mess of broken glass and blood and yank out her phone.

I pound the third adrenaline shot into my neck before dropping the syringe to the floor.

I can barely focus as I turn and surge back upstairs like Frankenstein's monster on a bender, ricocheting off the walls of the hallway until I crash back into the room where she's dying right in front of me.

"*Stay with me, solnishka,*" I growl, cupping her face and prying her eyes open as I hold the phone in front of them.

Mercifully, it unlocks.

"Stay the fuck with me, Eilish!" I roar. "Stay with me!!"

I hit the top number on her favorites.

"Hey! Welcome back, Blondie—"

"*GET. HERE,*" I roar like a monster into the phone.

That third hit of adrenaline is hitting me hard. Maybe too hard.

"*Gavan?!*" Castle yells. "What the fuck—"

"*GET. HERE. FUCKING. NOW!*"

My heart isn't slowing anymore. It's beating too fast. *Way* too fucking fast. I shouldn't have given myself that third shot of adrenaline. My arm starts to go numb, my breath coming ragged and shallow as my skin turns to fire.

Oh fuck.

I'm think I might be having a fucking heart attack.

"Gavan—"

"MY! HOUSE!" I bellow. *"HELP. EILISH. NOW!"*

He might not care about me, but he'll come for her.

The phone falls from my hand. My heart is beating so fucking fast it feels like it's going to explode from my chest. My jaw clenches, my eyes staring painfully wide as I slump on the couch next to her, shoving her bandaged wrist above her head and taking the other hand in mine.

"STAY WITH ME!!" I scream, choking as my breath comes too fast to manage. "EILISH…"

My left arm is numb. My chest is tight.

No.

No, goddammit, NO.

I pull myself close to her, panting like I've just run a marathon, my vision blurring as I touch my forehead to hers.

"I love you," I choke. *"I've loved you since the night I saw you."*

I wish I'd told her sooner than the second before we died.

34

EILISH

MY EYES BLINK OPEN, and I'm staring up at a familiar ceiling. My brows furrow, and I wince as I try and swallow. My throat is dry. I try again, my breath coming in a rasp.

"Here, try this."

I startle, whipping my head to the side as my vision slowly unblurs. Cillian smiles quietly from his chair beside the bed, his outstretched hand holding a glass of water with a straw in it.

"Where..." I focus on the room behind him, and around me.

Gavan's bedroom.

"Take a sip," Cillian says gently, guiding the straw into my mouth.

I sip gingerly, feeling the water trickle down my dry throat.

"I have the same reaction to saline drips," he grunts. "Mouth goes dry as a fucking bone." His eyes—green, just like mine—pierce into me. "Do you know where you are?"

I nod slowly. "Gavan's—"

Then it hits me. It *all* comes rushing back. I choke, bolting upright with a strangled scream before Cillian jumps up and grabs me.

"*Easy*. Easy, Eilish," he growls. "You're okay—"

"*Gavan*—"

"Is *fine*," he says firmly, taking my shoulders and guiding them back to the pillow behind me. "He's okay. Everyone's okay." His brow knits. "Well, everyone who matters."

"What…" I shake my head. "I blacked out. My wrist…" I glance down, shivering when I see the gauze and bandage wrapped tightly around my wrist.

"You nicked your radial artery." His jaw clenches. "I won't lie, we almost lost you, Eilish," he says quietly. "We might have, if Gavan hadn't—"

There's a soft snore from across the room, and I blink in surprise when I snap my head around and realize there's someone curled up asleep in the oversized easy chair in the corner of the bedroom.

Neve.

"She was sitting where I'm sitting right now for the last fourteen hours. Wouldn't leave your side." He smiles. "She only went over there to 'close her eyes for a second' because I threatened to kick her out if she didn't."

I grin, looking over at my sleeping sister before I turn back to Cillian. "Wait, did you say fourteen hours?" I frown. "Did I go to the hospital?"

Cillian shakes his head. "Castle called Dr. Blythe at the same time he was breaking land speed records racing to get here."

Through the fog in my head, I dimly remember that. Dr. Blythe is legit one of those mob doctors from the movies—a surgeon who sometimes operates out of veterinary clinics for patients with both cash and reasons not to go to the hospital.

Which, of course, is *exactly* how my uncle knows him.

"Castle kept you stable until Blythe got here and did his thing. Stitched you up, gave you a few transfusions, and then pumped you full of sedatives and saline so you could rest up."

I swallow, nodding as my eyes lock with Cillian's.

"Cil—"

"Gavan's okay, Eilish." He frowns. "It was only a small heart attack—"

"I'm sorry, *what?!*" I blurt loudly, my eyes flying wide open as I struggle to sit up.

Neve snores, shifting in her sleep before quieting again.

"A fucking *what?*" I hiss, softer this time.

He smirks, shaking his head. "He had a neurotoxin in his system that was gradually slowing his heart to the point it was about to fail. Apparently, he jabbed himself with *three* hits of adrenaline, which took his heart from slowing to a stop to beating about as fast as Usain Bolt running a race on crystal meth."

My face pales in horror. Cillian smiles as he reaches over and takes my hand in his comfortingly.

"But now, like I said, he's fine. He's *here*, resting, just like you."

"I want to see—"

"I know you do." Cillian frowns. "And you will, in just a minute. But…" His jaw grinds as he sucks on his teeth. "I want to talk to you first," he says gently.

"About?"

His eyes meet mine. "About what happened. With Svetlana, I mean," he adds quietly, squeezing my hand.

My throat bobs.

"I never in a thousand years wanted that for you."

"What?"

His eyes fill with sadness. "To take a life."

Something flickers between my eyes and his. I know what Cillian is. And I know, or at least I have a good idea about, the things he's done.

Does.

I draw in a slow breath. "She was going to kill him," I say quietly. "And probably me, too."

Cillian nods slowly, his eyes still locked on mine. "How does that make you feel?"

I know how it *should* make me feel. Horrified, maybe. Or full of self-loathing. Or consumed by fear and anxiety to the point of a panic attack. But I don't feel any of those things.

Honestly, I don't feel anything at all when I replay the moment when the gun exploded in my hand and that woman's eyes went dim.

"I'm fine," I say easily.

It's the truth. She was going to kill Gavan. There is zero part of me that wouldn't do it again.

Cillian nods as my brows furrow.

I'm fine. Wait—

"Does that make me…"

"Me?" he mutters, an amused smirk on his lips.

I blush. "That's not what I was going to say."

"No, but you were thinking it. I understand. Genetics, and all."

I swallow uncomfortably. Cillian smiles as he squeezes my hand again.

"You're not me, Eilish, and you never will be. Trust me. Not even *close*. You did what you had to do, that's all. Not everyone *could* have done it. But you could."

I nod, smiling a little before my smile falters.

"Cillian?"

He raises a brow.

"I…" I swallow. "I have to tell you something."

I look down at my fingers.

"*I killed him*," I murmur quietly, taking a shaky breath before I force myself to look him in the eyes. "I killed my dad."

Cillian is silent for a few seconds, his face utterly still and neutral.

"Explain."

"I mean…I didn't pull the trigger—"

"Eilish," he says gently. "I know you didn't. We all know who *did*—"

"But I filled his gun with blanks that night," I blurt, my eyes widening as it all just tumbles out. "I—I sent him to that meeting with *zero* chance to defend himself."

Cillian looks away and takes a deep breath in and out. My throat bobs heavily.

"Cillian, I'm *so* sorry—"

"You found out, didn't you."

I blink. "What?"

He turns back to me. "Your mother," he growls thinly. "You found out he killed Erin."

I stare at him. "You…you *knew?*"

"Only shortly before he himself died," he grunts. "I had my suspicions for a long time, of course. I knew about his affairs, or at least, some of them. And when Erin died so suddenly…" His green eyes turn a frighteningly dark shade, almost black, before he blinks it away. "She was a good person, your mother," he growls quietly. "She didn't deserve Declan and his bullshit."

He takes a deep breath, looking right into my eyes.

"Eilish, *you didn't kill your father*. He got himself killed. He was careless with the free and easy way he made enemies. If it hadn't been on that night, it would have been on another one soon after."

He pauses, sucking his teeth again.

"Do you know why your father and Vadim met, that night Declan shot him?"

I shake my head. Cillian's lips thin.

"Declan had been having an off and on affair with Svetlana, for *years*."

My eyes go wide. "I'm sorry, *what?*"

He nods. "Vadim wanted to confront him about it. I mean, she may have been a monster—and she was—but she *was* his sister, after all. When they met, things got heated, and your father pulled a gun. The rest you know."

I take a second to process that. Cillian squeezes my hand again, a wry smile on his lips.

"You're *not* like me, Eilish. And you're going to be okay. I promise you that."

I nod, biting my lip. "Can I see Gavan now?"

"I think that's a great idea."

I'm still a little wobbly as Cillian helps me down the stairs. Across the penthouse, through the glass doors leading outside, I can see Gavan wearing a bathrobe and sitting in a chair out on the veranda with Castle. Cillian pauses at the doorway and nods for me to go through. I'm barely two steps outside when Gavan hears me and his head whips around.

His shadowed face instantly lights up as a grin spreads all over it. There's no stopping the smile on my own face, either. Still unsteady on my feet, I rush to him anyway, choking out a sob as I collapse into his arms on his lap.

Tears stream down my face as I cup his, kissing his mouth, his cheeks, his nose, and his eyes as I cry with joy.

"I'm all right, Eilish," he grins, though he's still looking a little pale. He sighs, nodding past me. "Thanks to Castle."

I turn, and in a second, I'm jumping out of Gavan's lap and hugging Castle fiercely. He chuckles, holding me tight before he pulls back and giving me one of his signature smug, lopsided smiles.

"You came," I grin.

He laughs. "Told you. I'll always be your protector, Blondie."

I beam at him, hugging him again. "*Nobody puts Castle in the corner,*" I murmur under my breath in my terrible Patrick Swayze impression.

Behind me, Gavan sighs. "Man, I fucking love that movie."

Castle smirks, arching a brow at me as he leans close.

"Your boyfriend's not half bad, you know."

I grin. "He might sort of be more than just a boyfriend."

Castle's smile fades. "Well, *that's* a conversation—"

"Hey, Castle?"

Castle and I turn to look at Gavan. "As much as I want to keep on thanking you for the whole saving my life bit…"

Castle sighs, nodding. "I know. I'll give you two some alone time. I'll be inside with Cil." He turns to wink at me again. "Glad to help, kid."

"Thank you," I whisper back, giving him another big hug. When he steps inside and closes the glass door, I sink back onto Gavan's lap.

"I'm not sure how to break this to you…"

He frowns at my serious tone. "What's going on?" he growls, a worried urgency in his voice. When my face splits into a grin, he glares at me. "Really? *Now* is when you decide jokes with that kind of a setup are a good idea?"

I giggle. "I just wanted to be the first to tell you that you officially can't blackmail me anymore." I shrug. "I told Cillian about Declan."

He smiles quietly, reaching up to cup my face. "And?"

"And nothing. It's settled."

"So, you're saying my leverage over you is gone."

"Exactly. Tough break, sorry," I shrug.

Gavan grins. "I could always go with my secondary leverage."

I frown. "What the heck is that?"

"Threatening to show your family your internet search history."

I swallow, blushing fiercely. *"How do you know that,"* I mutter.

"Oh, *solnishka,*" he grins. "We haven't even *begun* to scratch the surface on the ways I've stalked you for almost two years."

My jaw drops as I stare at him. "I'm sorry, you *stalked me?*"

"Incessantly."

I shake my head in disbelief, somehow unable to stop smiling at his man.

"You creep!"

He shrugs. "Guilty as charged."

I look at him sideways. "Actually, that's kind of hot, in a really fucked up way."

"Right?"

I laugh, melting into him as he cups my jaw possessively.

"You saved my life," I whisper.

He shakes his head. "You saved mine."

"Does that mean we're even?"

"Not quite."

I shiver, my skin tingling all over and my pulse skyrocketing as his lips crash down possessively on mine.

EPILOGUE

GAVAN

Three weeks later:

ON A MOONLESS, cloudy night, the five of us stand stoically in a semicircle around the condemned. Yuri takes a deep breath, sweeping his eyes over the rest of us.

"We'll now take the final vote, yea or nay, concerning the execution of the condemned for high crimes against the other members of this Council, in direct violation of its guidelines."

I'm first. My lips curl into a sneer as my gaze stabs through the darkness of the construction site to where a gagged Abram Diduch is tied to a chair at the edge of a foundation pit. He struggles with his bonds and his eyes bulge, his face white, like the piece of shit is actually trying to plead with me for mercy.

Fuck that. He'll find *none* with me. And the fact that he's shaking like a coward now that his plot to burn the High

Council to the ground has been uncovered makes it even worse.

I fucking *hate* fake toughness and bravado that crumbles under pressure.

"Yea," I growl effortlessly.

Beside me, Viktor has a similarly merciless look on his face. And I don't blame him. The firebomb Abram set in his hotel room, trying to frame Drazen, could have very well killed Viktor's wife Fiona and their young son, Sasha.

"*Yea*," Viktor snarls. "A thousand yeas."

Yuri nods. "Also a yea from me."

All of us turn to Marko as he leans heavily on his new cane, his face permanently scarred and shiny in places from the explosion that almost killed him.

"*Yea*," he says in such an even tone that it's spooky.

Anastasia is last. Her answer comes just as easily as the rest of ours.

"*Yea*," she mutters, spitting on the ground for good measure.

I know now why she voted with Abram at the table before. That piece of shit had the young daughter of a friend of Anastasia's—her own goddaughter—held hostage. *That's* why.

This vote has ended, and it's unanimous. There are only five families left on the High Council now. The Diduch family will cease to have a chair in the next two minutes, once Abram is dead. Demyan Ozerov has been granted mercy— after all, you can't *really* blame someone for voting alongside family, even if that family member is a piece of garbage.

It was proven that the Ozerov family wasn't personally involved with any of the violence perpetrated by Abram, using Drazen's name and reputation as a cover, so Demyan himself is spared the same fate as his cousin. All the same, the Ozerov family has been stripped of its seat at the table.

Yuri clears his throat. "The council has spoken. Abram Diduch, you have been found guilty of crimes against your fellow Council members. The punishment is banishment from the table…" He draws himself up to his full height. "And death."

Abram squeals and sobs beneath his gag. But as Yuri just said, the council has spoken. Yuri turns and hands a Beretta fitted with a silencer to Marko—whom we unanimously agreed earlier should be the one who pulled the trigger if it came to that.

There's no pomp and circumstance, no fanfare. He simply raises the gun, glares at Abram, and squeezes the trigger. The silencer muffles the shot—necessary, given that we're in the middle of Soho. Abram's head snaps back, and his body and the chair it's tied to fall back heavily into the construction pit.

It's Dimitra Drakos who's so graciously donated this grave for us tonight. In a few hours, just before daybreak, the foreman of a Drakos-owned construction firm who's building this development will arrive and pour fresh cement without looking too hard into the pit first.

An inglorious grave for a disgraced and despicable man.

Good. He deserves it.

When it's done, we all shake hands. There'll be another High Council meeting in a few weeks to discuss the latest topic of the hour: Drazen Krylov and his bid for a seat at the table.

Honestly, he has a good shot at it.

He's got my vote, and everyone understands why: I've been very open about it. Curiously, though, he also has Yuri's and Viktor's vote—and those are just the ones I know about privately.

Since coming into his birthright—namely the Romanov crown jewels in the base of the Imperial Shield egg—Drazen has done exactly what he said he'd do. The Krylov Bratva is not quite a powerhouse yet, but it *is* going to be a force to be reckoned with.

It might even be a force that sits across the High Council table from me.

It was the contents of the dossier on Abram on Drazen's hard drive that convinced, and allowed, the council to take this action today. I've got to hand it to Drazen; he was *thorough* in his collection of information.

The hard drive had clear proof of everything: Abram's payoffs, the mercenaries he hired, the crimes he committed against the rest of us. He *was* bankrolling Svetlana's legal attack against me, which was his way of trying to take me out of the picture. He had plans for all of us, even Anastasia, despite her voting for him under duress. Even for his own *cousin*, Demyan.

Actually, it's the scope of the information on *all of us* that was on Drazen's hard drive that's going to convince most of the Council to vote him onto it. He had information on some of us that *nobody* knows.

Hell, he even knew about Declan Kildare murdering my father, God knows how. He knew they met that night because Vadim wanted to confront Declan about the ongoing affair he'd been having with Svetlana for years.

Apparently, there was even a child of that affair. I have no idea what became of it, since Declan obviously didn't raise it, and Svetlana sure as *fuck* didn't either.

But that child's identity or whereabouts is a mystery for another day.

After we all shake hands again and start to file away into the night, Marko Kalishnik stops me with a hand on my elbow.

"Gavan," he rasps, his vocal cords still damaged by the car bombing. "A moment, if I could?"

I nod. "Of course."

He shakes his head, smiling sadly to himself. "I owe you an apology."

"For?"

He shakes his head again. "For not knowing about your involvement with Eilish Kildare when I made my..." he shakes his head. "My suggestion concerning my daughter Milena." He scowls. "I was wrong to hold the idea of forming my own power bloc to counter Abram's over your head with a proposal like that. I felt cornered, and desperate, and I—"

"Marko," I smile warmly, clapping him on the shoulder. "I have nothing to forgive you for, because you have nothing to apologize for."

He smiles wryly. "Perhaps we can think of it as a foolish act from a desperate man."

"All I see is one tough son of a bitch who isn't going anywhere anytime soon. I don't see desperation at all."

He dips his head appreciatively as he reaches out and shakes my hand. "Vadim would be very proud of the man you have become. I hope you're aware of that."

When I finally get back to my car, the energy is surging inside of me. With that all over and done with, it's time for me to go home to Eilish.

And to our next chapter.

But one more thing first…

I smile darkly, my lips curling as I tap the contact in my phone and let it ring. Senator Harrison McKinnley is smart enough to answer quickly.

I'm going to enjoy this.

A *lot*.

"Mr. Tsarenko!" There's a forced cheeriness in Harrison's voice—the politician in him he can't ever turn off.

"I assume you received my note," I spit.

I feel no need to attempt any niceties with the man whose son I should *kill* for what he did to Eilish. The only reason I'm being so merciful is that blackmailing Brooks works better to influence his father than killing him.

Also, Eilish asked me to do it this way. *Not* because she feels mercy for him. But because she wants him to spend the rest of his life worrying about the day when I release what I have on him.

I swear, there's a fucking darkness in my *solnishka* that makes me love her even more.

Senator McKinnley clears his throat. "I...uh, yes. Yes, I did."

"Do we agree that the information I have on your son—his admission of a crime, and his disturbing, *illegal* tastes in pornography—would be catastrophic for both of you should it get out?"

He stammers. "Y-yes, of...of course, Mr. Tsarenko."

"And we are furthermore in agreement that the information I have on *you*—specifically, the names of the two college-aged staffers whom you got pregnant—would be just as catastrophic for you and your career if *it* got out?"

"*Please*, Mr. Tsarenko—"

"*Are we or are we fucking not in agreement,*" I snarl. "*Senator.*"

"We are," he blurts. "Complete, total agreement."

"Then I will not mince words," I spit. "As of this moment, I fucking *own you*. If you fuck with me, my organization, or any of the other Bratva organizations on the list I sent you—"

It's a list of all the High Council families. And the Krylov Bratva too, because it's always smart to plan for the future, right?

"—*Or* if you try to fuck with the Kildare family, or the Drakos family, then every scrap of information I have on both you and your disgusting son gets emailed to every newspaper editor on Earth. If you should ever quit your position as chair of the Organized Crime Senate Task Force, I will *also* release this information. Now, Senator, I will ask once and only once more: do we fully understand each other."

He doesn't hesitate.

"Of *course*, Mr. Tsarenko. We fully understand each other, and needless to say you have my total cooperation going forward—"

"Good."

I hang up without another word, grinning widely as the car takes me closer to home.

———

SHE'S asleep and the penthouse is dark when I get in.

Excellent.

I shower quietly and slip into the bedroom.

Our bedroom. Eilish lives here now, as of a week ago when she moved out of the house she grew up in on the Upper East Side. I don't think my place has ever felt more like home.

I leave something I brought with me on the edge of the bed before I slide under the covers at the foot of it. Eilish is asleep on her front. And when I realize she's gone to bed without a thing on, I growl to myself as my cock thickens.

Good girl.

My body slides up between her slightly spread legs, my muscled shoulders pushing them a little wider apart as my mouth closes in on its target. She doesn't immediately wake when I drag my tongue over her pussy.

But she *is* instantly wet. I groan, pushing my tongue deeper as my hands grip her ass. My tongue slides lower, to her clit, and when I take the throbbing nub between my lips, Eilish suddenly gasps awake.

"*Gavan...*" she moans, writhing and twisting as my tongue curls around her clit. I keep her pinned down exactly how I want her, my fingers digging into the soft flesh of her ass. My tongue plunges in again, swirling around to drink in her arousal. She whimpers and whines in pleasure, her ass lifting to press back against my mouth.

I don't let up. I keep teasing her, higher and higher, hotter and hotter, until she's actively and desperately thrusting her hips back against my tongue. Her moans get louder, her legs tighten on either side of my shoulders, and when I suck her clit back between my lips and flutter my tongue across the roaring nerves, she comes undone.

I growl into her cunt, tongue-fucking her throughout her orgasm as it shudders over her body. She's still quivering as I slide up over her. My knees shove her thighs apart, and just as she raises her ass, my swollen cock finds her slick, eager opening.

I grab a fistful of her hair at the nape of her neck, yanking her head back and making her gasp in pleasure as I sink into her sweet little pussy.

"Oh my *FUCK, Gavan!*" she shrieks, moaning and clawing at the bedsheets.

I roll my hips, slowly inching my thick cock back out from between her pink, swollen lips. Then I quickly ram back in, letting my balls slap her clit as she screams for more. My hips begin to pound faster, thrusting harder as my cock fucks her greedy, dripping, pretty pussy.

My hand tugs her hair harder, pulling her head all the way back, bringing her up on her knees with her back to my chest. I snarl into her neck, inhaling the scent of her and biting down on her soft skin.

My hands circle around her, cupping her breasts and twisting her nipples in my fingers before delving between her legs. Eilish moans as I stroke her puffy lips while I fuck her, rubbing her clit in slow circles as my swollen head sinks as deep as I can inside her.

I fuck her harder and faster, driving my cock in and out of her as Eilish begs for more, harder, deeper. She shudders, her head pulled back against my chest with my hand tight in her blonde locks. She reaches back like she loves to do, wrapping her arms around the back of my neck and all but hanging off me like a rag doll as I fuck the absolute hell out of her.

My own personal little free use fuck toy, begging and whimpering for more.

Eilish's moans get louder. Her body begins to stiffen and clench, and I can feel her pussy squeezing my cock like it's trying to milk the cum right out of my balls.

She's about to come.

Which is exactly when I reach back and grab what I left on the edge of the bed. I pop the box open, slowing my thrusts to a stop.

"*No...*" she whines, achy and desperate for release. She pushes back, thrusting her ass against me like she's going to fuck me even if I stay still. But I stop her with a firm, hand on her ass as the other brings the box up in front of her face.

The box with the gilded ring in it.

"*Marry me.*"

It's a command, not a question. But I didn't do this right before. I asked her, but it was—at least, I was telling myself it was—because of the wording in Vadim's will.

This time, it's for real. For *all* the right reasons.

I just got the ring back today from the master jeweler here in New York from whom I commissioned it—a master jeweler, I might add, who's a direct descendant of the Fabergé family.

The band is gold and slender, and it's adorned with delicate swirls, black engraved roses, and little yellow diamonds.

Lots and lots of diamonds. Specifically, the ones that once adorned the Imperial Shield egg, together with an enormous, square cut diamond—a thank you gift, or token of friendship, or maybe just a plain bribe—from Drazen, part of the collection of jewels now in his possession.

Eilish gasps, going still.

"*Gavan...*" she breathes. "Is...are those..."

"They are."

She starts to twist toward me, trying to pull away from where we're joined. Not happening. My muscles tense, keeping her right where she is as I start to grind into her again. Eilish moans, her eyes rolling back as her body comes alive against me.

"Do you want to come?"

"*Yes,*" she whines, begging as her pussy ripples up and down my shaft. "Yes, *please!*"

"Then there's a word you need to say. Answer me."

She groans, gasping as I teasingly grind my cock deep into her.

"That's...oh my *fuck*...Gavan, that's blackmail."

"That wasn't an answer."

She whimpers as I start to pull my cock out.

"*Wait.*"

She's shaking, hanging on the edge of orgasm as I keep still. One hand drops to gently tease her clit and her thighs with my fingertips as the other holds the box open in front of her.

"Marry me. Be my wife," I groan. "Be *mine*, Eilish."

"I already am," she moans.

"Well, you'd better fucking *say* it before I never let you come again—"

"*Yes!*" she blurts, twisting her head around and crushing her mouth to mine. She gasps, grinning and kissing me even harder as I toss the box away and slip the ring on her finger. I keep kissing her as my hips begin to rock, growling into her mouth as I start to fuck her again like she wants to be fucked.

Like she *needs* be fucked.

She clings to me—my fiancée—moaning into my lips with my band on her finger and my cock swelling so fucking hard and thick in her sweet little pussy.

"*Yes, Sir!*" she moans again. "Yes, yes, yes, yes, *yesssss!*"

She screams into my mouth as she comes, her pussy spasming and clenching tight around my cock. I groan, biting her lower lip as I drive in deep, my balls twitching as I spill rope after thick rope of hot cum deep in her greedy little cunt.

After we collapse onto the bed, I hold her in my arms as she snuggles back against me. My fingers entwine with hers, running over her new ring and grinning at what it means.

Mine.

Together for all eternity with the woman whose hidden darkness I love just as much as the golden grace and light she wraps herself in.

And the future we *both* deserve.

———

The Dark Hearts series continues with Castle's story in
Stolen Hearts.

Haven't gotten enough of Gavan and Eilish?
Get their extra scene here, or type this link into your browser: http://Bookhip.com/WMGVXDZ

This isn't an epilogue or continuation to *Twisted Hearts*. But this extra hot "follow-up" story is guaranteed to keep the steam going.

ALSO BY JAGGER COLE

Dark Hearts:

Deviant Hearts

Vicious Hearts

Sinful Hearts

Twisted Hearts

Stolen Hearts

Kings & Villains:

Dark Kingdom

Burned Cinder (Cinder Duet #1)

Empire of Ash (Cinder Duet #2)

The Hunter King (Hunted Duet # 1)

The Hunted Queen (Hunted Duet #2)

Prince of Hate

Savage Heirs:

Savage Heir

Dark Prince

Brutal King

Forbidden Crown

Broken God

Defiant Queen

Bratva's Claim:

Paying The Bratva's Debt

The Bratva's Stolen Bride

Hunted By The Bratva Beast

His Captive Bratva Princess

Owned By The Bratva King

The Bratva's Locked Up Love

The Scaliami Crime Family:

The Hitman's Obsession

The Boss's Temptation

The Bodyguard's Weakness

Power:

Tyrant

Outlaw

Warlord

Standalones:

Broken Lines

Bosshole

Grumpaholic

Stalker of Mine

ABOUT THE AUTHOR

A reader first and foremost, Jagger Cole cut his romance writing teeth penning various steamy fan-fiction stories years ago. After deciding to hang up his writing boots, Jagger worked in advertising pretending to be Don Draper. It worked enough to convince a woman way out of his league to marry him, though, which is a total win.

Now, Dad to two little princesses and King to a Queen, Jagger is thrilled to be back at the keyboard.

When not writing or reading romance books, he can be found woodworking, enjoying good whiskey, and grilling outside - rain or shine.

You can find all of his books at
www.jaggercolewrites.com

f 🐦 ⓘ

Printed in Great Britain
by Amazon

38398997R00225